"I ripped through *Winterkill*'s pages, desperate to know
the secrets behind this captivating world. Equal parts
creepy, thrilling, and touching, the book is a must-read,
and Emmeline is a character I won't soon forget."
—James Dashner, author of the bestselling
Maze Runner series

"An engrossing romance, set against a chillingly vivid
repressive society. *Winterkill* will haunt you."
—Julie Berry, author of Carnegie-shortlisted
All the Truth That's in Me

"Boorman's . . . protagonist speaks directly and powerfully
to a young adult experience." —*Publishers Weekly*

"The promise of forthcoming volumes should keep
antsy readers at bay." —*Booklist*

"Readers who have found themselves battling for their own
versions of righteous truth-seeking will cheer Emmeline's
grit." —*Bulletin of the Center for Children's Books*

ALSO BY KATE A. BOORMAN

Darkthaw

WINTERKILL

KATE A. BOORMAN

AMULET BOOKS   NEW YORK

The Library of Congress has catalogued the hardcover edition of this book as follows:

Boorman, Kate A.
Winterkill / Kate A. Boorman.
pages cm
Summary: When the revered leader of her settlement, a dark, isolated land with merciless winters and puritanical rulers, asks Emmeline for her hand, it is a rare opportunity, but not only does she love another man, she cannot ignore dreams that urge her into the dangerous and forbidden woods that took her grandmother's life and her family's reputation.
ISBN 978-1-4197-1235-7 (hardback)
[1. Fantasy. 2. Conduct of life—Fiction. 3. Love—Fiction. 4. Community life —Fiction.] I. Title.
PZ7.B
[Fic]—dc23
2014006378

ISBN for this edition: 978-1-4197-1673-7

Text copyright © 2014 Kate Boorman
Title page illustration copyright © 2014 Shane Rebenschied
Book design by Maria T. Middleton

Amulet Books and Amulet Paperbacks are registered trademarks of Harry N. Abrams, Inc.

Printed and bound in U.S.A.
10 9 8 7 6 5 4 3 2 1

THE ART OF BOOKS SINCE 1949
115 West 18th Street
New York, NY 10011
www.abramsbooks.com

1

OUT HERE, I CAN FEEL THE DEAD IN THE TREES. The Lost People rustle the leaves, muddy the shafts of light through the branches, whisper in my ear. They creep dusty fingers along my neck, tug at my braid, pull strands from my plait to tickle my face.

Or mayhap it's the wind.

I don't linger. I stuff the last of the spring beauty root in my satchel and push to my feet. I turn from my digging spot under the dogwood bushes and my bad foot catches on a clump of dirt. It sends a flare of fiery pain up my leg and into my hip.

"Almighty!" The curse leaves my lips before I can bite it back. I hold my breath and listen to the creaking poplars. I'm not in any real danger; it's not dusk for near three hours or more. But no good can come of taking His name in vain, alone in these woods.

When I get past the tangle of brush and onto the Watch flats, the air is warmer and the chill on my spine disappears.

The wooden walls of the fortification are poker straight from this distance. I cut a wide arc around the walls and head toward the east gates, where people from my quarter bend to work, drying mounds of berries on large hides. A group of youngsters chases crickets through the dust.

"Emmeline!" Tom leaves the hides and crosses toward me with giant strides, the smooth leather of his trousers whisking through the wild grasses.

A smile tugs at my lips.

Tom is my age, tall and lanky, with gentle-looking hands despite their being scalded by wax so often that they're forever scarred. He hooks two thumbs in his *ceinture* as he approaches, his head tilted in his thinking-hard way.

He's going to ask what I'm doing during free time. Often we venture to the river to fish or search for left-behinds from the Lost People. Nobody calls the Lost People that but me, and not many people find arrowheads or bones interesting anymore, but I hoard them. Those left-behinds tug at me, like they've got secrets etched in them.

Tom stops. "You weren't at Virtue Talks last night," he says.

I shift my sack of roots. Tom knows about my once-in-a-while truancy from settlement events. He must be teasing.

"I miss a new sermon? Some big fancy words?" I say.

He doesn't laugh.

"We going to the river today?" I say.

"Em . . ." Tom looks like he's searching for words. He never searches for words. His blue eyes are troubled, like the prairie sky with a storm brewing.

A hawk wheels above us, scouring for prey.

I look down and dig the toe of my bad foot into the soil, feeling a backward kind of relief as pain washes my leg. A beetle crawls across the stubble of prairie grasses.

"Brother Stockham's wondering about it."

My head snaps up. "Beg pardon?"

"You not being at Virtue Talks. My ma took a crate of candles to Council this morning, and he asked where you were last night."

A cold stone settles in my stomach. "Your ma came to you and asked after it?"

He nods.

"And you said?"

"The truth. Said I didn't know where you were."

I ignore the question there. "Why'd he notice? Six hundred—some people and he notices *I'm* missing?"

"Don't know." Tom runs a hand through his soft blond hair. "But Em? Make sure you're there tonight." His eyes are worried, not accusing-like.

I nod. I have no choice: one Wayward act earns a warning. But two? Two means you have to prove your virtues another way.

Like standing Watch on the fortification walls.

My skin goes prickly.

I'll be at Virtue Talks tonight.

"What's got, Em?" Tom's sister, Edith, pulls at my long shirt with one hand and jumps to snatch at my leather satchel with the other. It's a right pitiful gesture—a field mouse pestering a bison. Her smock is smudged with ash. No doubt Sister Ann—her and Tom's ma—shooed her out from underfoot but told her to stay close. Edith's the curious sort you need to keep an eye on.

Her eyes are too large in her scrawny face; at four she's painful thin. Some babies are blessed with fat, but they lose it soon as they're weaned. Not many have the chance to carry extra weight, and the children, all tag playing and rough and tumble, are no different.

We are equal in all things: affluence and destitution. We survive together, or we perish.

Brother Stockham reminds us of it each Virtue Talks. Except it's not exactly true. There's Council, who never look to be wanting for much, and Watch, who are rewarded with extra rations for the risk they take each night.

I brush her off. "Spring beauty root for Soeur Manon."

"From under the wood-dog?" she asks.

"Dogwood," I correct her.

She nods her blond head, serious, like we're speaking on the most important thing Almighty created. "Good job," she says.

I smile. Got a soft spot for Edith. It's not just that she's Tom's little sister—and Tom is my only true friend—it's that she's always asking after my work for Soeur Manon, like root digging is something special. She listens to my every word too. My brief trips to the edges of the Watch flats must sound real exciting. She's never been outside the gates, except for that once. But no one likes to talk about that, and she's too young to remember.

A cabbage moth flitters past and her eyes light up. She turns and gives chase, heading for the corner of our shared quarters building.

"Don't go far!" I call after her. "Your ma will be looking for you."

On cue, Sister Ann's voice comes from inside. "Edith? Edith!"

Before Sister Ann can poke her head out, I turn and head for the Healing House. A thin line wisps from the chimney of the weathered wooden building. My knock is answered by a gruff *"Entrez!"*

Soeur Manon is bent over the hearth stirring a pot of simmering herbs, her snow-white hair the one bright spot in her sooty kitchen.

"La racine." I gesture to my satchel, and she waves her hand at the table.

I gather for her poultices and rubs: horehound for birthings, sage for belly upsets, spring beauty root for bone setting and such. Thanks be, she still has a dusty old book she's guarded for years that has little pictures of the roots and herbs I'm to gather; otherwise I'd be bringing back every plant on Almighty's green earth, trying to match up what she describes in her hurried French. Sometimes I pretend I'm looking at her plants book and flip through the other books she has: the ones with pictures of people and animals I've never seen. I suspect some of those animals live far across the sea, or in someone's mind only. Some of them—horses and oxen—I know were real. They died alongside half the settlement when we arrived five generations ago.

I pull out the root and place it on the table, step back, and wait for something more. She adds dried leaves to the pot. Stirs. Finally she turns and sizes me up with her watery eyes.

Her face is lined with more creases than the river has fish, and her shoulders are thin.

"Emmeline," she says, *"ton pied. Tu l'as blessé aujourd'hui, non?"*

How could she know I hurt my foot? It hurts more than usual, all right, but I'm not moving on it funny. I always walk normal-like, or close to, around the fort. It gives me an awful dull ache in my leg, but Pa and me are already Stained; I'm not inclined to give people another reason to eyeball me. Limping around wouldn't do me any favors. Still, somehow she knows.

"Oui." I nod.

She gestures for me to take off my moccasin. When I do, she drops the ladle on the table, hobbles forward, and bends to gather my foot in her knobby hands.

She presses at my wool sock, peering at it this way and that, but, Almighty's grace, leaving my sock on. I don't like looking at the unnatural dark skin, the misshapen toes—and I like it less when others look.

She clucks her tongue. "You do this on purpose."

I stare at her. Again, she's right: snagging my foot in the woods was a mistake, but leaning on it in front of Tom was purposeful. He caught me unawares, though, with his Virtue Talks business; I can hardly be faulted for it. And hurting yourself isn't a Wayward act.

"Can I help you with something else?" If I can't, I want out of here, away from her eyes that see too much.

She levels me a look. *"Non, Emmeline."* She places my foot on the floor real gentle. "Do what you like."

+⇥ ⇤+

"We extend the Peace of the Almighty." Brother Stockham begins Virtue Talks, looming straight and tall behind the pulpit.

The air in the ceremonial hall smells of sweat and unwashed hair.

I'm wedged between two women from the north—the Watch quarter—tucked away from my pa's sad eyes. He beckoned to me when I showed up, but I pretended not to see, scuttled into the crowd away from him. I have enough to worry about right now without weathering his anxious look.

I turn to the bone-thin woman on my left and offer her the Peace, placing a hand across my chest and nodding my head. I recognize her haunted face; no one here is a total stranger. Her response is quick, though her eyes are low, like she might catch something if she looks on me too long.

The woman to my other side looks right knackered, her belly swollen with a child whose life no one will celebrate until it reaches its first year. So many children die that a celebration before their first life day is considered shortsighted and a waste of stores.

I want to ask her if she has to Watch in her state—if the extra rations are worth it—but of course I don't. I'm not in the habit of speaking to people I don't know well.

Brother Stockham calls us back to attention. "November tenth. The day our settlement formed, the day we learned to survive this harsh land. Next month we will celebrate that date at Affirmation. For three days we will give thanks, and affirm our commitments to the virtues and to our settlement, before *La Prise* is upon us."

The woman to my right stiffens at the words *"La Prise"*:

the deadly winter. It's plain she's thinking on that unborn child.

"Year round we work hard to survive. But these weeks before Affirmation will reveal our commitment to life, or to death."

There's a soft murmur through the crowd. *Our commitment to death.* It's a strange thing to say, though I suppose it might be a roundabout way of telling us to work hard, that anything less than upholding our virtues is courting disaster. And, like he's answering my thoughts, Brother Stockham launches into a sermon about the three virtues: Honesty, Bravery, Discovery.

Honesty is always telling the truth, following settlement rules like completing your duties, attending settlement events, staying inside the fortification borders. Bravery is doing what's asked, taking risks that benefit the whole and not jawing on about it when you do. Discovery is using the brains Almighty gave us to find ways to improve our lot— without risking everyone's safety.

I fail upholding Honesty every other day.

I try, but some of the things I wonder about make it hard. My thoughts fly back to gathering today, when it felt like the Lost People were hanging off the boughs and watching over me. The outer woods are forbidden, but some days I can't help but think about walking off into the trees, heading into that darkness beyond the first line of scrub where there are no wary stares.

There's an itch between my shoulder blades. I twist one arm behind my back and reach as far as I can. When I elbow the hard-looking woman to my left and receive a sharp look, I stop.

"The virtues have kept us safe thus far," Brother Stockham affirms in English, and again in French. His voice carries through the hall, through the mass of silent bodies. Even children hush up when Brother Stockham's speaking, even though we've all heard versions of the speech so many times it's beyond familiar, it's deadbore.

I know a lot of the women aren't even listening. They just look it because they're busy making moon-eyes at Brother Stockham. I spot Macy Davies doing just that—her big brown eyes wide like she's drinking in his every word, twisting a lock of her shiny copper hair in her fingers.

She's probably hoping he'll ask her to be his life mate. His position, given over by birth, makes him the most respected member of our settlement. And everyone wonders why he doesn't have a life mate yet. It is strange; he's easily twenty-five, mayhap twenty-six. Well beyond binding age. Mayhap he's too busy upholding his virtues. Can't say I think too hard on it. He's handsome, sure: tall with glossy black hair cut off just below his chin in sharp points. But something about his hawk eyes has always skittered me. Or mayhap it's that he can mete my punishment if I'm Wayward.

Brother Stockham's wondering about it.

My stomach gets tight. I'd rather gather roots at the Crossroads, under the hanging skeletons of the Waywards, than be punished with Watch.

I glance about the hall. Six Councilmen stand together at

the far side: vultures watching over carrion. I turn my head before I catch their eye. And spy a boy watching me. He's wedged in the crowd about ten bodies closer to the pulpit, but there's a gap that gives us sight of each other.

His eyes are big, making him seem young, but looking closer, I see he's my age. His hair is shaved close to his head, so he must be from the south quarter, Storages and Kitchens. Instead of looking like most of the south residents, though—missing an important feature, like a shorn sheep—his shaved head gives him a kind of stark beauty. A lone poplar against the prairie sky.

I lower my eyes, sure he'll do the same, then risk a quick look at him once more.

He's still looking at me, but it's not the usual wary stare—it's real friendly. The corner of his mouth curls into a secret-joke kind of smile, and then he's gone when a large man shifts his stance.

There's an unfamiliar fluttering in my chest.

I try to prick my ears to Brother Stockham's sermon, but it's near impossible. Silent, I curse the man between that boy and me. I don't consort much with anyone outside the east; until we turn sixteen and become eligible—of binding age— we're kept close to our quarters. And of course we're kept inside at dark. We don't have much chance to get friendly with people from other sections until we get older.

But I should know him: everyone knows everyone. I just don't recognize him because his head is shaved.

And then I place him.

He's the oldest Cariou boy, from the south quarter. *Kane.* As a child he was forever chasing his age-mates about the fortification, a tangle of bone-straight, dark hair streaming behind him. In the past three years since I've been gathering, I've seen him playing hoopball on the flats and hauling skins in past the gates. For years, he's been hidden in a group of boys, behind his hair, hovering on the outskirts of Virtue Talks.

His head is shaved now, which means he's turned sixteen and can work inside Storages and Kitchens, doing more important work.

When I turn sixteen in a few days, I'll start learning Soeur Manon's trade, how she makes her poultices and such, instead of just gathering for her. I'll also start delivering gatherings to Storages.

A thought lodges in my mind: I'll soon be seeing Kane regular.

My stomach flips over and I press my weight into my bad foot.

"Adherence to the virtues is our only hope," Brother Stockham says, his eyes sweeping over us. "Waywardness breeds chaos, and chaos brings destruction." His gaze rests on mine and for half a moment it seems he's talking right to me. "Remember and adhere to your virtues daily. For yourself, for your children, for our continued safety and prosperity." He puts a hand across his chest once more, and we are released.

I go slow, following the bony back of the Watch woman, hoping my pa won't wait. I'm in luck; as we shuffle from the hall, I can see him far ahead, heading back to our quarters with Tom's parents.

Someone appears at my elbow. I somehow know it's him

without looking, but when I do raise my eyes, my breath hitches.

Kane is a mite taller than me, but he's no longer the scrawny youngster who used to chase ground squirrels; working in Storages has filled him out. I can tell this by looking at the bare arm next to mine: his shirtsleeves are rolled to the elbows, which somehow feels terrible intimate. He smells of sage and woodsmoke.

"Emmeline, right?"

I nod, trying my hardest to walk normal-like. What does he want? Why is he speaking with me?

We step into the dusk, where the crowd is scattering. The north quarter is heading to Watch, lighting torches from the burn baskets.

He gestures to himself. "Kane."

We stop and turn toward one another. In the half-light, his eyes are black pools.

"I know."

He nods toward my quarters. "How're things?"

"All right."

"Mind if I ask how old you are, Emmeline?"

I feel a thrill hearing him say my name—the way he speaks! His voice is a lazy river, winding over to me, honeying my ears. We should be getting to our quarters, not bandying about, but I can't stop staring at him.

"Fifteen." I correct myself quick. "I mean, sixteen—next week."

"So I'll be seeing you at Storages soon." He's not asking.

"That's right." I'm trying to sound casual, but I know I

look like a cornered deer. It's like he was able to read the thoughts I was having moments ago at Virtue Talks.

His gaze is steady. "Mayhap we'll work together."

This levels me. Surely he knows I'm Stained? Ever since the Crossroads was built, there have been people who carry the shame of something a family member did to end up there. No way he doesn't know about my grandma'am. And it's addled enough we stand here jawing on while everyone prepares for dark, but to suggest that we should spend time together . . . in that inviting way . . .

My chest swells. I open my mouth to offer a response, but a voice from behind breaks in.

"Sister Emmeline, a word." It's Brother Stockham.

My blood freezes.

Oh, not here, not now.

Something flickers across Kane's amused face. I swallow before turning to face the good Brother.

He stands with his arms crossed in front of his dark cloak, his hair shining.

"Yes?"

"I have knowledge of your Waywardness. Skipping Virtue Talks is an offense."

My face flushes hot. I look to the ground, willing Kane away with all my might. People already think I'm more prone to Waywardness on account of my Stain. And now . . .

I clear my throat. "Apologies, Brother Stockham. I wasn't feeling so good."

"If you are unwell, you need to be seen by Soeur Manon."

"I should have told someone. I'm sorry."

"I'm sure you are. And I'm sure you are equally sorry for skipping the Thompson life day ceremony two weeks ago?"

The flush rushes over my entire body, my chest seizes with panic.

"This Waywardness requires penance."

I nod again, hoping with every inch of me that he doesn't mean—

"Watch on the fortification. Tonight."

My breath leaves me. "But I don't know how—"

"You will learn. Go to the north quarter. I will alert your father."

Pa's going to die a thousand deaths over. Being punished for two Wayward acts . . .

Brother Stockham puts a hand under my chin to raise my eyes to his. "Sister Emmeline. Never again. Do you understand?"

I want to answer, but my mouth is dry. I blink. Pa's sad eyes fade in my mind because there's something curious about the way Brother Stockham is touching me—is looking at me. He drops my chin and steps past, heading in the direction of our quarters.

A strange feeling shoots through me. Brother Stockham was irate, but there was something right gentle about his touch. I shiver. Then I remember Kane and hope he had the good grace to excuse himself from my tongue-lashing. I pivot and find nothing's going right.

Kane is still there, and his jaw is hanging open. "Why would you do that?"

For an addled moment I don't know if he means skip a life day ceremony or ponder Brother Stockham's touch.

"Two Wayward acts in two weeks?" There's something in his eyes that doesn't quite match his words. Like he's horrified *and* having a laugh at me. "You got a death wish?"

My temper flares. The only reason he knows about my Waywardness is because he's toying with it himself—waylaying me before Dark!

"No," I retort. "Just rather do Watch than work in Storages with the likes of you."

I spin on my heel and stride away before he can answer, trying to feel satisfied with the look of shock on his face. But around the corner of the weapons shack, I stop and wrap my arms close, angry tears biting my eyes. My heart leapt when he talked about us working together. Did I think for a moment that he wanted to spend time with me? He was probably sent to talk to me on a dare. His age-mates will have a good laugh now.

I stamp my bad foot hard on the earth, then clench my jaw and scrub my sleeve across my eyes, turning toward the north quarter. I'm still dreading Watch, but the humiliation burning in my body distracts me, dulling my fear.

Thank Almighty for that.

2

THE NIGHT AIR IS HEAVY WITH THE BITE OF autumn. I shift my weight off my bad foot slow, hoping Frère Andre won't notice me favor it.

We stand together on the fortification wall, my body a crushed sapling next to this hardened oak of a man. His beard lies in a wiry gray mass on his chest and his brimmed hat is battered. I think he's even older than my pa, but I don't ask. He's the senior Watcher, and surely not someone who wants to entertain foolish questions.

He has a spyglass and is scouring the torches that form a border about a hundred strides outside the high walls. They light the field surrounding the fortification, and each Watch post surveys a portion of the border. We're watching the west side of the fort, which faces the woods and the soft shadows of the coulees—the low, dry hills—beyond.

Andre's spyglass is for scanning the distance; I'm meant to watch along the walls with my naked eye. All of this I learned from Andre in a mix of broken English and quick

French in our first moments together. He hasn't spoken to me since, and I know it's not just because he's busy watching for the *malmaci*.

The sun set long ago, wild-rose pink bleeding out onto a bruise of swollen cloud hanging low on the hills. I've only ever seen the sky change colors from the courtyard, before we head inside until morning. Never seen the sunset from the walls before, never seen that big orange sun dip low and spread its golden rivers along the coulees, all through the cracks and valleys. My secret heart felt real full, looking on that.

Now, tendrils of mist curl across the flats toward us and my heart is tight. I can picture the river nearby steaming, releasing the day's heat into the cold night. The river, which winds along the east side of the fort, is flanked on the far side by steep earth walls that end with grassy plains as far as the eye can see. Those cliffs, pockmarked with tufts of scrub and sage, have deep cracks running down them like tear stains. Like the hills have been crying for thousands of years.

The coulees I'm watching are shadows now, but they have the same sad creases. Pockets of scrubby brush and poplars are huddled in their ravines, and tall spruce trees dot the low hills beyond. I gather for Soeur Manon in the first line of brush, where the Watcher in the tower can see me. A Taking in the day is rare, but it's Wayward to wander too far. It's also Wayward to miss important events such as life day ceremonies . . . Bleed it! Why did I get in my daydreaming way at the river that day?

I glance about the top of the fortification. The Watchers

on the far wall are small, dark shapes—the size of June beetles from here.

All of the Watchers are born into the north quarter, and I suspect they choose to stay and learn Watch as a matter of pride. Their rations are better in the north than in the rest of the quarters too, which is added reason to stay put.

Punishment with Watch is another story. It means doing the dangerous job without getting any reward for risking your neck. Proving my Bravery virtue tonight isn't a choice, because I failed in other ways. Even so, I can't help but wonder if the north quarter doesn't feel a mite insulted that my punishment is a turn doing their regular job.

I'm not about to ask Andre and get some cranky reply.

He's busy with the dark ritual now anyhow, staring through that spyglass and crossing himself with the other hand, muttering, *"Je suis Honnêteté. Je suis Courage. Je suis Découverte."*

I copy him in a half-whisper, crossing myself, my gaze tracing over the bare wood walls. *I am Honesty. I am Bravery. I am Discovery.*

Pa says by now we should all speak English and French perfect. We can't, so we're either stubborn as laying hens or clinging to our birth tongues because we're scared they're going to be taken from us, like everything else. We are a mélange—a mix—of three peoples trying desperate-like to get on together without losing ourselves. Most in the north quarter come from an Old World kingdom that spoke French. The east and west quarters have their roots in an English kingdom. The south are a mélange themselves, of French and First Peoples from the east—they're the only ones who speak both French and English well, and I've heard First Peoples' words in their speech too.

Pa says when we arrived there were also three religions, but the ungodliness of the *malmaci* banded people together in one understanding of the Almighty, and of how the virtues can keep us safe.

Pa. I'm grateful Brother Stockham sent me straight to Watch, that I didn't have to tell Pa myself and see that worry—that disappointment—in his eyes. I see it enough as it is.

A flicker of movement in the courtyard catches my eye. It's two Councilmen moving along the east wall, wearing their long, dark cloaks. Couldn't be anyone else; only Watch and Council would be outside after dark. I turn my eyes back to the bare walls, thankful they can't see who I am from this distance. I don't need them wandering over and fixing their stares on me. The fortification is big: everything of value— sheep, chickens, even the gardens—is kept inside the walls, and it takes me several minutes to walk one end to the other. But it never feels so small, so stifling, as when Council is around.

I shift, wriggling the toes on my good foot to keep them from freezing up. Andre is quiet, focusing on the woods. Watching, watching.

Some whisper the *malmaci* is half man, half bear—a nightmare mishmash of two creatures that destroys trespassers on its land. Others say it's a spirit, drifting on the night air like a death wind.

No one really knows, so we are watching for a *bête* or *fantôme* of some kind—although to my thinking, there's a world of difference between a beast and a ghost. Andre's rifle might do some damage to a beast; an apparition seems pretty bulletproof.

Course I don't get a gun. All the weapons are under lock and key, given to particular people at particular times, and the weapons shack key is hanging from Frère Andre's *ceinture fléchée*—the long woven sash we all wear and use for everything from wiping sweat to hauling things. Not even Councilmen carry weapons to enforce the law; Brother Stockham says common sense during conflict is better than a bullet. But I suspect it has more to do with the fact that bullets are so valuable he can't risk just anyone having their hands on them.

The woods beyond the Watch flats are silent and still. The ring of torches lights the first trees with a soft glow, but the shadows beneath the lowest branches are raven black. I risk a glance upward, away from the walls, hoping to see the stars now that dark has full fallen, but only a few are glimmering through the cloud cover.

Soeur Manon told me when she was a girl she saw them one night and there were so many it was as though *"Dieu répandit un peu d'argent sur un grande tissu noir"*: the Almighty had sprinkled tiny bits of silver upon a huge black cloth. I wonder if Soeur Manon saw them because she was forced to Watch. Wish the sky wasn't so cloudy.

I sigh and turn my eyes back to the walls—these looming walls standing at attention, keeping us safe from whatever lurks beyond. I watch and watch, until my toes are near frozen through my moccasins. By and by, despite the dark, it all becomes a mite deadbore. The backward part of me starts to hope something will happen. That we'll see *something*.

And then I've willed it upon us, because Andre sucks in his breath.

"Maudite," he curses in a whisper, his eye not leaving the spyglass. He points with a steady hand into the distance. I squint.

I see nothing outside the torch-lit ring but the brush. But there must be something, because I hear Andre bring the rifle to his shoulder with his free hand. My heart skips into my throat. He'll need to drop the spyglass to get a shot off. I scan the surrounding brush looking for movement.

There! There *is* something out there. It's slinking along the shadows, just outside the half circle of light. It's big—on all fours or two? When I fix my eyes on it, it stops dead, blending quick as a blink into the black of the woods. There's a pause where all I hear is my heart hammering in my ears.

It darts to the next tree, quiet and quick. It's on all fours— dark, but somehow shimmering in the moonlight . . .

I tear my eyes away and force my tongue to work. "What do we do?"

Frère Andre's face is grim. He brings the rifle to his eye and leans into it, training the barrel on the outskirts of the torchlight. The directive is calm, but I can see that his breath is coming fast. *"Sonnez la cloche."*

Ring the bell?

He jerks his head toward the Watchtower that stands six strides down the wall from us. There's a door facing us—the bell must be inside.

I push off my bad foot by mistake, but the shooting pain is swallowed by my fear. I run, asking the Almighty for steady steps. The *malmaci*'s never breached our walls; I can't be the reason it succeeds tonight. At the door my fingers scramble along the handle and I haul it open, feeling a slight give in the muscles under my shoulder blade.

Inside a single torch burns and a thick waxed rope hangs in the center of the circular room. I lurch forward, grab hold, and heave with all my might. The rope doesn't move. The dark cavern above me that houses the bell is silent, undisturbed.

I brace myself, ignoring the fire shooting through my leg, and heave again. My sweat-slicked hands slip, burning along the rough fibers. And then the right idiocy of this plan—sending the cripple to sound the alarm—makes me want to laugh.

Have I lost my senses?

I wipe my palms on my cloak, grasp the rope, and am about to heave again when something crashes into the room behind me.

"Arrête!" It's Andre. *"Soeur Emmeline, arrête!"*

I spin.

His eyes are wide, but one hand reaches toward me in a soothing, slow-down gesture. The other holds the rifle at his side. *"Ne le sonnez pas."*

Don't ring it. "Why not?"

"Mistake," he says.

Mistake? But I saw . . . I saw . . . I pause, thinking hard. That dark form slinking along the shadows.

"What was it?"

"Un loup." He shrugs, looking sheepish. *"Ce n'était pas un fantôme."*

A wolf. I stare at him, my heart slowing bit by bit, and then a curse bursts out: "Almighty! You scared the life out of me!"

He fiddles with the catch on his rifle. *"Je suis désolé."*

I wish he'd find another way to look sorry. I breathe again, the tight feeling in my chest easing up. Both my foot and shoulder are singing pain something awful, but I'm so relieved there's no attack, my anger melts away. "All right." I rub my rope-burned hands and take a step toward the door, expecting to follow him back to our post.

Andre doesn't move. "Emmeline," he says, "can you . . . not speak? Of this. To people. To Council."

I frown. He doesn't want me to tell anyone. Why? Sure, false alarms are Wayward acts. But we didn't raise the alarm.

"Mes yeux," he says. "They are not good now."

I study him. If his eyes aren't reliable, why hasn't he told Council as much? They'd release him from Watch, send him to a job where he wouldn't have to stand on this bleeding wall each night.

"Je ne comprends pas," I say.

He looks uncomfortable. "My family. They were healthy this year. The food."

And then I see. He doesn't want to give his position up because he'd be losing the extra rations.

My mind whirls. That's a Wayward act in itself: it's putting the settlement at risk. But there are other Watchers on the wall every night. And if he's doing it for his family . . .

I squish my eyes tight, trying to think.

A first offense gets a warning; a second means punishment. True Waywards end up hanging at the Crossroads, swaying in gibbets in a forbidden ravine due west of the fortification.

The last Waywards were sent years ago, when I was small. A south-quarter couple—the Thibaults—stole stores and hoarded them over the winter. To be sent to the Crossroads you have to fail your virtues pretty bad, like them. Or you have to do something truly awful, like my grandma'am.

Andre's watery eyes are worried. If Council knew he was unfit for Watch and hiding it . . . I wonder what family he's speaking on. A life mate, children . . . grandchildren?

The sole reason the settlement isn't in a ruckus right now is because my arms are the size of sparrows' kneecaps. And a little voice in my head wonders if Frère Andre is testing my virtues, wonders if he's trying to catch me promising something Wayward. He looks so worried, though.

I ignore the voice and shake my head no.

His shoulders relax. *"Merci."* He straightens. *"Viens."*

I follow, making my way through the tower and shutting the door. I wince as my shoulder hollers in protest. My foot answers with a dull throb.

Ahead of me, Andre's shoulders are back to a brave, straight line. I stomp on my foot, my insides all upside down. Did I just do something foolish? Suppose Brother Stockham finds out? This would be a third offense; would that warrant the Crossroads? I want to ask Tom about it, but I know he'd just worry himself sick. Tom is never Wayward. Not by choice, anyhow.

Back on the wall, the stars are dull through the clouds and the Watch flats are empty; there's no sign of the wolf.

It's as though the dark mist drifting toward the fortification swallowed the animal whole.

Oftentimes I wonder how it'd be if that darkness swallowed *me* whole.

Andre beckons to me to take my place beside him on the wall. He's looking on me real friendly, and I want to feel glad I reassured him.

But all I can do is pray to the Almighty word doesn't get back to Council about my good deed.

3

IN THE MORNING, I'M GATHERING OUT IN THE first line of trees to the north, trying hard not to think on my Watch shift last night. Paying no mind to my digging stick, I bark my knuckles on an unearthed stone. Bright red blood springs to the surface of my shredded skin. I suck at my dirt-caked hand, swallowing soil and iron.

Other gatherers sift around the Watch flats, picking the last of the berries on the edge of the woods. Some are just inside the trees to the west, gathering fodder for the penned sheep. I can see still others on the east side of the fort, in the willows near the banks, checking the rabbit snares. Most gatherers are inside the walls, harvesting the meager gardens.

I'm the only one who gathers for Soeur Manon, the only one who has to do this cursed root digging. I guess I should be grateful she took me on. Some people wouldn't want me working for them at all. Gathering gets me out of the fortification too, and today, the woods are heaps more inviting than the wary stares and the sad curve of my pa's spine.

Last night, Andre spent the rest of our shift schooling me in a number of things I've never wondered about: types of buckshot, knife whetting, nighttime birdcalls. I watched him careful-like, trying to figure if he was just playing at being kind because I did him that good turn. I wanted to warm to him. Just the idea of feeling a kinship with someone—I mean, besides Tom—felt real good.

That feeling lasted till I got home. Then Pa and me broke our fast in silence and Pa's defeated shoulders spoke plain. I fixed my eyes on the table while we ate, sure the disappointment on his face would set me to banging my foot against the table leg more times than it could bear. Helping Frère Andre didn't feel so good anymore, neither. My stomach was clenched real tight—near too tight for food—so I just filled my head with the song my ma used to sing to me at night.

Sleep, little one, with your secret heart,
Take to the night like the swallow.
When morning time brings what your secret heart sings,
Set your feet to the same path and follow.

I was real young when she died. Troubles after giving birth to a boy who didn't live. I didn't think on my ma much for a long while. Then this summer, when I was out at the river watching the swallows in the bank, one of the birds swung so close, it near brushed my eyelashes with its wings. And I remembered that song, remembered her singing it to me.

I like that "secret heart" bit. With all the eyeballing round here, I like the notion there's a part of me no one gets to know about if I don't want them to. But I don't speak on that kind of thing to anyone, not even Tom.

There was a time I might speak on it with my pa—back just after Ma died, when he'd try to cook stew the way she cooked it, or sing her songs though he can't sing a note. Back then, Pa would blink away the sadness of losing Ma and find a way to make me smile—carve me out a little birch dolly, or pick me some of the clover that grows near the rabbit snares. Back then, I might've told him some things.

But these days Pa's got a worry to him and we don't speak on much. He looks at me nervous-like and real sad, like the older I get, the more Stained I am. This morning it was plain as the scrubby brown beard on his face. I told him nothing about Watch, just ate and made myself scarce. I thought the fresh air would ease my thoughts, but Pa's worried eyes keep surfacing in my mind. Need to find a way to make that worry disappear . . .

A soft wind stirs the leaves above me. The Lost People drift through the branches, whispering to me, calling to me. My neck prickles, but I know that what I truly need to worry about is doing something unmindful—spilling my gatherings or such. The Watcher in the tower can see me if I need him to, and the larger beasts—wolves and bears—are far too skittish to venture close. And Takings in the daytime are rare.

But.

Mayhap my pa would be relieved if I didn't come back.

A stubborn piece of root bursts free in a shower of soil. I dust it off and drop it in my satchel, then sit back on my heels, wrapping my knuckles in the tail of my *ceinture*. I need three or four chunks of root to warrant my return; we need all the stores we can manage before *La Prise de Glaces*—the big Ice Up—arrives next month.

Each year, I feel it coming on the air like a poison breath. The birds escape in jagged lines across the sky and the woods get brittle and stark, waiting. When it strikes, *La Prise* sweeps down in ice-cold winds that burn and blistering snow that swirls so thick and fast, you need a rope to guide you from the kitchen to the woodshed. The sun wanes, the dark grows, and—the worst of it—we are all shut inside the fortification until the Thaw. Months of howling winter winds, months of nothing to do but attend pitiful bindings. When we finally stagger out into the springtime air, thinner still and half mad, we thank Almighty we've lived to see the trees bud out and the river swell.

Next Thaw, someone will come. No one says that out loud, and I suspect it's because no one believes it anymore. After eight decades of barely scratching out an existence here, the unsaid is louder, truer, than any declaration of hope: either everyone else is cut off, like us, or they're already dead.

I lift the cloth from my knuckles to make sure the bleeding has stopped, then scan the dirt for a new spot to dig. I'm not strong enough to get the rest of the root I unearthed. It's too far down, and besides, there are bound to be others nearer the surface. I rub at my brow absent-like and feel dirt smear across my forehead.

Oftentimes I wonder what they left behind for *this*. Pa says back years before we came, the *coureurs de bois* were the only ones traveling out this way, chasing after animal pelts. Then the animals those men were hunting got scarcer the further west they traveled, so they returned east to work the land.

But over decades, too many people arrived from the Old World; the colonies got crowded, relations with the First Peoples got tense. A few families—our ancestors—decided to press west. Pa says it was an odd assortment: English speakers looking for a better life, French speakers trying to escape being deported to the Old World, the offspring of French speakers and First Peoples who were tired of persecution for being of mixed blood. No way they all got along; I suspect the idea was to come in the safety of numbers, and spread out once they found suitable land.

But the emptiness should have warned them. Where were the First Peoples that were said to roam these lands? In the east, the First Peoples shared with the settlers from the Old World, taught them to survive on the new land; they mingled, had families together—became the mélange, whose blood remains in the people of the south quarter.

Here, just their ghosts remained, traces of people who had up and vanished. But where did they go? And why?

When the settlers halted in the woods just shy of the foothills, before the wall of Great Rock, they got an answer.

The *malmaci* had Taken those First Peoples. And then it came for them too.

It wiped out more than half those forest-dwelling settlers in a few short months, killed all the beasts of burden too. People would wake to find their loved ones' bloodied, blistered corpses, and their livestock ravaged the same. Terrified, twenty or so families shored up together in a settlement on the banks of the river. People who chanced the woods to the west or the plains to the east either never returned or were found torn apart, their eyes and ears bleeding rivers, their spilled-out insides swollen and black.

A Council of men, led by Brother Stockham's great-grandpa, formed to bring order and safety. They built the Crossroads for anyone who defied their rule. Anyone who breached the borders, anyone unwilling to comply with settlement rules was deemed Wayward because they put everyone at risk from what lurked in the woods beyond.

We survive together, or we perish.

Those who spoke French called it *le Mal*—the bad thing. Those with First Peoples in their blood called it the *maci-manitow*—the evil spirit.

Honesty, Bravery, Discovery: these virtues create a strength that keeps the evil—the *malmaci*—at bay.

I guess my grandma'am didn't have that strength.

Every day I ask my secret heart if everyone is right to look at me the way they do—like I don't have it, neither. Today, sitting across from my pa's sad eyes, it was trilling *Wayward girl, Wayward girl.*

I can see the Watchtower from where I'm sitting in the trees. It's supposed to make me feel safe, but suddenly my skin is crawling at the thought of someone up there, watching me with scornful eyes.

A flash of black at the gates catches my eye. A Councilman is coming out across the flats. Can't see who it is from the distance, but he won't be coming to help gather berries or roots; he'd never have to do something so menial.

My chest gets tight. I don't want to have to talk to who-ever it is, not after being punished with Watch, not after last night.

I push back into the bramble, away from the flats. I'm still visible, but when the Councilman stops halfway to the woods to talk to a woman headed toward the fort, I dart behind a tree.

I look around the forest. Leaves shimmer all shades of gold and red. Branches catch the soft breeze and sigh, like the woods are thinking on some fond memory.

The north-quarter people call these trees *les trembles*, which Pa says speaks to the way the leaves move in the breeze, all trembling. They make a soft tinkling sound that builds to a roar in a big wind. Feels like it's the Lost People, always whispering.

They're whispering real plain right now. *This way*, they're saying, *this way*.

I could duck down and keep searching for roots here, hidden from that Councilman's eyes. Instead, I take a deep breath and head a bit further in, brushing past white birch saplings gleaming in the sun. The forest is quiet and there's a prickle at my neck, but I go a little further, deep into the poplars.

Sunlight beams through the branches, tracing patterns on the forest floor. It's beautiful and dizzying; it coaxes me forward while putting a chill to my spine. I shouldn't go any further—it isn't safe. People who wander too far don't come back. People who wander too far are Taken.

But heading back means enduring Council's stares, may-hap getting questioned about last night. Frère Andre might've been testing me after all, and turned me in. And then what? I shiver deep, press into my bad foot to focus on the pain. I can't help but wonder if . . .

Pa would be relieved if I didn't come back.

I picture that sad crease in his brow, his shame over our Stain. I make it worse—getting in my daydreaming way, being punished with Watch. And now, a third offense . . .

This way.

I move forward. The grasses get higher, the scrub thicker, so I have to push my way into the tangle of dogwood and wild rose. Branches catch at my tunic and force me to duck under. Deadfall trips me up every other step. I bend and crash through until I have to pull up short.

The woods have given way to a small, dry ravine. There was a creek here once, that's plain, but now it's a rocky bed with slippery shale walls, near impossible to traverse without hurting my foot something fierce. It's my chance to turn back. I should turn back.

But I want my foot to hurt today.

I fumble down the steep bank to the dry creek bed and climb the other side. Every other tuft of grass tears away, so I use my fingernails, skinning my knuckles again as I scramble up the shale.

There's a jumble of logs inside this line of trees: four crumbling walls caked with lichen and dirt. A left-behind from the first generation. There are a few messes like this in the woods outside the fortification; soggy ruins after years of the woods creeping mossy fingers around them, pulling them into the soil. Some of the first settlers must've lived out here. Before they shored up inside the fort.

Before they knew about the *malmaci*.

Heart beating fast, I push into the woods, putting the ghostly jumble to my back and out of mind. I push deep and deeper until the brush gives way once more—this time to a grove. It's small; looks about thirty strides by twenty. The trees around it reach tall to the sky, and end in a circle of bright blue. The scrubby brush in the middle is scarce ankle-high.

I pause and listen hard. A white-throated sparrow trills in the bush and its mate answers. The breeze tinkles through the treetops, soft and sure. The woods around me teem with life I can't see, which is right skittering if I think on it too hard, but this . . .

This is a little secret haven tucked away from those unknowns.

My shame and anger drift away. Moving into the center, I close my eyes and breathe the earthy air.

Nobody has been out here in years—decades. Mayhap I'm the very first person to find this grove.

I like that. I like that it's just me out here. No wary eyes, no Pa, no shame.

A strange kind of peace fills me. *Les trembles* whisper with their tinkling voices, and both my feet feel solid, rooted into the forest floor like I'm a part of this grove, these woods. I breathe deep again. The Lost People are looking on me without judging. I can feel it on my skin.

The little voice in my head reminds me I'm addled. The Lost People were First Peoples, and they were Taken by the *malmaci* before our ancestors even arrived. The stories tell it that way, and Tom and I find their ancient traces—tools, bones—along the riverbank all the time. Only . . .

Only, deep down in my secret heart, I've always felt their absence as though it were a presence. As though they're still here, somehow—just . . . *lost*. Tom's the only one who knows I call them the Lost People, but he doesn't tease me about it.

Course, I don't tell him they call to me.

This way.

My eyes snap open.

A piece of sky is hanging from the brush on the far side. I squint.

No. A scrap of something.

I cross the grove to pull it from the tree. The cloth that comes off in my hands is beautiful, the color of an autumn sky. I turn it over, running my fingers along its strange smooth surface. And then my thoughts catch up to my hands.

Someone has been out here.

I grip the scrap real tight. Who? When?

A heady rush washes over me.

The last Taking happened before I was born. It was an old man from the south quarter; could this be what was left of him? Was he Taken in the night? Or in the day?

Suddenly the possibility of not returning to the fortification—ever—crashes into me. My throat gets tight and I need to take a few deep breaths to stop my head from spinning.

Think. Keep your head. Look around.

Beyond the tree I spot a broken branch, as though an animal has crashed through. Further on are more branches that look disturbed, but not recent. They aren't bleeding sap; they were broken long ago. I look off through the brush, following the swept-aside branches.

It's a path.

The grasses underfoot are tamped down by . . . footsteps?

But it can't be a trail. Gatherers and trappers don't come out this far anymore, haven't for years. Any trails made by the first or second generation would be long overgrown.

My heart races, but the little voice in my head slows me up. Could be an old trail, still used by animals. Deer? No. The branches are broken off too high for deer.

Looks as though a person's been through.

All right. Think.

The right thing to do would be to return and tell Council. They might send a group of armed Watchers to come explore.

But I can't. I'm out too far: it's Wayward, plain and simple. After last night, there's no telling what Brother Stockham might decide about me. I have to turn around right now and keep quiet, or risk it alone.

Takings in the daytime are rare.

I listen to the woods again. There's nothing but the tinkling of *les trembles* and the sparrow trill. But underneath it all the Lost People are calling to me, urging me forward.

I'll just follow it a little ways.

I start in, moving as quiet as I'm able. The path is slight; I have to look careful. But I'm creeping forward so slow my eyes start to blur on the path. I look up to rest them, scanning the woods beyond, when a tree ahead of me shifts.

I slow . . . Surely it was the breeze. The tree shifts again. I freeze.

That tree has a right human-like form.

I drop to a crouch behind a bush, my heart beating wild.

Did they see me?

There's a silence, so I rise on my haunches, risk a glance around the brush. The figure is dressed in dark clothes, a bison-skin cloak with hood, their back to me. Whoever it is stands still, glancing about.

I stay frozen, my breath caught.

Then the figure moves to turn and I duck once more. This withering cranberry bush is scarce cover; I pray my clothing blends in with the gray and brown. The damp smell of rot reaches my nose. The figure's head is turned to the ground, searching for something, the face hidden deep inside the hood.

When it turns in my direction, I pull further behind the bush. Silent, I shift to my knees, bow my head, and cower small as I can.

Twigs snap and the leaves rustle with footsteps—coming straight for my hiding place.

My heart! It's deafening, about to thump from my chest.

If they find me, I'm in a heap of trouble. Unless . . .

Unless it's not someone from our settlement.

Excitement shoots through my fear. It's not possible. How could they survive out here?

A thin fluting echoes through the forest. If it's a birdcall, it's no bird I know. It reminds me of the willow whistle some of the old men play. The rustling stops.

I pull my head up, slow, slow . . . and risk another look through the brush. I can't see proper, but the dark shape is about twenty strides from me now. They're turning away once more—this time in the direction of the sound that's trilling through the trees. They haven't seen me after all. My tongue works to free itself from the roof of my mouth to wet my lips.

My foot, crushed under my weight, hollers at me. I shift and rise ever so slight, to get a better view.

The figure is standing sideways to me, the head tilted in a listening way. Looking for something. The hood falls back. Pale skin, chin-length dark hair . . .

Brother Stockham.

No stranger at all. For half an addled moment I want to laugh—did I really think it wasn't one of us? But the next thought crashes in: what's he doing out this far?

The fluting sounds once more. He picks up his pace and disappears behind a jagged wall of trees. The whistle sounds again, softer, like it's retreating. And then the woods are silent.

I get to my feet. There's no way I can follow him through the brush quiet-like. My leg is singing with pain from climbing the ravine and crouching on it, and I'd be too slow without letting it drag.

I look to the sun. It's far across the sky to the west. It'll be dusk soon, and then dark. I should get back to the fort. Brother Stockham can move far faster than me, so he has more time to get back, once he's done whatever he's doing out here.

What could he be doing out here?

I give the trail one last glance, then I turn around and head back to the safety of the fortification. I'm back onto the Watch flats when I realize I traversed those woods without hardly thinking on it. I got back from the grove as though I'd been doing it all my life.

That night, my dreams are strange. I'm back on the trail and I'm trying to follow the path, but my feet are stuck to the forest floor. When I look down, I see they're not my own; the toes are perfect, the skin smooth. They're beautiful, but they don't work proper and I am frozen in place, unable to move forward or back. A hawk circles above me, slow.

And then snow swirls in and I can hear a keening on the wind. It's a wail, like the trees around me are calling and the sky is answering.

It's *La Prise* coming in, and I can't take shelter.

4

I WAKE FUZZY-HEADED FROM MY DREAMS AND still tired from my Watch shift two nights ago.

In the kitchen, Pa's real quiet again. His hair and scruffy beard need a trim and his shirt is rumpled. We eat in silence. I watch him scrape his bowl with his spoon, so careful. His hands have a slight tremor to them, like the constant shivering of *les trembles*. Never noticed that before. Those hands used to smooth my brow to sleep when I was young, but back then they were steady. Sure. They'd pull me close when I was scared or angry; when I'd had a nightmare, when an age-mate called me a bad name. They'd dance me around the kitchen to cheer me.

He'd sing to me. Listen to me. What's changed?

Is it that I've stopped talking?

"Pa, you ever go out past the first line of poplars?"

He looks up from his bowl, startled.

"When you trap, I mean." I fiddle with my spoon.

"What for?"

"Don't know," I say. "Better chance at getting animals?"

"There's lots of rabbit in the willows and the west snares are usually full." His brow creases. "What are you thinking on, Emmeline?"

His eyes are keen; he's interested in my answer. He hasn't looked on me this way for as long as I can remember. The words are burning my mouth, ready to burst forth: Brother Stockham out so far, that trail . . .

"Somebody been complaining about our gatherings?" The worry on his brow is back. No, not just worry—fear.

"No."

"You haven't been missing work at Soeur Manon's, have you?"

"No, Pa—"

"Because if people are talking about our contributions—"

"Pa! It's nothing like that!"

"So why are you asking?"

I swallow the words. "It's nothing. Just . . . never mind."

I grab our dishes and take them to the dish bucket, squeezing my eyes tight against the heavy feeling of tears as I scrub. What's changed isn't that I've stopped talking; it's that our Stain matters more than ever, and Pa doesn't trust I won't make it worse.

Course, mayhap he's right to worry.

I'm grateful to leave the kitchen to take our dishwater to the wastewater ditch. My shoulder is still stiff from Watch, and when I put the bucket on our stoop to get a better grasp, I'm caught just outside the door by Edith.

"Where going, Em?"

I gesture at my bucket.

"Sister Healer, after?"

I nod. "You stay here," I say, firm.

Edith's got this habit of chasing off after the nearest thing that takes her fancy. Usually it's harmless things—flying bugs or chickens or other children. It's only been a problem the once.

But once was enough.

It was two years ago and her ma, Sister Ann, was in charge of the gatherers bringing in the last of the garden harvests. The walls weren't fortified against the winter storms, though *La Prise* was heavy on the wind. When it's near, the underbelly of the air has an edge to it you recognize in your bones. It was there that day, but everyone had their heads to their tasks, trying desperate to get in the last of the stores before Affirmation started the next day. Two-year-old Edith was with the other youngsters in the garden corner near the south gates, close enough for the workers to keep an eye on. But she must've wandered away when Sister Ann's back was turned. Was twenty minutes or more before anyone noticed.

And then, so sudden, *La Prise* was howling around us in breath-stealing gusts of wind and snowflakes big as river stones. It came shrieking in over the walls, whipping our hair and cloaks about, blinding us.

Everyone gathered up the valuables and took cover, but Edith was nowhere. We searched for her, every corner of the fortification, but the snow was coming so furious it was hard to see two strides away. And when orders came to fortify the wall, to close the gates against the storm, Sister Ann was frantic.

I'd always known her as a virtues-upholding sort, but

I could see in her eyes that day she was thinking of defying Council by heading outside the gates. Her thin mouth was set in a line and her hands were shaking. It was awful, but watching Tom was worse. His face was so pale, eyes red-rimmed and wet. He knew his ma would have to risk punishment by death for a chance at finding Edith alive, and it was clear he didn't know who he could bear to lose.

And then a Watcher saved us all the anguish. While he was fortifying the south gates, he spotted Edith on the outside, cowering against a corner of the wall—near frozen in place.

Soeur Manon brought her round with healing broths, and in two days she was the same curious child we all knew. She was fine. Everything was fine. And there's no way she remembers it today; no way she remembers the terror and desperation.

But I remember.

And I don't mind when she wants to stand close and ask me about my day.

"Stay here," I say again. "I'll tell you about it after dinner."

A smile cracks her face wide. She nods and retreats inside.

I'm crossing toward the south quarter when I glimpse Kane, outside his quarters. He's helping a woman—his ma? —mend a barrel. His shirtsleeves are rolled back, and I can't help but stare a moment at his forearms. They're real strong, capable. I'm horrified to feel my heart race.

A small boy bangs out the door of their quarters—Kane's brother, I'm guessing. He sidles up to stand close and Kane smiles. It's not that funny smile he gave me at Talks; it's wide, certain. Then he gestures for the boy to hand him the rope on the ground, and when he glances over, he catches me looking. I duck my head, scowl at my bucket, and hurry off to the ditch.

Foolish.

I have to give my root sack to Soeur Manon half full. I can't figure if she thinks I left before finishing my chore yesterday or if she thinks there just aren't that many roots to be found, but she doesn't complain. She sends me for a few handfuls of the horsetail that grows around the flats. I scrub her hearth as she prepares a tea from the horsetail she says helps rid the body of *"trop de l'eau."* Then I take it to a family in the west quarter. When I'm done with my chores, I head to the riverbank to find Tom.

A Councilman—Brother Jameson—is standing outside Brother Stockham's quarters as I pass by. He's alone; no devout admirers cling to his cloak right now. Often he's standing in a crowd of followers waiting to hear him proclaim.

I swallow a spike of fear, set my jaw, and walk normal as I can. There are two dozen Councilmen, all men whose fathers before them were Council and, in some cases, their grandpas. There's a pecking order in the group, and Brother Jameson is at the top.

Council has usual duties like the rest of us, but not near so many. Most of their time is spent discussing settlement matters and hearing concerns. They impose order and enforce the law. They get the best rations and quarters, and they're called by their surnames as a show of respect.

It's not right to covet others' lots, but I know most people would trade their chores for a chance at being Council. No one tends to trade up to Watch, but if they could choose to be Council, they'd do it in a heartbeat.

I'd rather dig roots all day than be one of them. There's something right smug about the way they carry themselves. And Jameson eyeballs the rest of us like we're something to suffer—lost sheep that would use his rations and wander off cliffs if he wasn't here to set us straight. Always preaching on the virtues like we need the reminder.

He nods his jowly face at me, his ice-blue eyes unsmiling. I give a polite nod back, then duck my head and keep on. It takes an excruciating long time to get out the gates. I keep my eyes low until I'm halfway across the Watch flats.

I head to the river, the sun beating hot on my dark hair. Sandpipers are picking their way along the shallows. The cliffs on the far side of the river are buzzing with swallows swooping and diving from their nests in the banks. All these birds will be gone soon—fleeing *La Prise*. My eye traces the well-worn trail that heads diagonal up the bank to where the sheep are taken to graze in the day. They've pretty well eaten everything within safe traveling distance by this time of year, and we can't risk going further afield and grazing them out overnight, so there's no one up there right now, save mayhap a bison herd scout or two.

I glance at the tops of the cliffs, picturing the plains sweeping to the horizon in every direction. I've been up once to see, but I remember trembling along with the prairie grass. It was all unnatural large, unnatural empty.

Tom waves at me from the bank—he's got something in his hand.

"That a bone?" I get close.

He nods. "Bison," he says and hands it over. It's stained with dirt. I trace a finger along the smooth edge that ends in a sharpened point.

"Lost People."

He shrugs.

"This the only one?"

"Don't know. Just found it in the shale."

"Let's keep looking." I start down the bank, trying not to drag my bad foot, but when I don't hear him following me, I stop and look back.

Tom hooks his thumbs in his *ceinture*. "Where were you yesterday?"

We'd planned to meet at the river. We get a bit of free time almost every afternoon, and we always spend it together. I look at the bone, then scratch the point along my palm. "I forgot."

He steps past me, picks a stone from the shale and throws it at the river. "Doesn't answer the question."

I watch his face a moment. His head is tilted like he's thinking and his voice is mild, but his prairie-sky eyes are hard. Worried.

Two sets of eyes already today, worried about me, about what I'm up to. Couldn't tell my pa the truth, but Tom's different. Tom and I already share secrets.

"I—I was out in the woods."

His mouth pops open. "What? Why?"

"Don't know. Just . . ." I can't tell Tom about why. Can't tell him I was thinking it'd be better for my pa if I didn't come back; that it'd be better for him without a Wayward daughter to worry after. Tom wouldn't like that much, and

46

besides, I'm not sure I believe it now. I'm not so sure I wasn't being childish.

"I saw something out there." That isn't a lie.

"What?"

"A scrap of cloth."

Tom's eyebrows raise. "Lost People?"

"Don't know. But Tom, there was something else. A"—I look at the river as I say it—"a trail."

"A trail."

"In the woods."

He's quiet a moment. I look back at him. There's a flash of something in his eyes—something akin to longing. And then the worry clouds in. "You didn't follow it."

I rub my brow.

"Em?"

"Just a little ways."

"Almighty, Em! You were just on Watch for Waywardness. Why would you do that?"

"I don't know! It's . . ." I fumble for an explanation. "Sometimes I can't help myself."

Tom frowns. "That's not true, and you know it. You make a choice. There are things we can't help, but you chasing off into the woods isn't one of them."

I bite back a reply. I know what kinds of "things" he's speaking on. He's speaking on the secret he keeps: the thing that marks him Wayward without anyone but me knowing.

Soeur Manon calls them *ginup*, a First Peoples word for two-spirited: born with the medicines of both woman and man. Oftentimes a man will love another man, or a woman another woman. She told me when the people of the Old

Country arrived in the east, they imprisoned any of the First Peoples who were *ginup* the way they did their own people and forbade anyone to live that life. Nobody admits to being two-spirited; binding and producing children is a duty. And of course I keep Tom's secret. Soeur Manon doesn't know who I'm thinking of when I ask after it.

I know being *ginup* worries him. If Council knew . . . well, I'm not right sure what they'd do. Put him on more dangerous tasks than candle dipping, that's sure, hoping he'd end up in the Cleansing Waters, where all of our dead are cast. But would they send him to the Crossroads? He might be right that it's best to keep our heads down, but . . .

"But why would there be a trail there?"

"Could be an old trail that Council needs for something."

"Like what?"

Tom chews on his lip. "Guess I don't rightly know. But Em, whatever it is, it's none of our concern."

But Tom doesn't know how far into the woods I went. And if I want to tell him about Brother Stockham and how strange it was, I'll need to confess as much. I look him over. Oftentimes I wonder if he weren't already harboring a secret, he'd be less afraid of my wanderings, my daydreamings. He's keen to gather left-behinds and talk about them, sure, but telling him how bad I want to get back to that trail? It would only worry him sick.

Don't want that. He's the only person I ever feel truly easy around.

"All right," I say, taking the scarred hand that isn't holding the fishing line. "It's none of our concern."

He's quiet a moment. Then he gives me a smile, and squeezes my hand. "All right, then."

The river shimmers and dances—looks like a thousand trout flashing belly-up in the sun. Tom pulls a spool of gut line from inside his *ceinture*. He nods at the water. "Reckon we should fish?"

By the time we get back to our quarters, the river and Tom have put me back at ease. The sun was so hot he took off his moccasins, rolled up his leggings, and waded in. I took off my *ceinture* and rolled back my sleeves—wishing all the while I could take off my moccasins too. My bad foot could've used the cool, but then Tom would've had to see it.

Even so, it was real nice, sitting in the sun while Tom caught nothing.

I'm retying my belt and he's carrying his moccasins when his ma—Sister Ann—greets us outside their quarters door. She gives his bare feet a long look, then tosses her head in the direction of the sheep barns. "Your pa needs help with the feeding."

He nods and goes past her. I'm about to head to our door, but she stops me with a hand on my shoulder. Her gray eyes are serious. "Em, a moment." Edith appears behind her, looking eager. "Go inside," she says gentle.

Edith disappears, and Sister Ann closes the door and leads us away from the step.

Tom's ma knows the goings-on of our quarters. If Soeur Manon has nothing for me to do I come to her for chores. She's a force to be reckoned with, and the voice of command in Tom's family. She's been kind to me and my pa over the years, but she doesn't talk much to me. I can't figure what she might want to speak on now.

"Roll down your sleeves." Her tone isn't unkind, but I hurry to pull them over my forearms, embarrassed. She looks me over, her tight bun pulling at the sides of her thin face. "Emmeline, your sixteenth life day is in a few days."

I nod.

"And you will be eligible."

I force a nod again. Of binding age, she means. I'm meant to find a life mate within two years of my sixteenth life day. We don't bind young. That has to do with healthy birthings: young mothers are more prone to troubles in childbearing, and motherless children—like me—are a burden. We also don't bind old, for the same reason.

"And menfolk will start asking after you. Your pa will have some decisions."

I raise my eyebrows. What eligible man would want me for a life mate? I'm Stained for one, and then there's my foot. I look down at it, wriggling the gnarled toes.

She clasps her hands together. "I need to tell you that"— she pauses and takes a deep breath—"that you need to be careful. Of your mouth."

My head shoots up. "Beg pardon?"

"Your mouth," she says. "Menfolk find it . . ." She clears her throat. "Your smile. Men find it . . . attractive."

"But . . ." I still can't figure what she means; I don't often smile. I put a hand to my mouth and trace a finger along my bottom lip.

She looks at me serious-like. "You can't be bandying

about with your sleeves up. You aren't a child anymore. You need to watch who you're smiling at. Try not to draw too many eyes."

I stare at her. Since when do men notice my smile? Since when am I drawing their eyes? She must take my bewilderment for doubt because she crosses her arms and sets her jaw. "Emmeline, men's attentions are not helpful. Not for you, not for the settlement."

I know this. Women are modest and men are respectful. Both families agree upon bindings—not just the life mates—and unbound relations are forbidden. Disease, jealousy that leads to unrest: these things follow unbound relations. I just can't figure how Tom's ma thinks I could be in danger of that.

I look at my foot again, trace a finger over my lip. Mayhap Kane talked to me the other night because of my smile.

"Mind yourself," she says, breaking into my thoughts.

I look at her, see her hard eyes. And then I know.

My grandma'am. That's why she thinks I'm in danger.

"I will."

She nods, curt. "Heard the birth bell some time ago. You'll be needed at Soeur Manon's to help clean up." She turns and disappears into our quarters.

I touch my lips once more, then head for the Healing House.

5

THERE IS BLOOD EVERYWHERE. THE KITCHEN IS lit with tall candles, and splashes of crimson streak everything like long, dark shadows: the washbasin, the table, the bedclothes, Soeur Manon's arms up to her elbows. The woman on the bed in the corner is breathing loud; short and shallow. Her head is visible amidst the mound of bison skins and her face is unnatural white.

I throw my root satchel to the floor and cross through the dim space. The woman is the one I was standing near during Virtue Talks the other night.

Soeur Manon grabs up a small bundle of cloth and turns to me.

"*Il est allé à Dieu.*" She passes the bundle into my hands and I have to steel myself not to drop this thing that "went to the Almighty." My skin crawls away from the cold weight of the lifeless little body.

I've cleaned up birthings before, and birthings go wrong

as often as they go right, but I've never gotten used to the stillborns. I always expect the bundle to be warm and writhing.

"It come too soon," Soeur Manon says, wiping her hands with a cloth.

The woman on the bed moans, and I turn quick and bang out the door, taking in deep swallows of the fresh air outside.

Passing through the east gates, I make my way back to the river, heading north—downstream—to the Cleansing Waters. It's where we dispose of things we shouldn't bury on account of wild animals. Or worse.

During *La Prise,* when we're shut inside the fortification, we have to store anyone who passes on in the Hold, a tiny building with thin walls in the west corner. It keeps them frozen for the winter in a place that isn't life or rest. At first Thaw, Council is quick to get a hole chopped in the thinning river ice so they can be at peace. All our dead go to the Cleansing Waters—everyone but the Waywards.

I follow a curve in the bank and walk until the river gets narrow. The banks are steep here, and ahead two large boulders on either side of the river create a gate for a space no wider than three men lying head to toe. The water pushes through in a fierce rush; there are no eddies here to catch things and bring them back to shore.

The cold bundle feels like it's branding my fingers. I step as close to the edge as I dare, swing my arms, and cast it into the water. It plunges below the surface and bobs back up with a violent jerk, and for a heartbeat I'm terrified the cloth will come undone.

But then the river has it, grabbing it in a swirling torrent, rushing it past the boulders and carrying it off around the bend.

I'm standing there, muttering a plea to the Almighty to deliver that bundle to eternal peace, when a shadow falls on the bank beside me.

"Sister Emmeline, our sorrows are deep." Brother Stockham's voice rings out over the churning water.

I turn real slow. "Brother Stockham." I put a hand across my chest in the Peace of the Almighty, but my insides are jittering beetles. The bundle I threw downstream disappears from my thoughts; all that remains is the trail in the woods. Did he see me out there after all?

I risk a look at his face, but it's calm as he gazes past me, along the banks. Doesn't much seem he's here about my Waywardness.

"How many babies this summer?"

It takes me a moment to figure he's asking me how many birthings went wrong. I blink. I know his ma died in childbirth with him, just like my ma with the boy baby; is he asking because he's thinking on it?

"Mayhap four?" I'm not around for every birthing, but it seems there were a lot of stillborns these past months.

He clucks his tongue, and I can't help but stare at his face a moment; his jaw is strong and his cheekbones are high. He's good-looking, that's certain. And yet . . .

"Almighty, grant them peace . . ."

I finish his brief homily as I should: "This we pray."

His gaze swings toward me. "Don't you think it's unfortunate that all we can do is pray?"

"Beg pardon?"

"Don't you think it would be better if we could do something more than pray for these small souls?"

The river roars in my ears. Or mayhap it's my heart. I look at him careful; he's leaning forward, his head tilted at me. He's interested in my reply.

"Like somehow saving them before they're born still?" My voice is small.

"Indeed." He looks at me until I drop my head. I watch out the corner of my eye as he spreads his arms and gestures to the river and the willows that line the bank. "Sister Emmeline, our world is small. But the world around us is very large."

My brow furrows at this. Our ancestors made a long journey from the east to settle here, I know. Weeks—months, mayhap—crossing those lonely prairies. And the Old World beyond the east is further still, across vast waters. Pa told me so, and I've seen the ships in Soeur Manon's books. But the world around us is dangerous: the few people who ventured back east or further west never returned. We might even be the last ones left. What difference does it make if it's large?

"In our world, which would you say is the most important of the virtues?"

My thoughts dissolve as my stomach clenches. I broke my Honesty virtue twice since we've spoken last. He doesn't know that, though. Does he? "Well, I don't suppose Honesty or Bravery would've saved that baby."

He bows his head and rubs a hand over his jaw, and my stomach seizes again. Then he looks up and smiles. "A good answer."

I smile back in relief.

"Our survival lies in Honesty and Bravery. But our salvation lies in Discovery."

I swallow my smile, thinking about that scrap of cloth in the woods. What I did was Wayward, plain and simple. Going back there would be worse. Wouldn't it?

He studies my face, his thumb tracing his jaw. There's that sizing-up look in his eyes again. And something more. I twist my foot deliberate and feel a burst of fire.

"My grandfather wanted salvation."

I blink. Did I just hear him right?

"At the end of it all, he thought salvation mattered most. My father, though, always chose survival." He looks at the tear-stained cliffs. "But salvation and survival can be at odds, don't you think?"

I don't know what I think. Can't figure why we're talking at all. Brother Stockham has scarce said any more than a greeting to me in passing, yet here we stand, jawing like we're equals. For years I've felt his eyes on me with the rest of Council: watching me suspicious-like, finding me wanting. I've tried my best to stay out from under their gaze. Course, lately that hasn't gone so well.

Salvation and survival can be at odds.

I don't know what to say. But then I see he's not much waiting for an answer. He's gazing at the river now, his eyes lost in the currents.

"They were both strong leaders. They kept order, ensured the settlement's safety and survival. But they were not without their faults. No one is. Our ancestors made mistakes—you know this better than anyone."

A flush blooms on my neck. He's talking about my grand-ma'am. I carry the shame of her execution. But I'm not just Stained with her actions; I'm Wayward in my own right.

"But you are not the only one who lives with a family burden," he says soft.

I shift onto my bad foot and wash it in pain, focus on that.

"And there are ways to overcome."

An osprey circles high along the banks. The prey bird turns to the river, making its body into a tight line, and plunges. It hits the water with a slap but is back out in a heartbeat, carrying a fish in its talons and moving hard for the trees, its giant wings steady and sure.

We watch it go, and then Brother Stockham's eyes snap toward me. "Apologies, Sister Emmeline." He scrubs a hand over his face and smiles. "I'm feeling reflective today."

I shift off my bad foot.

"The river has that effect on me," he says. "It's hard to explain." Then he looks to me and I'm thrown, because he looks . . . uncertain.

I nod, flustered. "I like to come out here and think."

"I've noticed."

My heart skips and fear must register on my face because he continues, "There's no harm in thinking. On the contrary, I find it . . . appealing."

My heart skips again, straight into my throat. Does he mean thinking is appealing or *people* who think are appeal-ing? And why has he *noticed* me? I swallow hard.

He looks back to the rushing waters. "This river is so beautiful, but so deadly. It gives life and it takes life, but it never needs to deliberate on any of that—it only *is*." He frowns. "Would that meting reward and punishment was that easy."

He's talking about leading the settlement. Unthinking, I speak again. "You have tough choices." I recoil under his sharp glance. "Con-concerning people's well-being, I mean."

What am I saying? He's been learning to lead the community since he was a youngster—been leading it without his father's hand for five years now—surely he doesn't need my childish assurances.

He steps toward me, so close I can smell the bergamot soap on his skin, and places his hand on my arm. I fight the urge to recoil—I'm not used to being touched so casual. And certainly not by the leader.

"About Watch the other night," he begins.

Bleed it! Did Frère Andre tell him about me keeping his "secret" after all?

"I wanted you to know that I'm sorry about that. You know that I couldn't make an exception for your punishment, however much I wanted to. Settlement rules."

An exception? However much he *wanted* to? My thoughts are a mishmash of relief and confusion.

"Course," I stammer.

"I hope you can forgive me for my heavy hand."

My throat and mouth feel dry. "Nothing to forgive, Brother Stockham."

"Yes, well. I regret it all the same." He watches me real careful.

I stare back, the river roaring in my ears. Now I know I wasn't imagining that look in his eyes after Virtue Talks the other night. That tender look is back, but it's guarded. Like he's not sure he should be looking on me this way. Almighty! I need out of here before the air between us snaps in half.

"I should . . ." I look behind him toward the fortification.

"Of course," he says, removing his hand from my arm. "Dusk comes." He makes a sweeping gesture and stands aside.

I make sure not to brush against him as I go past, but as I make my way along the bank, the ghost of his hand burns into my arm. I don't want to think about the way he was looking at me, don't want to think about him finding me appealing.

It makes no sense, anyhow. After near ten years of being binding age, he'd never gaze about for a life mate and settle his eyes on the Stained cripple.

And yet . . . he seemed so sincere, talking about the river. Mayhap, for whatever reason, he thinks I'm someone he can speak plain with.

Our salvation lies in Discovery.

I think about him heading off through the trees. Could be Brother Stockham and me are more alike that I figured. Could be he was giving me permission to think, to wonder. Could be he was giving me permission to Discover.

But his talk about the past, about overcoming our family burdens, sets my skin to crawling. He was talking about my grandma'am, about me needing to be better than her, to not make her same mistakes.

All at once I want as much distance between him and me as possible. I pick up my pace and push hard for the fortification, my secret heart squeezed tight, like that fish in the osprey's claws.

6

THE REST OF THE WEEK I'M BUSY HELPING SOEUR Manon inside the Healing House and don't get back into the trees once. I dream about them every night, though: my perfect feet frozen in place, the woods silent and dark until the winds of *La Prise* sweep in and steal my breath.

The good thing about being so busy is that I don't do anything Wayward, and over the week my pa's spine straightens. That cloud of worry on his brow loses its thunderhead shape.

Friday is my sixteenth life day, and he trades some of our egg ration for a small life day cake from the Kitchens head, Sister Lucy. After early dinner, I sit at the table as Pa puts out the cake clumsy-like. His hands are trembling something fierce. Is he nervous?

I take a large bite. It's full of honey and saskatoon berries.

"You like it?" Pa asks from across the table.

"It's real good." I take another bite.

He smiles, and I feel a pang. Don't see that smile much.

"Thanks, Pa."

He smiles wider. Reminds me of when he used to smile at me when I was small and would tell him about something ordinary that I thought was special: the color of a caterpillar or some such.

"Finish up quick," he says. "Don't want to be late for the Harvest ceremony."

The memory dissolves. The Harvest ceremony marks the end of the growing-and-gathering season and is a break from our preparations for *La Prise*. There's music and dancing, and people mingle to jaw about nothing. It goes from early evening until dark falls. We're all meant to be inside by the time Watch takes their shift.

"You'll be dancing this year, I suppose?"

I don't answer, just chew more furious.

"Em?"

I swallow hard. Pa means I'll be dancing with *menfolk*. Harvest is a chance for eligible men and women to declare intentions. And then I understand why he's nervous.

Mind yourself. Sister Ann's words ring bright in my ears.

When I was a youngster, my ma and pa would dance me around our kitchen on their feet, humming songs I didn't know. I haven't danced at Harvest since my foot was crushed, but I can swallow the ache and dance. It's not my foot that'll stop me; I can dance well enough.

It's obvious Pa's worried about who I might be dancing with.

But I've got a plan for this, have for years. Tom and I talk about pretending to court one another—our families would think it natural and we wouldn't have to bind for another year, since Tom's fifteen. Living with Tom wouldn't be so bad. He'll never be allowed to love who he loves, and the chances of me being asked by someone I'd want . . .

I think of Kane; the look of shock on his face. And then I think of his perfect shaved head, his strong forearms.

My face flames. I put the last chunk of cake in my mouth. It feels dry as dust.

"Finish up"—Pa reaches over to pat my hand—"my girl."

When we enter the hall, the music is loud and lively, the dance floor awash with swirling skirts and twirling limbs. Groups of people laugh and talk, holding cups of saskatoon wine, a rare treat saved for Harvest. I count at least ten Councilmen. It skitters me, them mixing in and jawing on with the rest. Always feels they're waiting for us—for me— to slip up.

No one else seems to think on Council like I do, though— not even the sons of that Thibault couple. They were too young to understand what their parents had done wrong that winter, but they're Stained, everyone knows it. It's just . . . well, they're big, burly boys and in charge of the woodsheds. They're important.

And they don't seem prone to being Wayward like I am.

The air in the hall is plain summery next to the autumn evening outside. I'm wearing my ma's old dress—a real dress, not the leather leggings and long belted shirts every- one wears—with a tucked waist and puffy skirt. Not every woman has a dress, and I suppose I should be thankful I have my ma's old one. It's a dark river-stone color and near matches my hair, but the cloth is rougher than my bison- skin leggings and the waist makes my breath feel tight.

Macy Davies's copper hair is flashing on the dance floor. I look around the crowd for Tom.

I find Kane instead, standing in a group of age-mates. He's sideways to me and I can't help but study him a moment. I can see the First Peoples in his blood by the arch of his nose and curve of his brow. His shirt is a soft tan and fits him perfect. The twin boys beside him are from the south quarter; they haul water and feed to the sheep barns. The two girls in the group are unfamiliar, though their white skin tells me they work indoors. Must be from the west: the Shearing and Textiles quarter. They're all holding cups of wine and look easy with one another.

The blond girl standing beside Kane is talking to the group, but something about the way she holds herself tells me she's speaking mostly to Kane. His head tips forward like he's listening careful-like. I wonder what she could be telling him that would be interesting at all. That she carded a particular troublesome piece of wool today? But then she says something that makes him throw back his head and laugh and my stomach dives.

He takes a sip from his cup and turns, dark eyes searching the crowd. Before he can see me watching, I duck my head and hurry after my pa into a far corner of the hall.

"Wait here, Em." My pa disappears, leaving me with a group of east-quarter women who nod at me, their lips pressed tight.

I turn and stare at the dance floor, making sure I don't look for Kane again. The dancers twirl past in a flurry of quick steps. Everyone looks happy, like they've forgotten *La Prise* is only a month away. Does dancing do that to a person?

"Thought you'd want your first cup of saskatoon wine." Pa appears at my side, presenting the cup, shy and pleased. As I take it in my hand, all it reminds me of is my eligibility, how I'm supposed to be dancing.

I dip my nose toward the wine and breathe in. It smells so strange; berries and smoke and spice. When I take a large drink, it fills my lungs with a sweetness that burns. I cough and cough again, trying to clear my throat. Thanks be, the music is loud, and Pa is distracted by a group of trappers gathering in the corner.

My chest relaxes and the burning subsides. The taste lingering on my tongue is . . . actually, it's real nice. I try it again, just a little this time, and manage to keep from coughing. An unfamiliar warmth spreads in my chest where the tightness used to be.

"Good Harvest, Pa." I raise my glass.

"Good Harvest, Em," he says and heads off to the corner. I don't know if the men there are his friends. I don't want to know, and I turn away before I see what happens—whether they look at him with disdain or welcome him in.

I come face-to-face with Macy.

"Good Harvest, Em," she says. "Excited?" Macy is fifteen, but I know she's counting the days until her sixteenth life day. She wouldn't speak on it to me, but something in my gut tells me Macy is aching for a life mate . . . mayhap aching for children. She won't have to wait long. Macy looks like an angel from Soeur Manon's books: she has a dainty bow mouth and her hair always shines. As a daughter of a Councilman, she also manages to keep weight on her, which gives her a nice curvy look.

When I don't reply, she looks at me doe-eyed. "About your eligibility, I mean."

"I knew what you meant," I say. I take another drink.

"Oh." She looks at my foot. "I suppose you won't be dancing."

I bristle. A moment before I was loath to dance, but suddenly I want to. I want to show Macy I'm not going to be the one eligible girl here who has to stand in the crowd and watch.

And then, Almighty answering my silent prayer, a voice says in my ear, "Good Harvest, Em. Care to dance?"

I turn. Tom's straw-blond hair falls over one eye and he's wearing a shirt that is a mite too big—one of his father's good shirts, likely. My rescuer. He knows I'm meant to be dancing; I wonder if he overheard Macy and is giving me an opportunity to set her straight.

"Sure," I say.

His little sister, Edith, peers at me from behind him. She's got that look on her face: childish admiration.

Tom looks down. "Just have to keep an eye on her; found her 'making soup.'"

Edith's face falls. I raise my eyebrows.

"She was trying to put an acorn in someone's wine," Tom explains.

Edith's round eyes weigh my reaction to this. I can't help but smile.

She grins back in relief. "Pretty dress, Emmy."

I reach for her with my free hand. "Little mouse." I pull her toward me, lifting her arm and circling it so she spins in a clumsy circle and collapses into my legs. She giggles. I feel

Macy's eyes branding my skin through the back of my dress.

I down the rest of my wine, turn, and hand Macy my cup. She takes it, wide-eyed. I spin back to Tom. "Can you manage two girls?" I nod at Edith. Her eyes widen in delight.

"I'll do my best," he says, and whisks us onto the dance floor.

By the time we're finished, my cheeks hurt from laughing. I don't know what's wrong with me; I don't often laugh. But my head feels light and everything seems brighter, happier. I spin off the floor and Tom follows, carrying Edith on his hip.

Macy is waiting. "Good Harvest, Tom."

"Good Harvest, Macy," Tom returns her greeting. "Emmeline, save me another dance? I need to go find Ma." He tilts his head toward Edith.

I nod, my cheeks flushed. "Good dancing, mouse," I say to Edith.

They leave and Macy leans close to me. "I'm sorry. About what I said, I mean. You looked real good out there."

"It's fine, Macy," I say. I don't want her to talk about my foot. I don't want her to talk at all. I want to dance again.

"Was that a special dance?" Macy's eyes are bright.

"With Tom? We're quarter-mates."

"Oh," she says, her face dropping. Her eyes get bright again. "I danced with someone special. Henri Chavel from the north quarter." She sighs. "He has the *strongest* arms."

I frown. I'm not in the habit of noticing boys' arms, or whether they're strong or not. Especially boys from other quarters.

Except Kane.

And like that, he's back in my thoughts. I silence the little voice in my head and try to focus on Macy's chattering. Now she's telling me something about wanting to walk the riverbank with Henri. I have a hard time following because I keep fighting the urge to turn around and look through the crowd. It's plain addled: why should I care where Kane is and who he's dancing with?

The frenzied music slows then, becoming a waltz, and Macy pauses midchatter, her eyes wide. "The Choosing Song," she says. "I need to make sure Henri asks me!" She disappears.

The Choosing Song. Eligible young men are meant to ask eligible women to dance, though lots of people join in— fathers and daughters, bound couples. The song is so nice, it's hard to resist. Macy's eyeing up her prospects for when she's eligible next year. Her family will have to agree to the binding, though, so I can't quite figure what she thinks she's doing. Besides, it's just a song.

That pestering little voice wonders if I'd think that if Kane asked me to dance. And then I feel a hand on my shoulder.

I turn, cheeks flushing with the thought of being close to him again, and draw up short. It's not Kane. Panic seizes me as I stare into his gray eyes; has he come to discuss my Waywardness with my pa?

Brother Stockham offers his hand. He's in his Harvest finery, a shock white shirt and dark vest.

The light feeling in my head disappears. I throw a quick look behind me to make sure I'm not mistaking his intent. There's no one there but a group of older women who are all bound. They sneak glances at me from low-cast eyes.

I swallow my confusion and turn back. "Good Harvest,

Brother Stockham." I clear my throat. "I'm not much of a dancer."

"That's not true." His hand stays extended. "I saw you just moments ago."

Bleed it! Why did I have to dance with Tom? And why does he want to dance with me? The other day at the river flashes through my head.

He's waiting. I can't do much else but curtsy and let him lead me into the circle of dancers.

When we turn to face one another to begin the Choosing Dance steps, my stomach knots. I step hard on my foot, let the pain swamp my fear. We reach forward to clasp hands, and Brother Stockham holds my gaze and brings my hand to his lips. It's part of the dance, just one of the steps, but the way he is looking on me . . .

On the contrary, I find it . . . appealing.

His hair falls forward and brushes my knuckles. I scramble for a distraction. I pretend to catch someone's eye in the crowd and smile. Then I remember what Sister Ann said about my mouth and I drop the smile. My mind spins.

Brother Stockham pulls me toward him and we are whirling around the circle with the other couples. His left hand holds the small of my back tight and he guides me sure, unafraid of a misstep.

My heart is beating double time, all out of rhythm with the willow flutes and drum, but my steps follow along sure enough. My foot is hot, a pain that spreads up my leg and meets his fiery hand. He is dancing without pause, but he's not watching for other couples at all; I can feel his eyes on my face.

My room watching is getting impolite, has gone far beyond being modest. I glance up. "I didn't know you danced, Brother Stockham."

"On occasion."

"You dance real well."

The hand on my back tightens as he turns me around the outer edge of the circle. Halfway through the turn he presses me close and leans in, his mouth close to my jaw. "As do you." I expect us to break apart as the turn ends, but he keeps me close. "And now I suspect you do many things well."

I flush and miss a step, causing him to lose his grip. As I reclaim my distance, the corner of his full mouth pulls up.

"I enjoyed our talk the other day, Sister Emmeline," he says.

I swallow hard. "At the river?"

He nods. "It was refreshing. I . . . appreciated your point of view."

I don't remember having one. But the image of him out in the trees swims before my eyes. *Our salvation lies in Discovery*. Should I ask him? If I'm wrong . . .

"Brother Stockham, what you said that day . . . about Discovery."

His hand tightens on my back.

"What did you mean about it being our salvation?"

He takes a moment to answer. "Our virtues will always be the path to the settlement's prosperity."

"But you said the most important of the virtues was Discovery. The other day, you said that."

He pulls me closer. "Might we discuss this later?"

But the words are coming and I can't stop them. "You

always say our virtues ensure our survival. Council always says that. But how far should we go to prove our Discovery virtue? I mean, our borders, the woods"—I'm near babbling now—"you said the world around us is large. But how do we know just how large it is? And if our salvation lies in Discovery, shouldn't we want to find out?"

He looks at me sharp. "What are you asking?"

I picture him out in those woods. Take a breath. "Do you think exploring the woods could help prove your Discovery virtue?"

For the first time since we started the dance he breaks my gaze, casting a look about the room, smiling. Then he draws me close. "I don't go to the woods." His words are moth wings whispering in my ear.

I pull back and it's out of my mouth before I think: "Never said you did."

The smile vanishes.

Before I can think of anything to say, the song ends and couples break apart to clap and regroup. Brother Stockham takes me by the forearms and steps back but doesn't let go.

"Thank you." My voice is too high. Everyone watching the dance is looking at us, I can feel it.

He holds my gaze longer than he ought and I am frozen in his sharp eyes. Then he bows his head and the spell breaks. His hand brands my back once more as he takes me off the dance floor.

My pa is standing there looking pleased. The women beside him pretend to look on without interest, but their eyes are shiny.

Brother Stockham's gaze sweeps the group. "Good Harvest," he says. There is a murmur of polite response from the women, and a few raised cups.

"Brother Samuel." He offers my pa the Peace, and Pa does the same. "I hope it's all right to dance with your daughter? I should have asked beforehand, but you were nowhere to be found."

"Course, Brother Stockham," Pa says. His face is flushed.

No. I can't dance with him again. Can't have him looking at me that way—

"I thought you and I might dance, Pa," I say. "I would love a dance with you."

A shadow flicks across his eyes. "Em, you know I don't dance anymore."

"Well, then, Sister Emmeline"—Brother Stockham extends his hand once more—"it looks as though you are all mine."

The women titter again and I look at the outstretched fingers, my thoughts going every which way.

Brother Jameson appears from the crowd. He sweeps over to us in a large dark cloak and takes Brother Stockham's arm, pulling him out of earshot.

The music continues gaily, the dancers wash past, but it feels garish, all muddled. My ears ring with a silent bell as I watch the hazy scene.

Brother Jameson departs and Brother Stockham takes a step forward. "Apologies, Sisters"—he smiles—"there is a matter to which I must attend." He nods to me. "Emmeline."

It's all I can do to nod back. *Emmeline.* Not Sister Emmeline. Just Emmeline.

As soon as he is gone I want to disappear. I can't take everyone's eyes on me. I can take them for my Stain, but not for this. I pretend my foot hurts too much. "From the dancing," I explain to my pa. I ignore the disappointment in his eyes and scramble toward the doors, pushing through the crowd.

Kane stands near the dance floor with his arms folded across his chest. As I pass by I think, for one foolish heartbeat, that he's going to stop me, but then the blond girl appears at his elbow. I turn and brush through the bodies, clawing for the chill air outside.

It's dusk; the courtyard is washed with gray light. I think about the sunset the other night and I'm tempted to climb up and watch for it again, lose myself in its colors. I shouldn't do anything that could draw Brother Stockham's eyes, though, so I just head back to our quarters.

In my room I fumble under my bed for my favorite left-behind: a little clay four-legged animal that fits in my palm. I run my fingers over its surface, so perfect despite being buried in the shale for who knows how long. I try to lose myself in its mystery, but my thoughts won't stop going back to the hall.

Why was Brother Stockham lying about the woods? Why does he look at me like that—like he knows something about me I don't? Some secret part of me feels stripped bare, like a birch with the bark torn free.

I thought it was Kane's hand on my shoulder. I was hoping it was. Why would I want him to ask me to dance? I think about that smile he gave his brother as I passed by the other day. Think about him standing there, all easy with his agemates.

I close my eyes and grip the figure tight. I stay like that

a long while. I'm about to bank the fire and change into my nightdress when I hear a low pealing sound.

It's gaining in strength, ringing out across the courtyard, through the rawhide windows of our quarters.

It's the alarm bell.

We're under attack.

7

OUTSIDE IS A MASS OF PANIC. EVERYONE MUST'VE been headed back to their quarters after the dance, because the courtyard is full of people grabbing up any valuables still lying about—buckets, shovels, children. The sheep in the barns are bleating wild and there are shouts all around us.

"*Le malmaci!*"

"Hurry!"

"*À la salle sacrée!*"

I join the crowd scrambling back toward the ceremonial hall. It's the stronghold, the place we are meant to gather if the fortification is breached by the *malmaci*.

But it's never happened before.

I crane my neck, searching for my pa, but it's impossible to make out faces in the shadows. Only two burn baskets glow in the courtyard; the Watchers were obviously interrupted on their way to the walls. I pull my leg along. Bodies press against me on all sides, push ahead.

I'm one of the last to reach the hall. Andre stands at the doors, beckoning us in. *"Vite!"*

We press forward into the warmth and light. The gate-keepers call a loud warning once the last of us has siphoned through and begin to slide the massive wooden doors closed. The crowd murmurs in hushed tones, exclamations of fearful wonderment. I search the crowd again for my pa. But then, above the din, I hear a small voice crying out.

"Emmy!" It's far away, scared. And it's coming from beyond the hall doors.

I push to the front. A tiny form is cowering out beside the weapons shack. I am shot through with fear. Edith. Why is she alone? Where's Sister Ann?

I brush past Andre, putting a hand against one of the heavy doors. I have to go to her.

"Non!" Andre cries. *"Laissez-la!"*

I whirl back toward him. He shakes his head—a warning. But then he's distracted by a clamoring in the crowd. A bunch of people are in the center of the hall—Jameson's followers, no doubt—hollering about the Almighty's vengeance. Everyone turns toward the ruckus as Andre wades into the fray.

I look back to Edith's little form, half-lit by a nearby burn basket. I can't leave her, even though it's against settlement rules. If we come under attack, stragglers are meant to be left behind so as not to risk the entire settlement. I don't think another thought. I duck under the man beside me, slip through and break into a full limping run, feeling the doors close behind me, knowing I just left the last safe place in the fortification.

Edith and I won't stand a chance.

The doors bang shut. Bolts scream into place. My throat tightens at the sound, but I keep running.

When I reach the weapons shack, someone catches up to me. I glance back and see him pull up, casting a frantic look around the courtyard. My fear stalls a moment in confusion.

Kane. Where did he come from?

I grab Edith to me, feeling a wash of relief when her wet face presses into my shirt. I look back at the hall. The doors are bolted shut, our safety trapped inside.

"Over here!" Kane's just a form in the dark, beckoning toward the well.

I push Edith ahead of me as we scramble across the yard.

"In," he orders, pulling aside the wooden trap. "Climb as far as you can and hang on to the ladder."

"Edith can't climb."

"I know." He scoops her up and swings her around so that she clings to his back. He looks at me. I go. Down into the pitch-black space. The well is half empty, so I climb about fifteen feet down, until my feet get wet. Can the *malmaci* climb ladders? I want to be as far from the opening as I can, but going into the water is dangerous in this cold.

Kane climbs after me, sliding the trap back into place as best he can. I swing to the side to let him onto my ladder rung. Edith is clamped onto his back, shaking.

I'm not sure how long he can stay on the ladder, balanced that way. I'm also not sure if Edith could handle the slippery rungs, so I do the only thing I can: wrap one arm around both of them, and grasp the ladder on the other side. I press in, trying to give Edith my warmth.

We wait.

My heart thuds in my ears. Our breathing is ragged. The earth above us is quiet. No footfall, no noise.

We wait like that, locked together, trying to quiet our breath.

Why is Kane here? Did he see me running after Edith and come for us? I try to recall when he appeared at my side. He must've been outside the hall already.

But if that's true, he probably saw me leave. He knows what I did.

I close my eyes, try to calm my whirling thoughts. Need to keep my head. All that matters is that we survive this.

I count fifty of my rapid heartbeats. Do it again. And again. By the fourth time, it's slowing.

I feel Kane shift. My foot is on fire and the pain is spreading into my hip. I release my pins-and-needles arm and let him swing Edith to his hip between us. He switches hands on the ladder rung, steadies Edith with his elbow, unfolds his right arm, and pulls me close.

I suck into him like a moth to a candle flame. Never been this close to a boy before. Any other time I might feel nervous, but right now, with his arm so strong and sure around me, I'm so glad, so very glad, for him. Doubt I'd have thought of the well. And even if I had, there's no way I could hold Edith down here for this long. We huddle in silence.

And then, Edith begins to whimper. Soft at first, but I know her all-out-hissy oncoming when I hear it.

"Shh," I whisper, wracking my brains for something to calm her. "You want a song?"

She nods and whimpers again.

I put my mouth close to her ear and sing my mother's song:

Sleep, little one, with your secret heart,
Take to the night like the swallow.
When morning time brings what your secret heart sings,
Set your feet to the same path and follow.

She stops whimpering, one finger in the corner of her mouth. I keep whisper-singing, fearful her sudden quiet is the calm before the storm and unwilling to take the chance.

Edith's breathing slows. She's been so worked up she's fallen asleep. I draw my head back and look at Kane but can't make out his face clear and realize he can't see mine, neither.

Part of me is relieved. I don't want him to see the desperate gratitude in my eyes. I don't know how to repay him.

I press close again, rest my forehead on the rung of the ladder and let him tighten his grip.

It's quiet above and I fight the urge to doze. Almighty knows I need all of my wits about me to stay on this ladder. It's clear Kane is strong, but keeping hold of both Edith and me would be too much for anyone.

It's impossible to know how long we've been hiding here. I feel I'm about to lose my senses and fall backward into the water or scream the place down from plain aggravation when a slight scraping sound echoes.

And then the trap is ripped aside and light from a torch streams in from above.

A face looms down at us. "Almighty's grace!" It's Macy's

pa—Brother Davies. "We thought you were lost to us! What are you— How did you . . . ?"

Kane shifts a groggy Edith to his back and begins to climb. I follow, my legs shaking. We clamber out, squinting against the torch Brother Davies waves before him, checking us over.

Kane places Edith on the ground beside me and steps a respectable distance away.

Brother Davies flaps about. "Almighty's grace!" he says again.

I stare at Kane in the torchlight. His eyes are unreadable. He has his arms crossed over his chest like he's challenging me. I stand crooked, favoring my bad foot. We measure one another.

And then Brother Stockham arrives, striding over to us in a wash of black cloak.

Brother Davies shakes his head in disbelief. "By His grace alone."

"What happened here?" Brother Stockham demands.

It snaps Brother Davies to. "When we did the head count, these three were missing. We feared them Taken."

"Thank you, Brother Davies, you may go." Brother Stockham doesn't glance at the Councilman, who bows his head and disappears.

Brother Stockham turns to me. "What happened, Emmeline?"

My tongue works in my dry mouth. This is a Wayward act, clear and simple. And worse for Kane if he came after me; he's more valuable than a crippled girl.

Did Kane come after me?

My mind clicks over the last moments before the doors

shut. Who saw me leave the hall? Jameson's followers were creating that ruckus. Could it be everyone was distracted, too panicked, to notice me leave? They had to do the head count before they knew we were missing . . .

"We didn't make it before the hall was fortified." The lie comes natural-like. I avoid Kane's eyes.

Brother Stockham looks me over a long time, then turns to Kane. "Why not?"

Kane doesn't blink. "Didn't hear the bell until it was too late."

"And the child?"

"She was headed home with me," I offer quick. I have no idea where Edith was or why she was alone when the alarm sounded, but I hope he won't care enough to ask Tom's ma.

Brother Stockham looks between us, his jaw working. "You both need to get to your quarters."

He's right. Our families will be frantic. I search for Edith's hand and grasp it firm, trying to figure if Kane just lied to Brother Stockham too. I risk a look at his beautiful face, but Brother Stockham steps forward, blocking him from sight. He takes my arm and leans toward me.

"Emmeline, I'm so grateful you're safe." His shiny hair falls round his face, where there is relief, plain. "I thank the Almighty for this."

My heart stutters.

"I will escort you." He sweeps an arm around me. I hardly have time to glance back as I'm spun about, but I see Kane for a heartbeat, standing alone in the glow of the torches, arms hanging at his sides. I'm forced to turn my head and walk away.

8

NEXT MORNING, PA TELLS ME THE ATTACK WAS A false alarm. There was no breach of the fortification, no sighting of the *malmaci*—by anyone who'll admit it, anyhow.

Everyone has different ideas about what might have happened, but Pa says the most likely culprit is some foolish reveler who had too much saskatoon wine at Harvest.

Nobody knows for certain, though, and no one comes forward to admit their wrongdoing. Course, indulging in too much wine and then starting a false alarm? That would mean the Crossroads for certain.

Tom's ma was beside herself when she saw me with Edith. Edith had scampered away through the crowd heading out from the dance, and Sister Ann got caught at the back of the throng when the alarm rang. She believed my story, and I didn't need to repeat it to Council since they're far more interested in finding the offender who rang the alarm.

Thanks be, they'd never think to question the senior Watcher. Andre's the only one who knows what I did, and I don't need him giving me up in a bid to cover his own guilt.

Pa takes forever to leave in the morning, lingering over his porridge ration, looking on me far longer than I want. The false attack must have distracted him from my dancing with Brother Stockham—he doesn't speak on it. Eventually he goes and I finish my morning chores. Just as I'm about to head out, Edith pops into our kitchen through the common room that adjoins our quarters.

"You'd best get back to your ma," I warn.

She slips her hand in mine in answer.

Almighty! She's like a duckling following its ma now. I look into her round blue eyes, gazing at me like I'm something special.

Mayhap there are worse things.

I make a game of swinging her around me and hurry her back through the common room to her family's kitchen, where Sister Ann is making tallow. Sister Ann gives me a smile that's more friendly than usual. I return her smile, then duck out and head quick for the weapons shack.

There's a group of boys playing hoopball near the shearing pens, crashing about on the hard-packed earth. South-quarter boys. Each of the eight boys has a shaved head and bare chest.

One of the boys is Kane.

My stomach flips over and my thoughts fly back to the well. I can feel his body pressed close, shielding Edith and me.

Foolish.

I try to look anywhere but at his arms, the curve of his stomach above his leggings. Bare skin isn't new to me; I've seen bodies—men working the gardens and women in the washhouses—part undressed. But his entire torso ripples like the river as he catches the ball and passes it on. I stare at the ground and concentrate on passing without limping. Except now that I'm thinking on it, my foot feels heavier than ever, like it's *trying* to drag behind and catch Kane's eyes.

I pray he doesn't notice me. Still can't figure what he did last night. Last night . . .

The memory shifts, becomes a daydream. We're back pressed together so tight I can hardly breathe. Then he gives me breath with his beautiful mouth—grace!

I duck my head and push hard for the weapons shack. There's a tall Watcher sitting outside in the sun, oiling some kind of gun leather. He's got a scar that runs from his ear to his mouth, pulling the corner of it up in a bit of a sneer. He nods at me but keeps on his task.

Frère Andre greets me at the door. "Soeur Emmeline," he says, surprised.

I hesitate in the doorway.

"*Entrez.*" He waves me in. He lumbers toward the hearth, setting aside an arrow and a sharpening stone.

I close the door behind me and turn. The sight of the weapons overwhelms me. There are racks of bows and arrows. One wall lined with rifles and old muskets. Shelves of knives and rope. All of the weapons from the generations before are consolidated and stored here. It's Andre's job to make sure they're all in good working condition, and it's clear he takes it serious; the steel gleams. The precious few kegs of gunpowder are housed in a stone keep, outside the shack.

I clasp my hands together as he settles himself in a chair.

He squints up at me. Waiting. He's not going to make small talk, not this time.

I hesitate. I was so sure I needed to come here, to let him know that *I* know what he did. Now I can't get the words out.

We look at one another.

His barrel chest heaves with a sigh. "I know you leave the hall," he says.

I nod. "Yes." Blood rushes in my ears; I cast my eyes to the floorboards. "I . . ." But I can't say I'm sorry, because I'm not. "I couldn't leave her."

Silence. The air in the shack gets real warm.

"I don't tell," he says. I glance up.

He's watching me with soft eyes. *"Elle est un enfant."*

I let out a breath. "Yes. Just a child."

He cocks his head and scratches at his wiry beard. "You do wrong, *mais . . . c'etait Courage aussi.*"

He's saying I proved my Bravery virtue. My heart skips. "You mean that?"

"Oui," he says. *"C'etait Courage."*

I wrap my arms around myself, feeling pleased.

"Bien?" he asks, looking at the door. He expects me to go. The good feeling disappears. He thinks I got what I came for. Except I came to make sure he'd keep my secret by threatening him with what I know. I don't want that anymore, but I do want to know what he thinks he saw.

"Was it a wolf again?" I ask.

"Qua?"

"The false alarm. *C'etait un loup encore?*"

He shrugs. *"Je ne sais pas."*

"Then why did you ring the alarm?"

He shakes his head.

I try again. "I won't tell Council. I just . . . want to know why you did it."

"Ce n'etait pas moi," he says.

"Frère Andre," I say, "I won't tell Council."

"Because nothing to tell." He frowns at me. "Who send you?"

"No one," I stammer, thrown by the accusing look on his face. "I just"—I flounder for some explanation— "I thought I saw something strange in the trees. The other day." It sounds suspicious, even to my ears. My cheeks are going pink.

"Fait attention." His face is grave. He's telling me to be careful.

My heart drops. I didn't say *I* was out in the woods. "It might have been nothing, I was at the river—"

"You go to the river?"

I nod. That's not Wayward.

He squints. "You go to the woods?"

"Just to gather." *Forgive me.*

He stands and crosses to the table, picks up the arrow and examines it. Then he turns to me. "Yesterday," he says, "I shoot *cette fleche.*" He extends the arrow. *"J'ai vu un daim."*

Why does he look so skittered? He saw a deer and shot at it.

"Et when I go to . . . take *la fleche"*—his voice drops to a whisper—*"je pense que j'ai vu un homme."*

A man. Brother Stockham out in the woods?

"Qui?" I ask, but he waves me off.

"Ce n'etait pas un homme normal. Un . . ." His brow creases

and his eyes get distant. He's trying to put a name to something that has none. "Do you know what is *l'elephant?*"

An elephant. Seen pictures of them in Soeur Manon's
storybooks. They're the strangest animals—bigger than the
bison even, but without hair. She says they're real, but they
live in countries far away—further even than the Old Country.

I nod.

He looks at me meaningful.

"You think you saw an *elephant?*"

"*Non. Un* homme *comme l'elephant.*"

I draw back. A man like an elephant.

"Andre . . ."

"*S'il vous plait, Emmeline.* His face—a long, *comment
dit-on? Tronc.*" He gestures to his eyes with wide-spread
hands. "*Les yeux enormes. Mais . . . ,*" he whispers again, "*avec
vetements, les vetements d'homme.*"

A man in clothes with huge eyes and a trunk like an elephant. The skin on my neck crawls as I try to picture this
thing.

"With . . ." I put my hands to the sides of my head, mim-
ing large ears.

"*Non, pas des oreilles.*"

No ears. What on earth—"The *malmaci?*"

He shrugs, pacing away from me to the rifle rack, worrying the key ring hanging from his *ceinture*.

"Who else did you tell about this . . . Elephant Man?"

"Bette." Must be his life mate. "You."

And then I understand. I was there on Watch when his

eyes failed him. He's not sure what he saw. "Mayhap no one else for now."

He nods. Hesitates. Then he leans close. *"J'ai des reves de la bois."*

He dreams of the woods. Like me. I don't know what to say, so I'm glad when he shrugs and gestures toward the door.

I turn before I pull it open. "This isn't why you rang the alarm?"

He sighs. "I tell you already: *ce n'etait pas moi.*" I study his watery eyes. Mayhap he *is* telling the truth. He puts a hand to my shoulder. *"Que Dieu te protége."*

I don't go to the woods.

Almighty, protect me indeed.

That night I pull my feet from the dream forest floor. I wiggle my perfect toes, rock back onto my heels. I lean forward, feel the soil and spruce needles soft under my skin. The wind stirs my hair. This time, there is no hawk and *La Prise* doesn't come. This time the sound is quiet, a soft cry. A young girl's voice.

Find us, it calls.

I take a deep breath of the velvet air, and then I run.

9

THE RIVER SHINES IN THE AFTERNOON SUN, winding like a giant silver *ceinture* through the golden poplars. It's real warm for an after-Harvest day and the air is still, with no biting bugs to spoil it. The heat glances off the cliff walls and the heady smell of sage rises up in waves.

I can't enjoy it.

Not the river, not the warm air, not even Tom; I'm not at ease. And the longer I sit, the longer I watch Tom casting his gut-string line in the water, time and again, the more uneasy I get. Something's boiling up under the surface of everything: the river, my skin. I want to break something or run or scream. And Tom sitting there unknowing is starting to make me addled.

"It was so lucky you were there," he thinks aloud for what seems the hundredth time. He won't stop talking about Harvest. I didn't set him straight about what happened, just let him believe what I'd told everyone else.

I jump up and walk to the river's edge.

"Edith would've been so scared all alone," he muses.

I pace back and forth on the sandy shore.

"Was just so lucky."

"It wasn't real anyway," I say.

"Still," he says. He tosses his line and looks back over his shoulder at me. "You ready to try?"

"No."

"They're not biting anymore, anyhow." He pulls the line in, gathers it on his spool and turns to face me. "You want to spot jays? We got time before dinner."

I shake my head and keep pacing.

Tom fiddles with the spool and fishing line, his brow creased. "You got an idea of something to do?"

I want to shout at him. Instead, I press into my bad foot and pull at a loose thread on my belt. "Let's just walk," I say.

We make our way along the rocky shoreline, keeping quiet. I stare hard at the shimmering river, but Brother Stockham's eyes swim up and out of the ripples, so I scrunch my eyes shut.

And trip on a stone.

"Easy." Tom catches my arm gentle-like and rights me.

There's a giant fallen tree several paces ahead; we'll need to climb the bank to get around it. I turn back to the river, pick up a stone, and skip it hard along the silvery water. Tom sets the fishing spool aside to join me and we skip rocks in silence—Tom tossing them easy and making six or seven skips, me whipping them as though to tear the waves in half and only making three or four.

After a few minutes, Tom speaks. "Before the alarm, you left the dance quick." He says it in an offhand way, but there's a question there.

I whip a rock and land it with a huge splash. "Yep."

"Before we could dance again."

"I was tired."

"Oh." He skips a rock. "Well, I guess that's good, because if you hadn't been tired, then Edith would've—"

"Can we stop talking about it?"

He looks at me, startled.

"Please." I don't want to think about any of it. Not about my Wayward act, not about Kane being there. Certainly not about the dance. Or Brother Stockham looking on me strange, lying to me.

"Something's bothering you," he says. He worries the rock in his scarred hands.

I throw my rock at the river.

"You're not thinking about that trail in the woods, are you?" I watch him turn the rock over and over. "You're not thinking about going back there?" His voice sounds a mite wistful.

I think about the girl's voice in my dreams. About running toward her . . .

"Em?"

What can I tell him? I don't want to lie to him again, but I need to stop the questions. I look around for a distraction and settle on his hands. "You must be the worst candle dipper in the history of the settlement."

Tom's cheeks flush. I close my eyes. Why did I choose *that?* I know why Tom's hands are scarred; it's the same reason my foot hurts so bad certain days. Fighting yourself is torture, and it's better to harness the pain than drown in it. And he and I don't speak on that kind of thing.

"S-s-sorry." I fumble the word. "Don't know why I said that."

"It's all right," he says, but he doesn't meet my eyes.

"No, it isn't. I just—don't know what's wrong with me."

He looks up and watches me awhile. "You looked real happy at Harvest. Dancing."

I throw another rock.

"Looked like you'd forgotten to worry about your Stain."

I shake my head. "Doesn't matter much if I forget about it; everyone else remembers."

"Not half as many people as you figure."

"That's not true."

"Isn't it? Edith's real fond of you."

"Edith's a child."

"She sees you for you," he says. "Soeur Manon does too. Lots of people do."

I snort and wave him off.

"You're always too worried about the people who look on us unkindly in the first place."

"You mean Jameson."

"Jameson, sure. Council."

"They watch me closer than most."

"So what if they watch you close? They watch you because they think you're apt to do something Wayward. But only you can decide what you do, Em."

His words send a spike of cold through me. I study the water a moment.

"I don't think I'll fish today," I say.

Tom nods. "Mayhap tomorrow."

I turn to head up the bank.

"Em?"

I look back at him.

"Was good to see you smiling like that."

I pretend to head back to the fortification, but when I reach the dirt path that crosses the flats I keep going, heading north along the stream. Tom's wrong about the others. He doesn't know how it feels to be eyeballed the way I do, to have Stockham's eyes on me all these years. But I don't mind that he's wrong. He's the one person who cares that I'm happy, the one person who doesn't mind about my Stain. He and I watch out for one another. That's something.

I traverse the bank as far as I can until it jumps up steep and I know I'm approaching the Cleansing Waters. I sit and stretch long on a sun-warmed rock, closing my eyes, trying to wipe my mind clean of everything: the dance with Brother Stockham, Andre's Elephant Man.

A shadow falls across the sun.

I squint and find someone blocking out the sky, the sun a blue ring of light behind them. Brother Stockham? I scramble up.

Kane. He's standing on the rocks, his shirt open at the neck, sleeves rolled back.

"Oh." I sit back down, trying to look easy, but my thoughts fly back to him playing hoopball yesterday. With no shirt.

"Afternoon, Em."

I nod, my eyes to the ground.

"*C'est belle,*" he says. "Beautiful."

It takes me an unbearable moment to realize he means the day, the river. I nod again.

"You like coming out here, hey?"

I glance at him. He's looking over the river all casual, but there's something about it that seems a bit put-on. Like he didn't just happen on me here; like he was mayhap . . . looking for me?

I decide not to answer him direct. "Just resting a minute."

He settles himself on a rock nearby, picks up a pebble. The other night hangs between us, heavy and unspoken. It's addled, us sitting here like nothing after being pressed tight together in that well, but I pray he doesn't bring it up. Don't want to speak on it, especially if he knows I lied to Brother Stockham.

"Nice enough to go in." He nods at the river.

"It'd be cold," I say.

He shrugs. "Cold's all right by me. Could be the last chance before *La Prise*."

I stare down at my moccasin. Not about to take it off in front of him. "I don't swim."

"Someone should teach you someday." His lazy-river voice tugs at me. I look over at him, at his easy smile. He tosses the pebble in the air and catches it, over and over. "I've been swimming since I was a youngster. Taught my brothers to swim too."

Are we making chitchat? I fumble for something to say. "How old are they?"

"Four and six, but believe me, you're never too old to learn."

Does he mean *he* could teach me? My secret heart swells. I watch the river. The whine of the crickets grows. The scrub along the bank has turned; the leaves are pink-orange and bright yellow. Days like these, it's hard to imagine *La Prise* sweeping in, cloaking the world in ice. Comes so fast, though, you could be standing in the river one day and in knee-deep snow the next.

The animals aren't fooled. Above us, a flock of geese heads south, honking. Wispy white clouds scud across the yawn of blue sky. I watch the birds awhile. A thought pops from my mouth: "You ever see that blue color anywhere? I mean, besides the sky?" It's the color of that scrap of fabric I found in the woods. It occurs to me I've never seen it in our fabric dyes.

He stops tossing the rock and looks over. "No," he says. "But can't say I've been looking." He raises an eyebrow. "Why?"

I shake my head like it's nothing.

He goes back to catching the rock. Toss, catch. Toss. "It's nice here. Real peaceful," he says.

I nod.

"Can see why you'd want to come out here."

This time I can't help but smile over at him.

He fumbles the catch. Real quick, he snatches the pebble from where it lands and tosses it at the river. Clears his throat.

"So. You keeping out of trouble?"

"Beg pardon?"

"Keeping in the good books?"

"I think so," I say, willing him to drop it.

"Hide in any damp wells lately?" He says it joking, but my heart gets tight. Does he want me to admit I lied?

"Don't you have somewhere to be?"

"Umm . . . no?"

"Well, what do you want?"

"What do you mean?"

I hop up. "I'm needed at Soeur Manon's. So unless you have something important to speak on, I'll be on my way." The words come out in a rush, my throat too tight. I sound like a treed squirrel. It's just . . . he's speaking easy. Looks easy. But seems like he might be trying to catch me in some sort of trap.

He runs one hand over his shaved head, back and forth, and nods, eyes fixed on my face. "All right. I just . . . wanted to talk." He shrugs. "Ask if mayhap you want to . . . play hoopball sometime?"

I stare at him. "Girls don't play hoopball."

"Regular girls, no. Thought mayhap you . . . " He trails off.

I flush to the roots of my hair. "Can't. Got some *irregular* things to do." I say it with as much bite as I can muster.

He bursts out laughing.

And then I realize how addled I sound. For an instant I want the ground to swallow me whole, but his laugh is so good-natured it's catching. I frown to hide a smile.

He puts a hand to his chest in the Peace. "Emmeline. *Un plaisir, toujours.*"

Always a pleasure. I bite down on my bottom lip as I head up shore.

What does he truly want? If he knows I lied to Brother Stockham, then he's guilty like me for keeping my secret. If he doesn't know, why does he want to talk about my Waywardness? And what was he doing outside the doors during the false attack, anyway?

The only thing that's certain in all of this is that I'd best mind my tongue around him.

But that's what's so skittering. Something in me wants to spill my secrets when I see him. His eyes are so warm and calm.

It's unsettling. *He's* unsettling.

And I'm already full up to the brim with worry.

That night at dinner my pa looks skittish. I serve the turnip stew quick, hoping to get dinner over with, but he lingers over his bowl.

I don't like the way he's looking at me and I truly hope he's not thinking about jawing over the false attack. I take out my jar of arrowheads and start sorting through them, positioning them on the table smallest to big.

"Got some things to speak on," he says as he scrapes his bowl clean. "First matter is new chores. Now you're sixteen, you're meant to be learning Soeur Manon's skills."

I nod.

"You'll practice her tinctures and medicines. She's in charge of you now."

My ears prick up at this. The woods. With Soeur Manon in charge, might there be more chances for me to get out there?

"But remember to mind Sister Ann—she'll need you for chores now and again, mostly to run gatherings to the south quarter for storage."

I nod again and hope my skin doesn't give me away at the words "south quarter." I adjust the arrowheads. My thoughts flash back to Kane sitting on the riverbank, forearms on his knees, dark eyes fixed on my face—

"—paid a visit." Pa pushes aside his bowl and my thoughts

snap back to the room. I think I just heard Brother Stockham's name. "Thanks be, this time, it was a good visit." Now Pa is surely nervous; he's twisting his hands together. If Brother Stockham visited and it wasn't about my Waywardness, why is he jittering?

"It was about your eligibility."

I stare at him. "Sorry, Pa—beg pardon? Did you say *Brother Stockham* paid a visit?"

"I did." He takes a breath. "Em, this morning the good Brother visited about your eligibility."

"What about it?" My head feels stuffed with wool and my tongue works slow. I can't put together the who and the what in my pa's words. Because if he called about that . . .

"He asked for your hand."

My hand? I stare stupidly at Pa. He's smiling wide. Haven't seen that big a smile on him for as long as I can remember.

"Whatever for?"

His smile dies. "What do you mean 'whatever for'?"

"Well, I mean, I know why . . . why someone asks for . . . for someone's hand, but . . ." I'm stuttering, trying to find the words and losing all my thoughts.

"He wants you for a life mate. He came to ask." He leans forward, his hands clasped on the table. His eyes get shiny. "It's a real good thing, Em. Think on it: You bound to the good Brother would mean you could forget about chores, forget about taking on that old woman's trade. Almighty, Em, you'd never have to gather again, never have to go near the woods. You could rest up that foot, mayhap . . . heal a bit—"

The guilt in his voice near undoes me.

"It's a real good thing."

He's right: me bound to Brother Stockham could change things for us. But my head swims because . . . because why me? Why in Almighty's name would the revered leader want a Stained for a life mate? After all these years he could have chosen someone?

I thank the Almighty for this.

My skin feels hot and tight. Brother Stockham looking at me as though he knows something. The familiar way he touches me—those hawk eyes and determined hands . . .

I don't go to the woods.

The hope in my pa's eyes is so bright, it's burning a hole in my heart.

"The good Brother wants our answer by Affirmation," he says. "Says until then, we'll keep the proposal quiet."

Three weeks from now. Affirmation is a three-day ceremony: one day for giving thanks, one day for affirming our commitment to the virtues, one day for declaring bindings. Once the Ice Up arrives we're all stuck inside the walls with not much else to do but attend those bindings.

"Why does he want to keep it quiet?"

The shine in Pa's eyes dulls a bit. We both know why. No one on Council will be too pleased he's asked for me, knowing my grandma'am's legacy. They might even wonder if I've done something untoward to get him to ask.

No. They'll *surely* wonder. All these years of being eligible without a life mate? He doesn't want to have to weather the jawing and hard looks about proposing to a Stained, not unless our binding is certain. What I can't figure is why he'd want me at all.

"No sense in ruffling feathers just yet," Pa says quiet.

"Course," I say quick. But the "just yet" tells me Pa thinks the decision is made. And why wouldn't it be? Neither of us thought I'd be asked to bind to anyone at all, much less Brother Stockham. What can I say? Something about him skitters me? I saw him in the woods and he won't admit to it?

There's this Cariou boy . . .

Pa's sitting straighter, like someone just told him *La Prise* won't be coming this year after all. He reaches across the table and squeezes my wrist with one hand. "My girl," he says.

I'm of two minds: one to flinch and throw his hand away, the other to bury my face in his scrawny chest. I do neither, just get up from the table and scrape the arrowheads back into the jar. They clatter against the clay.

"Goodnight, Pa." My voice is raw. I'm doing my best to look grateful, but as I cross the room and escape to our sleeping quarters, I feel the walls of our home, the entire fortification, crushing in on me. I set the jar near my bed, hoping it brings me some comfort.

Tonight, though, sleep is a long time coming.

10

IN MY DREAM, I'M RUNNING AGAIN, QUIET AND sure. The woods whip past in a blur of greens and browns and the air is soft on my skin. The girl's voice is calling to me as I run. *Find us*. But I can't figure which direction it's coming from. I stop under *les trembles* and listen for her, listen to the tinkling leaves. I see a piece of sky-blue cloth, a trail leading up a hill—but then it's too late. The ice winds of *La Prise* rush in and deafen me.

When I open my eyes, the morning is bright and warm. The dream lingers.

That girl's voice. Is she . . . could she be my Lost People? Are my dreams telling me to find her before it's too late? Before *La Prise*—

Brother Stockham's proposal shatters my thoughts.

I hurry through my porridge. I can tell by the look in my pa's eyes that he expects we'll speak on the proposal again soon, and I don't want to. Guilt cuts me, seeing him all puffed up and proud. The worry in his eyes is all but disappeared.

Thanks be, he's on his way to chores. A herd of bison was spotted close to the fortification, and every able east-quarter man is needed to help with the kill. Using both arrow and the odd precious rifle, they usually only pull down two dozen before the herd spooks and disappears for another week or so. Pa has to go; we need the stores. And he'll be busy for days skinning and cutting and curing, so there'll be no time for speaking on the proposal.

I'm headed to the Healing House for chores that afternoon when I spy Brother Jameson gathering his crowd in a corner of the courtyard. He's talking loud—on the virtues again, no doubt. I'd have to duck back around the barns to avoid him and I'm half thinking on it when he looks up and sees me.

I swallow and keep walking. As I get close, I can hear him plain.

"Though the dangers are great, we survive. *Nous survivons le malmaci.* But it waits for us to make mistakes, and punishment for those who would make those mistakes must be swift." His eyes sweep his followers, who are murmuring assent. His brow shines with sweat. Most times he's cold as a river rock, but these speeches light a fire in his eyes.

"The *malmaci* is cunning; it is an ancient evil. It Takes, it rends bodies limb from limb, it causes sickness we have never seen. And we do not know for certain what it is truly capable of." His voice gets low. "But sometimes, Brothers and Sisters, I wonder if it hasn't found a way into some of our minds and hearts. I wonder if it doesn't already live among us." He pauses.

And stares straight at me.

Several heads in the crowd turn my way. I stop dead, heat coursing up my toes to my brow. I'm frozen in their stare, want the ground to open wide and swallow me whole.

"Emmeline!" It's Soeur Manon, peering out her door. *"Viens ici. Maintenant!"* She sounds real cross.

I don't think twice. I turn away and limp fast for the Healing House.

She shuts the door behind me and presses her back to it. I can't think what I've done wrong, but I'm so relieved I decide I won't mind a tongue-lashing. She looks at me a long time, saying nothing.

I shift.

"You gather today." She's giving me my task.

I nod. Wait.

"Alors." She crosses to the table toward a book, starts flipping through the pages.

I cross the room, trying to figure if she's angry, trying to shut Jameson's voice from my mind.

I wonder if it doesn't already live among us.

"They trouble you?" She flips the pages, tilts her head to the door. She means Jameson, the crowd.

"No," I say quick. I straighten and try to look unconcerned.

She stops and sizes me up another long while. Finally she points to some late-harvest mushrooms in one of her books and sends me out. I skirt the Healing House and head through the gates, out of sight of the crowd.

As I'm crossing the Watch flats, the fever under my skin starts to simmer.

I know I should stay gathering. Shouldn't go back out to that trail. Not after Andre's warning. Not after Jameson eyeballing me that way and Soeur Manon cross about something. I should just find the mushrooms and get back. But . . .

My dream with the girl calling to me—it won't stop running through my head.

And that trail leads somewhere and Brother Stockham lied about it. Could it lead to her? To what she needs me to see?

Might we talk about this later?

Would Brother Stockham tell me the truth about it if we were alone?

A chill shoots through me. I don't want to be alone with him. If I want to find out about that trail, I'll have to go see with my own eyes.

I linger just inside the scrub line, my eyes scouring the deadfall, hoping to get my task over quick. But I can find hardly a handful of the bleeding mushrooms Soeur Manon wants. My satchel stays near empty as I move further into the trees. Several minutes of searching later, I find another handful growing on the side of a fallen log. They're right next to a bunch of withering bittersweet. I make sure not to touch the poison berries as I pull the mushrooms from the log. When I straighten, I realize I'm out of sight of the Watchtower.

I forget searching for more mushrooms.

I go. Fast as I can. Even so, it takes me a good ten minutes to get back to the grove. It's quiet and still, like the other day. Like it's been waiting for me to return. The piece of cloth lies where I dropped it, next to the trail.

This time I'm quiet on the path, moving real slow, watching for any shifting trees. The woods are still; no strange fluting noise this time. *Les trembles* drop silent, gold leaves around me.

I pass the spot where I saw Brother Stockham. I want to head the way he did the other day, but the sensible part of me wonders if I'd get lost out here with no markers to look for. Everything in these parts of the woods looks the same: thick underbrush and row after row of golden poplars. The sun glimmers through the boughs ahead of me, so I can tell I'm still headed west. I squint hard for the trail—a snapped branch here, a flattened piece of earth there.

Concentrating on following it takes over my senses; the seconds and minutes blur and disappear into the damp smell of the forest.

Finally I can see the brush part and empty into a clearing. My heart skips a beat. I've reached something; I can feel it. I burst from the bushes.

And stop dead.

The woods have given way to a clearing, flanked on three sides by high earth walls. A long birch pole is set in the middle of the space. Tied to it is a single red cloth.

I know this place. I've never been here—have only visited in my mind when Brother Stockham speaks on it, warning us away—but I know it. This red flag is a signal that I'm approaching a place I should never hope to see.

The Crossroads.

The bodies of the Waywards are there, set high off the earth in precious metal cages so their souls never have rest. Council sends the Waywards there alive, hoping it might appease the *malmaci*'s appetite, dissuade it from Taking the innocent, the good.

I should go. I should turn around and head back down the path and finish my mushroom gathering and head home. But my feet refuse it. I stand in the grove, aware the sun is dead ahead of me. The shadow of the flagpole stretches long.

A birch flagpole marks the path to the Crossroads. If you should ever be unfortunate enough to see it, pray to the Almighty for His grace and mercy.

Why haven't I turned around yet?

My grandma'am.

The Crossroads lies just over the first hill at an intersecting path, and her remains will be swinging there. Right *there.*

This path leads to my past, not my future. I close my eyes and grit my teeth against my disappointment. And then I'm washed with anger.

I need to see her. I need to see this woman who had such disregard for the virtues and the reputation of our family that she courted her own death.

I take a step forward. And then another. And another.

I brush past the pole—it catches at my sleeve as though it is willing me to stay put. I set my jaw and throw myself into climbing the sloping mound before me. It's slow going—I have to find handholds and sturdy brush to haul myself up the cracked wall of the coulee. My hands scrabble in the rock and my leg drags behind me, begging me to turn around.

When I crest the top, I'm faced with more hills and rock shelves marred by pockets of trees, reaching off into the distance. But at the bottom of this hill, dead center of a sizeable valley, it's plain as day. A circle of eight tall structures— shorn poplar trees pushed into the ground like arrows, shorter beams lashed to them at right angles, and dangling from those, the gibbets.

I force my feet ahead, picking up speed as I hobble down the hill. A flame burning inside my heart spurs me on. I slip in the shale, sending a hail of rocks and dust around me, and reach the gibbets, breathing ragged.

Some of the bodies in the cages are near crumbled to dust—small jumbles of bones that the ice winds of *La Prise* have preserved. Scraps of clothing remain. The skulls are the best put-together—empty eyes staring into space, teeth bared in grins. Waywards from before my grandma'am's time, I guess. Two of the skeletons are intact, so they must be the Thibault couple. I think again of their sons, who nobody seems to look on with the same scorn as me and my pa. Doesn't seem fair. Course . . .

Course that couple didn't do what my grandma'am did.

A soft breeze comes up and one of the gibbets twists slightly. The iron lets out a soft groan. I pass between them, my eyes scouring the bones, searching.

There.

I don't know how I know, but I do. The skeleton is a jumble, forehead resting on the gibbet, a hand extended, missing bones. Shreds of brown cloth still cling to the sun-blasted carcass. I step forward for a closer look. The gibbets hang a good man's length above me, but I can see her plain enough.

My grandma'am's empty eye sockets size me up.

Wayward. Miscreant. Harlot. Whispers that describe my grandma'am. They bite into me, pierce me like a poison, but I know those words aren't unfounded. I know she wandered the woods, failed her virtues.

And I know she propositioned a married man—the leader of the community, no less.

I step hard on my bad foot, wash myself in the pain. And the day my Stain came visible—that day rushes in on me, cold and merciless.

It was a warm late-summer day, my ma dead a year already. We were playing in the courtyard, barefoot and bareheaded, shooting stones in the dust. The adults were slaughtering chickens. I knocked one of the older east-quarter girls' point rock out of the circle.

I did it again. And again.

"Wayward," she spat. "Nobody wants you to play."

It was the worst name we knew. "Am not."

"Are too. Your grandma'am was Wayward."

"She was not!"

"Ask anyone here."

The circle of children had low-cast eyes; they all knew something I didn't.

"Mayhap it's a family curse. You should leave before we catch it from you."

I stood, my fists clenched. "Take that back!"

The girl stepped over our stones. "Or what?"

Rage in my chest, my hands landed on her shoulders and shoved her backward a step. Her face went dark. She put her hands on my chest and shoved. Hard. I staggered back a few steps; she kept coming. She shoved me again, harder still, and I stumbled back near the slaughtering blocks right when Brother Giles dropped his axe.

I push that foot into the earth. The blunt end came down first, thanks be, or I'd be short my toes, but the axe was heavy and my foot was small, and some of the bones were crushed to near nothing straightaway.

I stare at the skull, a dull anger throbbing in my head.

Even if Brother Giles had never dropped his axe, I'd still be different. My child's eyes hadn't noticed the shifting glances when my pa and I arrived at settlement events. But I noticed them after that. Been noticing ever since.

A rage rushes in and roars in my ears. I look to the few stones scattered about, grab the nearest one, and lob it at the iron cage with all my might.

It bangs the metal bottom with a clank that echoes off the coulees around me. I grab another stone and hurl that. And another, and another. With each throw I curse my grandma'am's name: *Clara*. Smash. *Clara*. Smash. But it's not near enough to satisfy my rage.

I find a large rock, one twice the size of my fists, that takes both hands to lift. I don't have the strength to hurl it overhand and so I brace my bad foot, then heave it upward from between my knees. It crashes against the bottom of the cage with a satisfying bang that splits the air, echoing through the Crossroads. The impact loosens the decrepit body from its rigid perch, and the bones shift, dropping to one side and knocking the skull against the cage with a hollow crack.

Something drops from the cage into the dust before me. I scramble forward to snatch it up. A ring. I run my fingers over the tarnished gold band, picking away crusts of dirt and Almighty knows what else.

I hold it before my eyes. My grandma'am's wedding band? A family ring? No one wears jewels anymore—not even family heirlooms—since they're reminders of useless wealth. I gaze at its perfect circle. And then I see a reddish-brown stain on the rock wall beyond.

I close the ring inside my fist and step closer.

There are figures etched into the rock in black and reddish-brown colors. I look along the rock face and see the entire wall is full of them, near blending into the earth. The drawings are simple—not like the figures I've seen in Soeur Manon's books—but it's plain they're people and animals, scratched into the surface with something sharp and hard.

I've seen something like this before—there's one on a rock near the riverbank that Tom and I found years ago. A left-behind from the Lost People.

My hands trace along the figures as I skirt the walls, outside the circle of gibbets.

I've never seen so many left-behinds in one spot. The pictures are a few hands' widths from each other: people next to a big herd of animals, people standing with animals below their feet, fire, sun, great swirls of black and red and brown along the top of the rock.

There's one part of the wall where the drawings get muddy and jumbled, like the scene was scratched in, smoothed over, and scratched in again. It's people, standing in a group. Beyond them, several more lie on the ground. Above that is an animal—several times bigger than the people—with horns, like those in the great herds. It has a long tail, like nothing I've ever seen, and clawed feet. It's standing on two legs.

The air in the valley gets real still.

The malmaci.

I hold my breath. The heat bounces off the rock in waves, making the picture dance. A buzzing fills my ears as I watch it shimmer, come to life. Then the beast is lunging forward through the pile of dead, grabbing the next person in its claws. I choke back a cry as it opens its maw and closes jagged teeth around its victim, gnashing and tearing the flesh.

The light shifts and the scene goes still. I blink. It's just a dusty etching.

I throw a quick look behind me, toward the gibbets. My grandma'am's bones are leaning awkward in a heap. But her skull is against the cage, and her eye sockets are on me. The glare of the sun behind her blinds me a moment, and when I drop my eyes I notice the long shadows on the ground, reaching across the space with greedy fingers. My breath leaves me in a rush. It's dusk.

Less than an hour before dark.

I stuff the ring inside my *ceinture* and spin around. A wind rushes in from over the coulees, snaking around me, through the Crossroads. The gibbets rock and sway, throwing frantic shadows on the hills. The creaking of the cages becomes an ear-splitting whine, drowning my thoughts.

I pitch forward, back the way I've come, stumbling through the swaying bones, hugging my arms tight around myself. I am halfway through this place of death when I feel the caged bones shift, come alive. They're reaching for me, grasping with brittle fingers. They're going to pull me up with them, into those cages of starvation where the sun blisters the skin and flies feed on oozing eyes. Where death comes quick if you are lucky—

I run.

Stumbling, pulling my leg along, scrambling up the hill, down again, past the flagpole, and into the brush. The woods are a muted shade of gray, the sun's rays just slices of red peeking through the poplar boughs. My eyes strain to find the path, but it is gone. Each tree looks like the next, shadows loom at me from each side, and I am running, running, following only my instinct now.

The *malmaci* breathes hot on my neck, the Lost People urge me to hurry. Branches whip at my face, catch my hair, tear at my arms as I go. I hit the ravine unawares and near pitch down the bank. Catching myself in time, I slide, then tear my fingernails as I claw for the top. A rosebush tears at my cheek as I burst into the bramble, and then I'm running again. I'm nearing the Watch flats. I steady my breath and keep going, limping, dragging my foot. I'll make it back to the fortification, but . . .

How will I get in past the Watch? If they don't shoot me on site, mistaking me for the *malmaci,* they'll surely turn me over to Council. No one is allowed beyond the fortification after dusk.

The last of the sun disappears behind me, but I'm so close now. I could make it before they close the gates. I burst through the last of the scrub, into the thin birch trees, and find the torches already blazing. The Watch fires are being set atop the walls, and I can hear shouts as Watchers prepare to take their posts. The doors on this side of the fortification are already creaking shut.

My heart sinks as I watch the fort close up for the night—a rock daisy folding its petals tight to wait for the morning sun.

I stand at the edge of the woods and the dark rushes in around me. My leg aches. The heat of the autumn day has been snuffed out with the sun. If the *malmaci* doesn't find me, I'll catch the fever out here for sure. But if I'm turned over to Council . . .

The trees at my back creak, reaching for me with tangled arms. My mind wants to splinter, but I force myself to blow out my breath. Think. I remember standing on those walls the other night. How scared I was at first. The other night . . .

I get an idea. It's risky, but it's all I can manage. Hopefully he'll be far more careful about what he's firing at after his near-mistake.

I cut a wide arc, far enough outside the circle of torches that I remain in shadows. I head to the corner of the wall I patrolled. I can see a Watcher taking position on the corner near the Watchtower.

Almighty, let it be Andre.

I swallow hard, then step into the light of the torch and wave my arms, praying the response is not a swift bullet to my chest.

I can't see the Watcher's face, but the person stops moving. Then I see a flash of glass—a spyglass? Whoever it is will have clear view of me any second—

"Soeur Emmeline!" It's a hiss, thanks be, not a shout.

I scour the walls for other Watchers taking their positions, but, Almighty's grace above, Andre is first to his post on this section. I take a breath and limp across the lighted area to the shadow of the wall. When I look up, Andre is squinting at me, his face distorted with shock.

I make a frantic, helpless gesture.

He glances about quick. Then he straightens, crosses away from me, and disappears into the tower.

For an awful moment I wait for the alarm to sound. *Way-ward!* I press myself against the rough wall, trying to blend into the shadows.

Then Andre is back with a rope. It snakes down to me. I have no idea if I'm strong enough to hold on to this rough lifeline, but I'll tear all of my arm muscles trying.

I wrap the rope once around my right hand and grab tight. Then I nod up to him.

Andre may be old, and his eyesight is right crumbly, but the man is strong. He has me over the side of the fortification before my hands begin to burn.

He drops me abrupt-like to the ground, then quickly coils the rope. I climb to my feet.

He stares at me. *"Que faisiez-vous?"*

I swallow hard. *Forgive me.* "I was gathering." I gesture to my root sack. "Lost track of the sun."

"C'etait trop dangereux!" He shakes his head. *"Cette fois-ci, il n'y avait pas de garçon pour te sauver."*

No boy to rescue me this time? Kane? The silence stretches between us in the dark. I can see in Andre's eyes he's figuring something. *Please.*

"You must go home," he says finally.

Relief floods me. *"Merci,* Andre." Tears brim in my eyes and I blink them away, embarrassed.

He ducks his head and waves his hand toward the east quarter. *"Allez,"* he says, gruff. But his eyes look a mite pleased.

I go as fast as my foot can bear.

11

FOR DAYS I KEEP MY HEAD REAL LOW. I LEARN poultices from Soeur Manon, gather from the barns, run things to the Kitchens, keep my eyes ahead and my walk normal. I show at Virtue Talks and stand near the back, then leave quick-like for bed, before Brother Stockham can catch my eye. Before Pa can get around to speaking on anything.

That night of the Crossroads I made up a tale about losing the time at the barns and missing dinner. Pa was so starry-eyed about Brother Stockham's proposal, he didn't seem to mind. I can't decide the worst of it: being untruthful to Pa or heading knowingly to the Crossroads, to the clutches of the *malmaci*.

"Emmeline." Soeur Manon's voice jolts me from my thoughts.

I glance up from a yellowed page of her plants book. She holds a ladle in one hand, a fistful of rose hips in the other. "It is the season of *le fievre*." The fever. "You learn a healing broth."

We bend over her pot on the hearth and I listen to her mutter, *"Ca c'est bon pour le fievre."* She adds a sprig of spruce needles. *"L'épicéa."*

I know now I was seeing things at the Crossroads: the drawings and the skeletons in the gibbets coming alive—it was all a trick of my fearful mind. But I'm still angry, only now it's at myself. What was I thinking on? What did I hope to gain by brazening it out with someone long dead? I almost got caught outside the fortification at dark. My hopes the Lost People weren't Taken by the *malmaci* were crushed to nothing by those drawings on the rock wall.

Worst of all: that trail leads nowhere but the Crossroads.

"Emmeline!" I snap my eyes to Soeur Manon's weathered face. *"Attention!"*

I nod, trying to fix my eyes on her hands.

She straightens and looks at me. *"Viens,"* she says, gesturing to the bench at her table. She settles herself across from me, her eyes raking over me head to misshapen toe.

"It bothers you," she says.

I look at my foot. "I guess."

"Non, pas ton pied." She touches her brow. *"Ta tête."*

I frown.

"Tu as les rêves etranges."

She's right: my dreams are strange. The girl's voice that now calls to me, me running so fast and sure through the woods. I stare at Soeur Manon's creased face, my eyes so wide they're drying up. "Sometimes."

"How do they look?"

For half an addled moment I think she means the Crossroads, but then I see she's asking after my dreams.

"Jumbled."

She tilts her snow-white head, waiting for me to continue.

"I'm—I'm in the woods. And sometimes *La Prise* comes, and sometimes it doesn't. And there are voices that call to me." I stop, my face going red. "They're just foolish dreams."

"You are sure?"

"Well, I can't figure what they could mean."

"Ask them."

"The voices?"

Her toothless mouth pulls into a smile. "*Non.* The woods."

As I cross the courtyard away from the Healing House, I feel for my grandma'am's gold band tucked inside my *ceinture fléchée* and worry the smooth, warm surface. What would the woods say about me stealing from the Crossroads? What would Soeur Manon say?

She never says much at all, and I figure that's because she's taken me on in the Healing House as an act of mercy: helping the Stained girl learn an important task. Still, she doesn't seem to mind too much when I talk about odd things or ask strange questions.

And it was like she was urging me to listen to my dreams. Mayhap she understands.

Or mayhap she's so old she's losing her senses.

I spot Kane in the southwest corner of the yard, near the shearing pens. I don't have to pass that way to get to our quarters, but I pretend I'm headed somewhere else and swing past. He's on free time, throwing a knife at a fence post from round about thirty strides away. His brow creases as he holds the tip of the knife just so and then lets fly. His aim is dead sure. He walks forward and pulls the knife from the post, jogs back to his place.

I can't help but stop and watch. It's another warm autumn day and his shirt laces are open at the neck, almost to the middle of his chest. I try not to stare at his collarbone, the way his chest flexes as he draws the knife back behind his neck, elbow high, and then whips it forward. The knife thunks into the fence post—looks to be the exact same spot. He's concentrating so hard he doesn't notice me.

Pas de garçon pour te sauver.

Did Frère Andre mean Kane left the hall and came *after* Edith and me during the false attack?

My thoughts stall as I notice someone else watching. On the far side of the pens, the Council building looming at his back, Brother Stockham is looking on. My stomach drops.

Kane sees him as he retrieves the knife. He puts the knife in his left hand and offers him the Peace. Brother Stockham raises his eyebrows and nods, then shifts his eyes to me again.

Kane follows his gaze. For half a foolish second, I'm frozen in their stares. Brother Stockham's proposal. I haven't seen him face-to-face since I got word . . .

Kane looks to Brother Stockham. Then he tosses the knife back to his right hand and stabs it into the fence post. Hard. He turns and begins striding over to me, like we're going to have a talk. He's smiling, but it doesn't reach his eyes.

I turn and start walking normal as I can for the other side of the fort.

"Emmeline!"

The fence boards creak. He's scaling the pen, I know it. I

pick up my pace but am pulled up short as he grabs my arm. I whirl, snatching it away.

He draws back, and the forced smile breaks into a grin. "Easy," he says.

I glance back at the pens, but Brother Stockham has disappeared.

"Where are you going?" he says casual, like we just happened upon one another.

"Home."

"Oh." He laces his hands at the back of his neck. His shirt opens and I look away again. "You're going the wrong way," he points out.

"I—I know," I stammer. "I'm . . . going the long way. For a walk."

He cocks his head, his mouth turning up in that half smile. "All right. I'll walk with you."

My heart leaps. I'm trying hard to keep my eyes from resting on his collarbone, the top of his chest. "Why?"

He shrugs. "Why not?"

The proposal is why not. If it were common news, he'd know what he's doing is frowned upon. Consorting with another man's chosen? A warmth creeps into my cheeks. I let myself believe that for a second: that he knows about the proposal and is choosing to speak to me anyhow.

"Need to talk to Brother Harold about the smokehouse," he adds.

Grace. Course he needs to do something chore related. Course he wasn't *consorting* with me. I'm about to open my mouth and accept when a clamor comes from the center of the courtyard.

"Brothers and Sisters!"

It's Jameson and his followers, spilling out from behind the weapons shack, a dark sickness in a furl of cloaks. They're right wound about something: talking amongst themselves, staring at the woman walking beside Jameson, in the middle.

"Brothers and Sisters!" Jameson calls again, his voice ringing out across the courtyard. He's drawing a crowd. People appear out of the buildings, the Kitchens. Tom and his pa emerge from the barns and follow. Even Andre is joining, wandering along with the tall Watcher who was outside his door the other day.

Kane turns from the ruckus and raises an eyebrow at me. "What do you suppose?"

"Don't know." I glance around. I want to make myself scarce without Jameson noticing, but they're coming straight for us.

"Should we make a run for it?"

"Course not!" I snap my head to Kane's face, a sliver of panic shooting through me that he knew what I was thinking.

There's laughter in his dark eyes. "All right, then," he says and tilts his head at the crowd.

They're slowing at the pens, veering off toward the Council building. Jameson starts up the stairs with the woman. We venture closer, but I hang near the back, cabbage moths flitting in my stomach.

"Brothers and Sisters," Jameson says from the stairs. "We are here to acknowledge and laud Discovery." His jowly face is satisfied, his eyes lit with that spark he gets when speaking on our virtues.

Everyone hushes.

He points to the woman standing beside him. It's one of the Woods girls, from Shearing and Textiles. She's tall and thin, with narrow-set eyes. "Sister Sarah has proven her Discovery virtue."

The man beside me leans forward.

Our salvation lies in Discovery.

I look around for Brother Stockham. We haven't had a true Discovery in years, not since Jasper Hayes figured out a way to make better tick curry combs for the sheep. It was a big Discovery, I suppose, since every spring and every fall there's a tick surge, and we can't risk the herd getting sick. I'm hoping Brother Stockham won't appear, but surely he'd want to see this?

Jameson reaches into his cloak for a small leather satchel. He dips a hand into it and brings out a pinched thumb and forefinger.

"This"—he rubs his fingers together and a fine sheen of powder sprinkles through the air. It's yellow; the color of goldenrod—"is crushed lichen. When added to red ochre, it creates one of the most beautiful oranges I have ever seen." He spreads the dust through the air, anointing the crowd. He looks to Sarah, appraising. Her cheeks go pink. "We will be proud to wear this brilliant color, Sister Sarah."

Dye for the *ceinture fléchée.*

The women ahead of me put their heads together, talking excited-like, but I feel a pang of disappointment. Surely our salvation can't lie in the brilliance of an orange thread?

I turn away from the crowd and find Kane studying me.

"Unimpressed?" he says quiet.

Why can he read my thoughts like that? I look around, but the crowd is too busy with Jameson and Sister Sarah—some people are pushing forward to get a look at that powder.

"I just thought . . ." I shrug. "Thought it might be something different." As the words leave my mouth I realize how it sounds. My eyes fly to his face. If he thinks my answer is shameful, his eyes don't say it. But he's looking at me hard.

"I have to get home." I turn and leave quick, before he can offer to come with me again.

Hurrying through the courtyard, I shift weight onto my bad foot and focus on the spike of pain.

My dream self is running fast and quiet through the woods again, slipping down and up ravines, my perfect feet barely touching the ground. The wind is blowing, but this time I can hear her voice beneath it plain as day: *Find us*. I follow that sound to the base of a low hill dotted with spruce trees. I want to climb it, need to see what's on the other side, but movement makes me look to the sky. The hawk is above, circling slow, its eyes seeing into my soul.

12

NEXT MORNING I'M CROSSING TO SOEUR MANON'S when I hear a ruckus at the west gates. Council has a man tied up, just inside the walls. I can tell by his clothes he's a shearer. His hands are bound behind his back and his mouth is gagged.

I've never seen this before, but I've heard tales; I know what's happening.

They're sending him to the Crossroads.

There's a small crowd forming around the spectacle. Brother Davies is standing with his arms out, keeping the onlookers back. The shearer makes muffled sounds through the gag, fighting them. His eyes bulge and his tunic is stained with dirt from scuffling about on the earth. There's a smear of blood on his brow, just below his fire-red hair. He thrashes so hard, it takes two of the bigger Councilmen to hold him.

Brother Stockham stands, watching on.

I stop. I don't want to, but I can't look away—my eyes are drinking it in even as my mind tries to shut it out. All at once his name comes to me: Jacob. Jacob Brigston, from the west quarter.

They're trying to bind his feet, but he's moving so furious they can't grab hold. Finally one of the Councilmen throws him face-first to the earth and another kneels on the backs of his legs, wrapping a piece of twine around them. He's about to cinch it when Jacob twists his body and kicks out. The Councilman pitches forward and when Jacob kicks again, it catches him in the jaw. Three Councilmen—one of them is Brother Jameson—leap at him and everything is a flurry of cloaks and limbs and shouts.

The crowd is murmuring, getting agitated, and more people keep showing up. There's now a semicircle of curious faces watching it all unfold. Jameson's followers huddle together, craning their necks to see. I'm far enough away I can see the whole thing plain.

"Jacob!" A panicked shout.

A woman with a mane of red hair is hurrying across the courtyard toward us. His sister? Her face is real scared and she's aiming to bust right through the crowd.

The Councilmen have Jacob on his knees, and Brother Jameson has put the twine around his neck and he's pulling at it. Jacob's not thrashing anymore, just making a horrible, strangled cry.

The crowd is getting louder. Some people see his sister and move aside.

"Brother Stockham?" Brother Davies's voice booms across the clamor of the crowd. He waves his arms, warning the crowd to give the Councilmen space.

Brother Stockham's arms are folded across his chest, but

there is a muscle moving in his jaw. His eyes flick to the woman running across the yard, then to the crowd that's surging forward, then to Jacob. There's a moment his eyes look pained, like they're looking on the saddest thing.

He won't let them kill Jacob here. He couldn't possibly—

But his eyes harden and he nods to Brother Davies. Once. No remorse now.

Brother Davies barks over his shoulder at Brother Jameson: "Do it."

Jameson tightens his grip by shortening the rope, making Jacob's eyes go even wider. His cry is coming out more like a whine now, like his breath has closed off fully and it's all he can do to make any sound at all.

There are more exclamations from the crowd, but they're retreating now, away from the scene, and the woman is fighting her way through. "No!" she cries, clawing her way to the front. Brother Davies wades into the fray to grab her.

Jacob's not making that sound anymore.

Brother Stockham's eyes sweep the crowd and rest on me, his face expectant—like he's daring me to say something. The crowd is murmuring, crossing themselves. A woman utters: "Almighty's will be done."

I force a step backward. *Move, Em, move.* It's long moments before my syrup-slow body answers. I turn and take several stumbling steps toward the east quarter. I'm almost to our door when I stop and give up my stomach onto the hard-packed earth.

By afternoon, everyone's heard about Jacob and everyone's talking about it in hushed whispers. I close my ears to it all and put my head down. But I can't stop a picture forming in my mind: Council has me tied up, and I'm begging and thrashing and fighting for all I'm worth while Brother Stockham looks on.

I'm standing around back of our quarters, pulling the dried river grass from Pa's mattress to replace it, when a shadow falls on the wall before me.

It's long, the way shadows get this time of year, but the way it moves is unmistakable. I swallow a sour taste of fear and wait for him to speak my name.

"Emmeline." It's not a punishing voice. Not happy, neither.

I turn and find him standing with his arms folded, cloak washing around him.

I drop the grass in my hand and offer him the Peace. "Brother Stockham."

"I don't mean to interrupt." He nods at the mattress.

"You're not." I lay it against the wall.

There's a heavy pause as I wait for him to speak. I tell my heart to beat slow.

"I came because . . . " He stops, then unfolds his arms. For the second time I've ever seen, he looks like he's not real sure what to say.

"My pa told me. About the proposal." I speak quick.

"Yes," he says.

"I'm—I'm real flattered," I say. "And I know not to say anything before Affirmation."

He smiles thin. "The settlement—Council—can be . . . difficult. But I think you know this."

A chill takes me. After years of enduring his hard stare, him speaking this familiar unnerves me. Unless . . .

Unless that's not why he was looking on me all that time. I shove the thought down deep.

He studies me a moment and I realize the proposal isn't why he's here. I look to my hands. Will my skin to stay cool.

"That was unfortunate. Today."

My eyes snap to his face.

"It was upsetting," he says.

Is he checking to see how upset I am? Can he see my guilt? "I'm all right," I say. But my stomach clenches again at the memory of the Councilmen wrestling Jacob to the ground. My mouth waters and for a heartbeat I'm sure I'm going to lose my stomach again. I close my eyes and take a deep breath.

"I wish you hadn't been there to see it."

My eyes fly open. He's staring at me, but now his eyes aren't so hawk-like. They're wide and full of something like . . . worry.

I should reassure him; it would cover my guilt. But images spill into my head: Jacob's eyes, his sister struggling, Stockham's cold nod, giving the order . . .

I can't meet his eyes. I focus instead on his neck, on a small part of skin between his jaw and his cloak. There's a thin line: pink, raised. A scar.

"My father taught me many lessons," he says soft. "Ensuring our survival at all costs was the most important." He's speaking on Jacob, that's plain, but the way he's looking at me says he means something more. "He . . . he had no use for anything that might compromise order."

I swallow. He means me. My Stain. My Wayward legacy. His father would have no use for me.

"He was a strong leader," he says, "but he may have been wrong about some things."

"Like punishments?" I say before I lose my nerve. I risk a look at his face. He knows what I'm asking.

He speaks quiet. "What would you have had me do, back there?"

I have no idea what Jacob did, no idea what he deserved or what choices Brother Stockham had. "I . . . don't know." My heart's beating fast now.

He stares at me a while longer, but it's not a disapproving stare; there's no ire at my brazenness. "You don't know what it's like to wonder about the wisdom, the choices, of your father," he says. "To want to carve your own path."

But of course I know. I know exactly. But what I think my pa is wrong about—that Stockham and I should be bound—I can't share. And what I can't figure is what kind of path Stockham's hoping to carve by binding to the Stained girl.

"But I hope you can understand that I still have a duty to uphold." He hesitates, then steps closer. "Because I need you."

My breath is tight in my throat. He's standing so close now, if someone came around the corner and saw us—

A flash of black catches my eye. It's a Councilman moving along behind the stables. Brother Stockham follows my gaze and the moment breaks. He steps back, drawing himself up. He looks every inch the all-important leader, but I can see it: there's a spark of something desperate in his eyes.

Then he turns on his heel and walks away. The day at the river comes rushing back, his words:

You are not the only one who lives with a family burden.

13

SISTER ANN SENDS TOM AND ME TO GATHER EGGS that evening, before the hens roost for the night. We walk quick between the shacks, our breath making clouds in the cooling air. The days are getting shorter and now, when the sun gets low, the cold of night rushes in quick.

Tom's quiet—I suspect it's because he's thinking on Jacob Brigston. My insides are still in knots from the afternoon.

I bend my head to collecting eggs quick as I can. I'm halfway done my side of the coop when I find a hen already nesting. I reach forward to move her from her perch, and she bobs and pecks the top of my hand, drawing blood.

"Almighty!" I curse, flinging her from her perch. She squawks as she hits the floor and Tom swings round, his blue eyes wide. I duck my head and grab the egg the hen was guarding so stubborn.

"Everything all right?"

"Just fine," I mutter, looking in the next box and finding

nothing. I complete the row and turn, hoping that Tom can't see my red cheeks. I pass him, heading for the coop door.

He puts a hand on my arm, stopping me midstride.

"What's going on, Em?"

"Nothing. I don't know. I just—" I close my eyes and grit my teeth. "Got some things on my mind is all."

"That why you don't want to meet at the river anymore?"

The hurt in his voice pierces me straight through. I open my eyes. His face is anxious, sad. So that's why he's been quiet. I need to tell him. I don't want him thinking something's the matter with him, with our friendship.

"Course not." I say. "Just been busy with Soeur Manon."

His brow creases.

"Truly. Been out gathering and such."

"You find anything new?" There's that look again. Longing. Just for a heartbeat.

"No."

"'Cause you're looking unwell, Em."

I swallow. "Saw that shearer being sent to the Crossroads today."

Tom's face blanches. "You were there?"

I nod.

"You know why they sent him?"

I shake my head.

"Was it awful?"

"Real awful." I hesitate. "He didn't . . . he didn't make it there. He was fighting so hard they put a rope around his neck in the courtyard . . . They choked him . . . They . . ." And I'm crying, tears blurring my sight, my face hot with shame. I stumble, looking for something to lean against.

Tom grabs my shoulders, puts his arms around me, and pulls me close. I cry into his shirt, trying to wipe Jacob from my mind. His wide, scared eyes—and the Councilman pulling the noose tighter . . . until he just stopped moving.

It takes me a long while to get hold of myself. Tom smoothes my hair as I pull back. I lean into his touch. Glad, so glad, he's here. He takes my hands in his scarred ones and clears his throat. "Well, at least we're all still safe."

Still safe.

"Em?" He squeezes my hands. "What's wrong?"

I'm going to burst if I don't tell him. "Last week I missed the gates."

"You what?"

"I missed the closing of the gates."

He drops my hands. "How on Almighty's green earth did you manage to do that?"

"I lost the time—"

"How?" His eyes narrow.

"I . . . I was out gathering and got in my daydreaming way and . . ." I think about that day on the riverbank, him talking about my "choices." I'll have to tell him I went down that trail, after I said I wouldn't. I scramble for an explanation. "And I fell asleep." *Almighty forgive me.*

"How'd you get in?"

"One of the Watchers."

Tom waits.

"I said I wouldn't say who."

He raises his eyebrows. It's plain he's clear unimpressed with me and whoever my secret helper was. "That was real dangerous."

He's got no idea how dangerous. "I know." I look at the basket between us. I can feel his eyes sizing me up.

"Does Brother Stockham know?"

"No."

"Thank the Almighty for that."

I should tell him about the proposal, but I don't want to explain all that right now. I just want reassurance. A friend. I nod. "But . . . I have these dreams. About the woods. I feel like I need to go out there."

"Dreams."

I nod. "And after seeing Jacob, I'm . . . I'm scared."

Tom weighs my words a long time. "You don't have to be scared," he says finally. I wait for him to tell me no one will ever know. "You can stop."

I draw back. "Stop?"

He holds my gaze, his jaw tight.

"I can't control what I dream, Tom."

"I don't mean your dreams," he says. "I mean all of this." He tilts his head. "I think you do these things on purpose."

"Beg pardon?"

"You mean to do it."

I frown. "Why would I *mean* to be Wayward?"

"Because you think it's all you can be. Because you think you're good for nothing else."

"That's addled."

"Is it? Are you sure you're not punishing yourself for the Stain you didn't ask for?"

"Like your hands?"

Pain flashes in Tom's prairie-sky eyes. Then those skies turn black. He shakes his head, turns on his heel, and bangs through the coop door. I've done it now. Just twisted the knife where his pain is deepest.

Come back.

But I can't say it. I'm stinging too hard from his words. He's wrong—I don't do Wayward things because I think it's all I'm good for.

Do I?

I grab the basket, realizing too late I'm right wound. One of the eggs totters, then falls and lands with a crack. The yellow yolk that oozes onto the coop floor looks like Jacob's bulging eyes.

On my way back from delivering eggs to the Kitchens, I see a group of age-mates gathering in a corner of the courtyard. It's dusk and dew is settling on my bare arms; we'll need to be getting inside soon.

"Emmeline!" Macy beckons me over to her group. I recognize the girls from the dance—the west-quarter Textile workers—but the boys have their backs to me. I know two are south quarter; the rest I can't tell. They're surely speaking on Jacob and the Crossroads; everyone's been speaking on it all day.

I glance around, thinking on a way out.

"Emmeline!" Macy insists.

As I join the group I realize one of the south-quarter boys is Kane.

"This is Henri," Macy says all meaningful, and gestures toward a nice-looking boy across from me. She's risking a talking-to or worse; she's not even sixteen yet and she's hanging about with age-mates from other quarters. Mayhap she thinks she can get away with it because her pa's a Councilman.

I mumble a hello. The rest of the group does quick introductions—the Textile girls' names are Annabell and Mirabell. Bad luck, those names. There's Charlie Jameson, Brother Jameson's son. He's like his pa: suspicious, thinks he's above the rest of us. My eyes linger on Kane's face by accident, and the corner of his mouth twists into that funny smile.

I hide mine.

The other boy from the south quarter, who introduced himself as Robert, speaks up. "Anyone know what he did, then?"

They *are* speaking on Jacob. I don't want to be here, don't want to even be thinking on it . . .

Macy seems real pleased to be in the know. "He was already being watched for not showing at settlement events. Stole some eggs beginning of summer. Then last week got in a scuffle with another shearer." She's repeating what her pa told her no doubt, but the way she's telling it—it makes my skin crawl. Like she's happy he was found out. I didn't know Jacob, sure, but the way he fought . . . "The last straw?" She pauses for effect. "He forced himself on a bound woman from the south quarter." She throws a quick look my way.

My face goes hot.

"But they killed him? I mean, before putting him at the Crossroads?" Robert asks. He either doesn't know exactly how my grandma'am was Wayward or he's more interested in the awful details, because he doesn't look my way. "Why'd they do that?"

"Had to," Macy states. "He was putting up a fight and there was a crowd. It was for the best."

For the best. Was Council worried they couldn't control the crowd?

"I heard it was awful," Annabell or Mirabell says, eyes too big.

"I heard it was right skittering." The other -abell shudders.

Charlie smirks. "I heard he choked like an overfed ram."

"Oh!" Macy's mouth drops.

Jacob swims before my eyes, clawing at his throat, screaming that horrible, garbled cry.

Charlie's smirk gets wider. "He must've looked like a trussed chicken by the end."

Bulging eyes, struggling in the dirt. I close my eyes for a heartbeat, trying to wipe the picture clean.

"Bleed it, Charlie," someone curses. My eyes fly open and I see Robert frowning. I wonder how Kane feels about this; his face isn't letting on, it's all closed.

"What? It's misfortunate is all." Charlie looks around the circle defiantly, then jerks his chin at me. "Macy heard you saw it, Emmeline."

I nod slow. "I saw it."

"And?"

"And what?"

"What'd the shearer look like?"

"His name was Jacob," I say.

Kane's eyebrows raise.

"Well, then, what did *Jacob* look like?"

Scared eyes, that horrible, desperate cry . . . "I'm not one for speaking on that kind of thing."

"Why? Your kind stick together?"

Jacob vanishes. There's a pause, like the whole group takes a breath.

"Beg pardon?"

"Your kind: Wayward." Charlie smiles, but his eyes are all bite.

I raise my chin and look round the circle. Macy drops her eyes and digs a toe in the dirt. Henri and Robert look off into the distance and AnnaMirabell titter. And then I meet Kane's eyes. He's watching for my answer.

I turn to Charlie. "Don't know what you mean."

"Doesn't much seem you think that shearer deserved what he got. Mayhap you don't think your grandma'am deserved it, neither." His eyes narrow, but his mouth is curved in that mean smile. "Your Stain's showing, Emmeline."

The words slap at me like *La Prise*.

"Shut your maw, Charlie." Everyone looks to Kane, who is standing with his arms crossed. He's staring at Charlie real calm, but his face is dark.

The girls shift.

"Say again?"

"Shut. Your. Maw." Kane's voice is low, but there's a river of violence in it. "I need to tell you another way?"

Charlie's smirk falters. He looks around the group. No one is meeting anyone's eyes. "What if I said you do?"

Kane cocks his head to the side. "*Are* you saying that?"

No one speaks.

Charlie barks a forced laugh. "Settle down. I'm just having one over on Emmeline, here."

Kane's eyes don't leave Charlie's face.

"Don't have to get prickly." Charlie looks to Henri, but Henri just stares at the ground. The ground has become right interesting to most of the group, as a matter of fact.

Kane doesn't drop his gaze, doesn't move.

Charlie snorts again, then turns around and stalks away.

There's another silence, and then Anna- or Mirabell speaks. "We'd better get home."

Robert makes a similar declaration and the three melt away. In a few quick seconds it's just Henri, Macy, Kane, and me left. Kane's arms are still crossed, but he's softened his stance; he's not full to bursting with anger anymore. Henri and Macy are lingering—obviously hoping to speak together alone for a moment. Shame is bright in my chest. And something else too—something for Kane . . .

I don't want to owe him a debt, and I don't want his pity.

But when I look at him, those concerns wash away. His mouth is in that funny twist again, like we're sharing a secret joke. Like the secret joke is Charlie.

I wrap my arms around my waist and nod at the ground, but as I turn to go, I can't stop my mouth from echoing his smile.

"Affirmation is in less than two weeks, Em," Pa says.

I stoke the fire. "I know."

"You been thinking on the proposal, then?"

I nod, keeping my eyes on the flames.

"And?"

I turn to look at him. We didn't speak on the Wayward shearer. He doesn't even know I saw it. I think he prefers to think on what gives him hope—and all that gives him hope these days is Brother Stockham's proposal. He's sitting at the table with wary eyes. With his scruffy hair sticking this way and that he looks like a ruffled-up barn owl.

I remember another time he looked at me that way—like he was begging me to understand his meaning. It was the day my foot was crushed. He visited me at the Healing House, tried to explain what the east-quarter girl who'd pushed me was accusing. I sat there with my foot in an herb bath, watching my pa fumble with the word, watching him tell me my grandma'am was Wayward for something I couldn't understand at the time.

But when I asked him how him and Ma ended up bound, his eyes had gone wide, remembering. He said he chose her for her smile, didn't care what everyone else thought. He said that Ma was kind and brave, that he knew it would be the right choice. He looked so hopeful when he said it. He hasn't looked that hopeful again until now.

He followed his heart when he chose Ma. A flicker of hope springs to life in my chest. "Pa, I know it'd be real good for us. But . . ." I swallow. "I'm not so sure."

There's a long pause. The fire pops and crackles in the hearth. I turn back to him, force my eyes to meet his gaze, and see how wrong I am. In his eyes there is despair so deep, it's going to drown me.

"But why, Em?"

Jacob flashes into my mind. Brother Stockham's eyes. *I need you.* I trip on my words. "I'm—I'm not sure. I feel like . . . like there are other things that could be good for us."

"Like what?" He looks at my bad foot.

I try to stand straighter. What can I tell him? What will he hear?

"Sometimes it's hard to see what's best, my girl." He looks at me, his eyes full. Warning me to take his meaning.

And at once I can see what Pa thinks is best. I can see he wants so bad for my Stain to be washed away, he'd rather I bind to a man I don't want. It's plain on his face.

"We'll talk again, all right?"

I nod. It's childish to feel betrayed. Pa hasn't known my mind for years. Even so, I must've been holding out hope he'd understand me because I can feel a piece of my secret heart—the part that keeps my child's memories of a pa who danced me around the kitchen—dying a slow, icy death.

Feels like the winds of *La Prise* railing in my chest.

14

IN THE MORNING I CHOP AT THE WATER BUCKET with an axe. *La Prise* is heavy on the wind. I suffer through morning chores, Charlie's voice ringing in my ears.

Your Stain's showing, Emmeline.

Shame curdles with rage in my stomach. Tom's wrong about me caring more about my Stain than other people do. He's wrong about me worrying too much over Council watching me. I think about Brother Stockham, watching me for years.

And there it is. My way out of all of this. Binding to Brother Stockham—it's the one thing that'll change the way people look at me.

I put the thought in a box in my mind and bury it deep.

I focus careful on Soeur Manon's instructions for making medicines today. Can't let myself think on much else.

I'm banging out the hearth rug back at our quarters before free time when Sister Ann appears, Edith trailing behind.

"These bundles of sage go to the Kitchens." Her pinched

face looks more tired than usual. She offers some cursory instructions about where and who to deliver them to and dumps the bundles on the ground, then heads back inside.

Edith lingers, her round blue eyes watching me.

"What do you want, little mouse?"

She puts a finger in the corner of her mouth and smiles.

I smile back. "Scoot." I nod at her ma's retreating back.

On my way I meet a runner who is also heading for the Kitchens.

Inside, large vats sit on tabletops waiting on heating or spicing. There are three clay ovens and, judging by the blazing heat in the Kitchens, each is stocked full of wood. Sister Lucy, alone, mixes something on the center prep table. Her workers must be at the barns. The runner heads toward her with his message.

I make my way through the loops of drying root vegetables toward the far wall, where someone is waiting outside the Storages tunnel.

It's Kane, leaning against the wall easy-like, with a soft smile. Like he's waiting on me. He pushes off the wall as I approach.

"Sage," I say, tossing one bundle at his feet.

He nods. "Obliged. Been waiting."

I drop the second bundle.

"But I was expecting the usual runner. This is a good surprise; Matthew's a little hard on the eyes."

I bite my lip to fight a smile. "Need help taking them to Storages?" Bleed it! Course he doesn't need help.

"It can wait. I'm on free time now." He leans against the wall again. "You?"

"Emmeline! Kane!" Sister Lucy calls from the center of the kitchen. Coarse speckled flour covers her apron and hands to her elbows. She gestures to the large bowl before her. "These life day cakes need to be baked by noon." She wipes her hands on her apron and nods at the runner beside her. "There's a problem with the curing and I need to see to it. You can handle this task—it'll go faster with two. Mix it well. The saskatoons are there." She gestures to a clay bowl. "Waste nothing."

She bustles out.

I shrug out of my cloak and walk over to the washbowl.

Kane appears beside me, rolling up his sleeves. As I dry my hands, he washes, and I drop my eyes. Why are his hands and forearms unsettling? I've seen him without a shirt—

I close my eyes and push the thought from my mind.

We take our places at the prep table. The dough stares back at me from the bowl, lifeless. I hate baking. I throw a handful of rough flour at the table, sprinkling the surface.

"Not exactly how I was picturing free time," he comments, watching me stir the thick dough with a wooden spoon.

"I'll say."

"What were you going to do?"

I shrug and turn the dough onto the wooden surface.

"I was going to play hoopball," he offers.

"I'm sure," I say, sprinkling more flour on the dough.

"Thought you might want to join."

The other day on the riverbank floods in. "Pass me the berries." I nod at the bowl in front of him.

He passes it slow. I can feel his eyes on me. "So . . . no?"

"Why are you asking?" I snap, my eyes on the table. "I

mean, I know I'm not a *regular* girl . . ." I swallow and grab the slab of dough, pulling it rough into two pieces. I shove one piece at Kane and punch the dough hard.

"That's certain," he says. "Never met anyone like you."

Punch. "Count your blessings."

"Why would I do that?"

I punch again. "Less chance of being caught in the fray when punishment comes down."

I want him to say he came after me and Edith that night of Harvest. Him sticking up for me yesterday shifted something in me, and I want it to be true. I risk a look at him. He's frowning, like he can't figure my meaning.

The silence stretches between us. Then his eyebrows raise. "Ah. Virtue Talks," he says, misunderstanding. "That first night we talked."

"What of it?"

"You think I was appalled. About your offenses."

Well, that is true. That exchange still fills me with shame when I think on it. I keep my eyes on the dough.

"Is that why you're so prickly with me?"

"What?"

"Prickly."

"I am not!" But as it leaves my mouth, I realize how prickly it sounds. I swallow and focus back on the dough.

"Look, what I said that night . . . ," he says, "it came out all wrong."

"Which part?"

"After Brother Stockham told you to head to Watch. It sounded like I was angry. At you." He's trying to get me to look at him.

"I was being punished for Wayward acts." I push and knead nervous-like.

"Sure." His shifts and falls silent again. "It's just . . . I've thought about skipping those things—life day ceremonies and such—before. Never quite had the nerve."

My heart skips and I falter in my rough handling of the dough. Kane turns his attention on his portion, adding half of the berries.

I try not to watch his forearms as he kneads. I sprinkle the rest of the berries on my portion and knead again, then grab the roller and attack. A large chunk breaks off and I have to pat it back into place.

"You ever made life day cake?" Kane asks, sounding amused.

I feel the heat rise in my cheeks. "No. I'm only ever at the Kitchens for delivery."

"Well, here." He places his hands on the roller, on top of mine.

He moves our hands, rolling the dough into a circle in a few quick strokes.

We are shoulder to shoulder and the heat from his body sears right through my side, his rough hands warm over mine. I keep my gaze low, sure I'll blush to my toes if our eyes meet. Can't quite figure his know-how at this task. It seems so unlike something he'd want to be good at.

His hands linger a moment. "There."

When he straightens and lets go, I miss his touch straight-away. I watch him do the same to his portion. Then he crosses to an oven and opens the doors wide. The fire roars back at us. Grabbing a large wooden paddle from underneath the prep table, he clears his throat and asks, "So what's gathering for Soeur Manon like?"

I'm short for breath and take a moment to answer. "All right." I shrug like I'm feeling easy, which I'm not. "She's got all these old books of interesting things."

"What things?"

"Plants and animals and such. Wish I could read them." I feel the heat rise in my cheeks again. I'm not ashamed I can't read, not many people can, but admitting I'd *like* to feels like uncovering a part of my secret heart to him.

"Could you show me the books someday?" He shoves the board under the dough, concentrating more than he ought.

"Why?"

He shoves the paddle in the oven, shakes the dough off onto the rocks. "Because . . . I've read all my ma's books."

Kane can read. He turns toward me but doesn't meet my eyes. Is he embarrassed? I scramble to speak. "Sure! I mean, course—someday on free time or whenever you have a moment, or . . ."

Stop jabbering.

He drops the paddle on the table and smiles. "That's good of you, Em."

"How'd you learn?"

"Ma taught me during *La Prise*. She says it's a good thing to know."

My pa can't read. I wonder if my ma could? I wonder if she would've taught me.

"And I think it *is* a good thing; reading always gets me thinking."

"Thinking on what?" I say, a mite eager. But that tiny flare of hope that Kane is a wonderer, like me, is burning bright now.

"Ways to figure things."

"Like what?" *Stop asking questions!*

He shrugs. "Settlement goings-on. Sometimes I think there must be a better way to hunt those bison herds. Mayhap if I were allowed to join the hunt I could find it."

"I've seen you practicing knife throwing. Like that?"

"Knife throwing's just something to try to get good at," he says. "But . . . just sometimes I wonder about things, if it could be different. You ever think that?"

"All the time," I say, thinking about the woods, how high my hopes were for that trail.

"That why you're always thinking on something?"

"Beg pardon?"

"When I see you on chores, you're either thinking hard with your head down, or gazing beyond the Watch flats like you see something the rest of us don't."

A flush of pleasure washes me. Kane's noticed me that much?

He steps close, reaches out, and touches two fingers to my brow. "What goes on in there?"

I have to close my eyes a moment against the dizzy feeling.

"You got some big wish for your years ahead?"

My eyes fly open. I pull my head back. He doesn't know about the proposal. How could he? It won't be common news until Affirmation. He's waiting for an answer.

"That I won't be in the east quarter forever," I say. "That I get out."

"Oh?" He laughs again. "Well, take me with you when you go."

Warmth creeps up my chest and into my cheeks again. His face is so open, so inviting, like he's asking me to lay my thoughts full bare. My conversation with Tom about my Stain comes flooding in, about people seeing me for me. *There are others too.* All at once I want to tell someone— no, I want to tell *him*—and the words tumble from me. "I've already been out."

"Sure." He grabs the paddle again and turns toward the oven. "Gathering. Across the flats."

"No. I mean, *out.*"

He stops and turns back. The oven casts an orange glow behind him so I can't see his face plain, mostly just the whites of his eyes.

"Where?" he asks.

"The Crossroads."

His eyes get wide. The air grows thick. I look down and trace a finger in the leftover flour. I don't know what I expected him to say, but all at once I'm less sure it was a good idea to confess so much. I try not to lean on my foot, try to stay calm without the pain.

"Why?" He breathes so quiet I barely hear him over the roar of the oven. He stands real still.

"I don't know *why*," I stammer. "It was on accident, sort of. I lost track of time and it got to be dusk—"

"*Dusk?*" Impossibly, his eyes get bigger.

"I mean, I saw the flag and knew I shouldn't be there, I just . . ." I shake my head. "I needed to *see.*"

"Em, that was—" he starts, but I cut him off.

"Please don't say anything to Council! I shouldn't have done it; I know that. But I don't have a *death wish*." I throw his words back at him with some heat. "I know you think it was foolish."

"No." He takes a breath, like he's short for it. His eyes are wary, but there's a softness in them. "I wasn't going to say 'foolish'—"

Whatever he *was* going to say is cut off by the main door banging open and Sister Lucy appearing.

"Thank you, Kane, Emmeline. You may go."

I hurry to grab up my cloak.

"Em!" Kane calls as I head out the Kitchens door and into the courtyard. "Wait!"

I turn back but draw up short.

Three Councilmen are coming round the wall of the Kitchens. Kane follows my gaze, then turns back to me and nods. *Go,* he mouths. Then he turns and heads straight for them.

"Brothers," he calls out, like he has business with them. Can't imagine what he'll dream up to say, but it's clear he's buying me a moment to escape. My secret heart swells.

I turn and make myself scarce.

15

I DON'T SEE KANE THE NEXT DAY, OR THE NEXT. It seems our chores are suddenly at odds, because I'm sent to Storages and Kitchens several times in those two days and each time I go—cabbage moths aflutter in my stomach—I run into everyone but Kane.

I spot him from afar at Virtue Talks, but something tells me consorting with him in front of Brother Stockham is a bad idea. And whatever he said the other day must've caught their fancy, because the Councilmen are forever hanging near him.

I can't get the other day—his last words—out of my head: *I wasn't going to say "foolish."* And his face when I told him about being at the Crossroads: I've seen that look before. On Tom. That curious part of Tom, the part that would let him wonder about things if he weren't so afraid: it was plain as day in Kane's eyes. He's not afraid to follow me.

The thought of binding to Brother Stockham now is just impossible. I think about him out in the woods that day;

what if he were doing something contrary to his virtues? Surely I wouldn't be expected to bind to him *then*.

I can't leave the idea alone; I turn it over and over in my mind. I need to get back out there, only this time I need to do it without losing my way and stumbling on the Crossroads instead.

In my dreams that night, I'm climbing that spruce-covered hill, and the trees are full of bright-colored threads. The girl's voice is calling to me, urging me forward. In one hand I have a little leather book, cracked and falling apart. In the other hand, my grandma'am's ring burns bright on my finger. There's a light coming from the other side of the hill. If I can only reach the top . . .

I wake to a kill frost.

When I go for gathering duties, Soeur Manon tells me there's nothing to gather anymore, that I should come back tomorrow to learn some poultices. It means I have the day to myself, and everyone else is busy with their tasks.

It's a sign. Has to be. My dreams have given me a way to search those woods without getting lost. I have to go.

Back at our quarters, I wait until Tom's ma has left for the barns, then I enter the common room attached to our kitchen. I pull her fabric basket from its place on the shelf and dig through the wool threads. She's been saving them to make Tom's pa a new *ceinture fléchée,* but she doesn't have near enough yet. She won't be working on it for a while, and surely won't notice a few of the brightest pieces are missing for a day.

"What's got, Em?"

I jump. Edith is standing in the common room, her fingers

twisting a lock of her blond hair. I stick my hands behind my back, hiding the threads away from her curious gaze.

"What are you doing, little mouse? Who's watching you?" I back away from her, through the common room to our kitchen door.

"Me." Tom appears at the door that joins their quarters to the common room. He looks at me cautious-like. We haven't been on chores together since that day in the coop.

"Morning," I say, keeping my hands hidden.

"Morning." He hesitates, his eyes guarded. Then his shoulders soften. "I—I wanted to say sorry, for the other day. I shouldn't have said those things." He offers the Peace by way of apology.

Relief washes me. "Me, neither," I say quick. But I can't move my hand to offer the Peace back, not with the threads in them.

He smiles, a bit uncertain. "Where are you off to?"

My heart sinks; I have to lie to him. Again. I can't pull him out of Edith's earshot and tell him the truth. He cares for me, but burdening him with my secrets doesn't do either of us much good; that much was made plain the other day. "Just running something to Soeur Manon."

"I come wif?" Edith takes a step toward me.

"Don't think so, mouse." My fingers fumble for the latch on the door behind me.

"Stop by when you're back? Found some late-harvest mint. We could make tea," Tom says.

"I'll try," I say, and his eyes dull. Bleed it! I want to say yes, it's just I don't know how long I'll be out in the woods.

Tom steps forward and takes Edith's hand. "Come on,

Edith." Tugging her behind him, he disappears into their quarters.

Inside my room, I put on my wool socks and moccasins and wrap up in a winter cloak, swallowing a pang of guilt. I want to apologize proper to Tom. I want him to make tea and talk about nothing like we used to.

But going to the grove can't wait.

Hoping it looks like I'm on some errand, I head through the west gates. In the south end of the fort, a few gatherers are pulling the last of the squash from the garden. Outside the walls a few women are banging out hides and rugs. The wind whistles across the Watch flats, cold but not death-cold. Not yet.

In the scrub there's a dead smell in the air. I push in past the bramble to where the woods give way to *les trembles*. Fallen leaves lie in wet clumps around their trunks. Less leaves means less cover for things to hide in, but somehow the rows and rows of shedding poplars are more skittering.

Everything looks the same: sentenced, lifeless.

Another week and these woods will be blanketed white, signaling *La Prise* and everything that follows.

I make it to the ravine and labor up it as quiet as I can. My skin gets prickly as I approach the grove and pass through. I go several paces along the Crossroads path, but when I reach the place where I spotted Brother Stockham, I stop and close my eyes a minute. He'd walked off to the . . . northwest. I fish around in my satchel, bring out a few bright pieces of thread, and tie them on the nearest branch. Then I set my feet toward the northwest and push ahead, moving slow.

For such a dead bit of forest, it sure feels alive. I keep checking behind me as I walk, so it's slow going. Round about every forty strides, I tie new threads to a tree. I've walked for five or so minutes when I come upon a tree-covered hill.

My heart speeds. It's the one in my dreams.

I stop and listen careful.

Silence.

I'm taking a step forward when something bursts from the bush on my right. I leap back, panic shooting through my body. Then I see the grouse. It's flapping off through the woods in a heart-stopping flurry of feathers.

Foolish.

I take a deep breath, try to slow the racing in my chest.

Forcing my feet forward, I climb through the spruce and push for the top. I feel the way I did the other day when I came upon the Crossroads flag, like I'm about to see something I need to see. I pick up my pace, eager.

But as I crest the hill, the scene below stops me dead. The hill slopes downward, the trees thin out and become low scrub, emptying into a gully.

In the middle of the gully is a cabin.

Not a ruined cabin like the others around the fortification, not an abandoned jumble of old decaying logs and moss sinking back into the earth. No. These log walls are clean of moss, chinked perfect. The thatched roof is intact. It's a proper cabin.

I stand there stupidly, trying to reconcile the sight. Then it dawns on me I am full exposed; if anyone were to step out of the cabin, they'd see me in an instant. I dart behind a tree and sink to the ground, my heart thudding in my ears. The spruce trees on this hill are spindly, with scrubby branches that begin a foot above my head—scarce cover from someone inside the cabin.

But who would be inside?

My mind whirls. I need to get down the hill unseen. I can't be sure anyone is around, but my skin is prickling like I'm being watched. Peering around the tree, I risk a better look at the cabin. I can't shake the feeling I'm not alone.

There are no windows and no sound is coming from inside.

I crawl out from behind the tree, keeping close to the ground, aiming for another sizeable tree a few strides away so I can get a mite closer. I start down the hill that way, moving from one tree to another. I'm halfway toward the next spruce when the door swings wide.

I flatten to the ground, praying to the Almighty my cloak and dark hair blend in with the leaves and deadfall.

I wait with my face to the earth. Dead still. Can't stay here. Need to leave before whoever that is sees me. Sees me and climbs over here, hauls me to my feet, drags me back to Council—my thoughts start to splinter. I wait for a hand to grab my cloak . . .

Nothing. Inching my head back up, I see a figure with dark hair disappearing back into the shack. Brother Stockham? I scramble back behind the tree.

There's a little fire burning in my gut. I have to get inside. But how long can I wait? What if someone realizes I'm not working for Soeur Manon today and they can't find me? Won't they report me to Council? What should I do?

I can be careful. I can at least get within listening distance of whatever is going on in there.

What in Almighty's name *could* be going on in there? It's so strange that I wonder if I'm imagining it all. I pinch the skin on the top of my left hand. It smarts. I'm not dreaming. Am I?

One way to find out.

I'm about to get to my feet when I hear something in the woods to my right. It's coming through the trees in the distance, careful but not real quiet.

Could be a deer. Or a wolf.

Or something else.

The thin spruces that cover this side of the hill are no cover at all. I have to choose the side of the hill with the cabin and go quick—too quick to be secret-like—or head back to the grove. Or . . . or risk meeting whatever that is coming upon me. *L'homme comme l'elephant.* Andre's words ring around in my head.

I can get a look inside the cabin later.

I crawl backward from the crest of the hill, then turn and hurry as quiet as I can back toward the Crossroads trail, stepping hard on my bad foot even when I try not to. I rip the threads from the branches as I go.

One bunch of threads is troublesome and I have to stop to use some force. My last footfall, whispering through the fallen leaves, quiets—but the sound comes a heartbeat later than it should, it seems.

I move to the next mark of threads and stop. The woods are silent. I start walking, then stop abrupt. My noise goes silent—again, too late.

Something is following me.

I am almost to the grove, but I can feel that something

behind me. Not too near, but I'm right certain it's following my path. Mayhap even hanging back on purpose.

No.

That's addled. What could be tracking me that wouldn't want to get too close?

I force my legs to stop. I stand quiet in the middle of the woods, my ears pricked for any sound. But it's quiet all around me—no footsteps, no cracking branches.

A prickle touches my neck. I pick up my pace as I head through the trees to the ravine. I need to talk to Andre.

I find him oiling rifles in the weapons shack with that tall Watcher with the fearsome scar. Andre glances up in surprise, squinting at my flushed cheeks and unkempt hair.

"Luc," he says to the Watcher, jerking his head toward the door. Luc gives me a long look before setting down a rifle and making himself scarce. Andre gestures for me to sit beside him.

I'm still breathing hard from the trek, so it takes me a moment to get the words out. "Brother Andre, about the other week. That day of the Harvest ceremony."

He holds up a hand; I stop talking. He watches the door a moment, listening. Then he speaks in a hushed tone. *"Oui?"*

I drop my voice too. "What you saw in the woods: *l'homme comme l'elephant.* Are you sure it wasn't . . ."

Andre's eyes widen and he leans closer still.

"Brother Stockham?" He draws back, but I carry on: "Think he might"—I search for the words—"go walking in the woods. Think I just saw him there."

Andre looks at me for a moment. Then he gets to his feet

and paces away from me, toward the door. *"Non, pas Frère Stockham. C'est pas possible."*

"You're sure you didn't see him."

"Non, I am sure *you* did not see him."

I pause. "I did. A little while ago." I stand and follow him.

"Mais, Soeur Emmeline, il est ici."

"Where?"

"Avec Council." Andre pushes open the door and gestures to the Council building. It looms opposite the weapons shack, casting a large shadow on the main courtyard.

I am about to protest again, but the building's front doors open and a clean-dressed Brother Stockham steps out. He speaks a moment with the Councilman outside the doors, then looks up and meets my gaze.

I snap my gaping maw shut and force my body to move, lifting my hand and giving a halfhearted nod. His eyes measure me for a heartbeat. He nods. Descending the steps, he heads for the ceremonial hall. Councilmen appear at the doors and as I watch them follow him, I realize Kane is with them. I have a fleeting fuddled thought for him.

"Tu comprends?" Andre puts a hand on my shoulder.

"I . . ." I stare after the group, trying to get my fuzzy thoughts in order.

"Emmeline? What did you see?"

I snap to and find Andre staring at me, eyes wide. "No one. I guess."

"Peut etre la même chose de moi?" He means the same thing he saw: the Elephant Man.

Feeling dazed, I shake my head. "No."

"You are sure?"

"Yes. Why?"

"Parce que je l'ai revue."

He saw it again.

"Where?"

"Le bois."

"Why were you in the woods this time?"

He hesitates.

"Please," I say.

He scratches at his beard again. *"C'est difficil—"* He pauses and searches for the English words. "I have this feeling. To be out there." He peers at me. *"J'ai des rêves. D'un don de Dieu."*

He dreams about a gift of God. I think about my dreams of running through the woods, the Lost People calling to me, my burning curiosity to follow that trail—

"Un don de Dieu en le bois. So I go to see. But I find . . . I find *l'homme d'elephant encore.* He disappear. No noise."

I stare at him. He has a thin sheen of sweat on his brow. It's plain he saw something he can't explain. Again. I murmur reassurances and leave quick. Before I reach our quarters, I have to stop and put my hands on my knees: my head is spinning.

Who *did* I see? It was no Elephant Man, that's certain. No *gift of God.* Mayhap Andre is old and seeing things. Mayhap he's seeing what he wants to; what he thinks his dreams are telling him.

Mayhap I am too?

No. That cabin was real and someone was there. I breathe deep and force myself to consider the only explanations: either Brother Stockham can be in two places at once, or someone else knows about that cabin.

16

NEXT DAY I BREAK MY FAST WITH PA, FEELING like a caged animal. He's eyeballing me in a spooky way. Either he knows I was out in the woods yesterday, or . . .

He wipes his hands on his *ceinture fléchée* as he pushes back from the table. "Emmeline, can you change your clothes?"

I look down at my tunic and leggings. "What for?"

"Brother Stockham's paying a visit. Soeur Manon knows you won't be in until later on."

"It's . . . a courting visit?"

"Course." Pa nods at my leggings and tunic. "You'll need to be dressed proper."

Fear squeezes my throat. Brother Stockham. Looking at me. Looking through to my thoughts.

"Your ma's dress would look real nice."

Brother Stockham stands in the doorway, tidy and calm. His dark hair is tucked behind his ears, his tunic spotless.

"Brother Stockham, please." Pa beckons him in through the door.

Brother Stockham doesn't move. "I thought Emmeline might enjoy some fresh air." He offers his arm. "Care to walk?"

I throw a look to Pa, hoping he'll insist Brother Stockham stay put—where a proper courting visit should take place. My pa's eyes are uncertain a moment, then he straightens his shoulders and smiles.

"Course she would. Wouldn't you, Em?"

Brother Stockham sweeps his arm toward the courtyard. "We'll return within the hour."

I cast my eyes low and step out beside him. Inside, I'm in a cold sweat. The fabric of my ma's dress itches at me everywhere.

As we walk, Brother Stockham speaks. "Your father is a very virtuous man."

I nod.

"He works very hard," he says.

"He has—" I stop. "Yes."

"You were going to say 'He has to.'"

"I only meant . . . well, on account of our Stain. He works hard because—"

"I understand."

We approach the Healing House. Soeur Manon is at the door, sweeping out her kitchen. As we pass, she looks at us with her watery eyes and goes still. Brother Stockham inclines his head and she offers the Peace in return.

"You gather for Soeur Manon."

"No," I say quick, my thoughts flying to the woods. He

tilts his head. "I mean, yes. But I'm learning her poultices now. Her broths and such."

He raises an eyebrow but says nothing, guiding me along like he's got someplace to be, like getting fresh air is the last thing on his mind. I realize with a start that we're headed for the ceremonial hall.

Inside it's empty, dead quiet. With no windows to let in the autumn sunshine, everything falls pitch black when he shuts the door. For a heartbeat there is just the sound of our breathing. Mine is coming too fast.

What are we doing here?

He strikes a flint. "After you," he says, gesturing toward the pulpit at the front of the hall.

He lights the torches as we make our way to the front and soon the space is pockmarked with circles of yellow light. The shadows from the ceremonial table, with its wooden box and candles, stretch tall to the thatched ceiling above us.

We climb the stairs to the table, my heart beating hard. At the top he turns me toward him. I remember that prey bird plucking the walleye from the river right in front of us. I swallow and meet his eyes—praying to Almighty I look nervous like any young girl with a suitor would, not nervous like I know something about him I shouldn't.

He tucks a lock of his hair behind his ear. "Thank you for accompanying me here."

"Course," I say, wondering what choice I had.

"I'm keeping you from your work, no doubt," he says.

I shrug, trying to look easy. "The poultices can wait."

"And the gathering?"

Why is he asking after that? I feel my cheeks start to pink. "Not much to gather these days."

"But you often head outside the fortification."

My insides freeze over. I'm back in the woods, face pressed to the earth on that hill . . .

Go with something close to the truth.

I think about the arrowheads and bone tools tucked under my bed. "I spend my free time on the riverbank, looking for left-behinds."

"You have a fascination with such things, don't you?"

"Tom and I've been gathering left-behinds since we were children."

"Since you were children. But"—he leans close—"you are no longer a child, Emmeline."

I swallow. "I'm just interested."

"And interesting." His gaze traces over my face and lingers on my mouth. I want to clap my hands over it. I look around for something—anything—to look at, and settle on the locked wooden box on the ceremonial table beside us.

He notices. "The sacraments."

I nod. I know the sacraments for the virtues commitment ceremony at Affirmation lie inside: a sacred plate and cup, a cloth. But I've always wondered, "Why is it locked?"

"Because what's inside is much more than a ceremony symbol."

My eyebrows raise.

"Inside is our commitment to life, or to death. What we decide for the days ahead." He looks across the hall, to the dancing flames of the torches. When he looks back at me, that strange, uncertain look is back in his eyes. "Emmeline, could you . . . tell me your ideas for the days ahead?"

"Days ahead." I repeat his words, trying to figure them. Is he speaking on the proposal or something else? I don't want to address the proposal so I hedge with the something else: "I . . . I want to prove my Discovery virtue."

A pause. "Do you."

"I want to prove it so everyone knows I'm . . . worthy."

"I already find you worthy." His gaze makes the room suddenly smaller, the walls tunneling in around us. It's not proper: him and me alone together, in this dark hall.

I have to drop my eyes—I can feel my cheeks growing hot—as I fumble for something to say. "It's just . . . you said our salvation lies in Discovery. And I believe that too. But I'm not always certain proving Discovery is possible without disobeying Council." His eyes narrow.

Grace!

"I mean, we can't risk the safety of the settlement, I know that. But how will we ever know what can help us if we don't venture out, if we don't . . ."

What am I saying? I'm making it worse. I trail off, a trout gasping for air on the riverbank.

But he smiles. "You are a thinker, Emmeline. I admire that."

I duck my head. The leader admiring me? He can't mean it.

"Discovery is something I have thought long and hard about. To what lengths should we go in order to uphold that virtue? How can we be sure the risk will result in a better life for our people?" He rubs a hand over his jaw. "It's something my grandfather wrestled with. My father had no use for such ponderings; he thought my grandfather was a doddering fool."

That squirmy feeling is back in the pit of my stomach. What risk is he speaking on? How does he know what his grandpa thought about?

"My father's idea of leadership was clear. He had no use for decisions made from impulse, from desire"—he pauses and holds my gaze—"from love."

I swallow hard.

"He taught me that I could lead, or I could desire. But never both." His hands go to the ties of his cloak. "I have been waiting for nearly ten years, wondering if it was possible to prove him wrong. Thinking. Praying."

Then he does something I'm not prepared for. He undoes the tie of his cloak and lets it billow to the floor at his feet.

My breath stops as he grabs the leather ties at the neck of his shirt and pulls them loose in one quick motion, jerking the fabric aside, revealing a bare shoulder.

My face burns. I should drop my eyes, I should look away. But I can't.

I can't because I can see the deep, violent marks snaking over his shoulder and onto his chest. He turns away from me, drawing his shirt back further. The scars continue down his back, disappear under the shirt.

Seeing his damaged skin . . . my stomach hollows out. The scars dance in the candlelight, twisting, winding. Without thinking I reach toward his back—my fingers want to trace those scars.

He freezes.

I drop my hand, press into my bad foot. Hard.

He turns around and tugs his shirt back in place.

"That—"I swallow. "*That* helped you learn his teachings?"

A muscle twitches in his jaw. He doesn't reply, but that unguarded look in his eyes is back. Like he's answering me. Like he could only ever speak this plain with me. The pressure of his pa's expectations is plain. And I understand.

The torches flicker long shadows around us.

He leans forward and lifts a hand to my face, brushing a wisp of hair from my cheek. "Tell me what you do out there. Outside the walls." His fingers trail to rest on my collarbone.

My Wayward acts scream around my head. I want to lie, but the look in his eyes . . . it's like he's seeing my thoughts plain. Images tear through my mind: Brother Jameson strangling that shearer, the bone-filled gibbets, the cabin. What does he want to hear? Why has he been waiting near ten years?

I can feel a flush starting up my neck. "I . . . well, I look for left-behinds."

He waits, his eyes liquid. Hopeful.

"And . . . I listen."

He is mesmerized. His fingers start to travel upward, beyond the collar of my dress to my bare neck. "What do you listen to?"

"Everything. The river, the wind, the birds. I mean, it sounds addled, but"—I swallow—"sometimes it seems the woods are talking to me."

His fingers stop. "I've—I've often felt that way."

We stare at one another in the half-light. Then his fingers burn a single line as they trace to my chin. He tilts my face toward him, his chiseled face, shining dark hair. "But I don't know what they say."

"I think I know."

He leans close. That hope in his eyes—it makes me want to lean close too.

My voice is a whisper. "They say *Find us.*"

He stops dead. For a moment I think that he's going to pull away. But then something flashes across his face—excitement? Relief? He leans forward to put his lips to my brow. The kiss brands my skin, sends hot pins and needles everywhere.

He steps back, looking me over. "You are very much like her."

I take a short, hiccupy breath. "Who?"

"Your grandmother."

I draw back, the pins and needles turning to ice. "How can you possibly know that?"

His smile falters.

"Brother Stockham." We both jump. Brother Jameson appears from nowhere, stepping out from a dark corner of the hall.

Oh, for the grace! When did he come in?

His hand is across his chest in the Peace of the Almighty, but there's no peace in his eyes. "This is a most unusual sight."

My eyes fly to Brother Stockham, stepping away from me. The laces of his shirt are undone, his cloak lies around our feet. Blood rushes loud through my ears, heating my face.

"Brother Jameson," Brother Stockham says, "I didn't see you there."

Brother Jameson walks toward us, his hands clasped behind his back. He's leveling me a look I'm well used to. I want to disappear.

Brother Jameson raises his eyebrows. "I am interrupting."

"Nonsense."

There's a silence. The hall creaks around us, the torches flicker.

Brother Jameson stops. "You've taken to giving Virtue Talks privately?"

"This is a courting visit."

Brother Jameson's eyes go wide with shock. Then they narrow with disdain. "Is it." He's looking at me like I'm not fit to clean the sheep pens.

"It is." Brother Stockham's face is pleasant enough, but there's a warning in his voice.

"And when were you going to inform Council you had chosen a life mate? That you'd chosen a . . . Stained?"

"I'm telling you now." They stare at one another, shadows dancing on the walls, on their faces. Something real strange passes between them.

I'm used to being eyeballed, but a part of me wants Brother Stockham to set Brother Jameson straight, tell him to speak to me with more respect. Another part of me wants to scream that the proposal's not a done deal, not yet.

Brother Jameson straightens. "Well, then, I will tell Council the good news." He turns on his heel and sweeps out. The door bangs shut behind him, echoing in the hall.

Bleeding Almighty! Everyone will know about the proposal within a day. My secret heart dies a thousand deaths right there.

I turn to Brother Stockham, my cheeks hot. "I have to go. Soeur Manon needs all the rose hips I can find." Bleed it! I already told him there was nothing left to gather.

But he just says, "Of course," and I can see his thoughts are elsewhere. His eyes trace over the wooden box behind me.

I swallow and turn to start down the steps, but he catches hold of my hand.

I'm brought up short, and as I turn back, he brings my hand to his mouth, places a kiss on my knuckles. His eyes are piercing. "We will prove him wrong."

I don't know who he's speaking on: Jameson or his pa. A sick flush washes me. I nod and remove my hand careful, then all but throw myself down the steps and out the hall doors.

Our quarters are empty, thanks be. I dash into my room, thinking to look for one of my left-behinds, thinking mayhap that little clay figure might soothe me. Instead, my hands move as if of their own accord, and I grab my grandma'am's ring from under my pillow. Then I tuck it into my moccasin. A wave of exhaustion sweeps me and for a minute I think about lying down, burying my face in the pillow. But I need out of here. Out of these walls. I need to get back to that cabin.

I slip out the side door, turn at the corner of our quarters, and head for the west gates.

Once I get past the Watch flats and into the first line of trees, I run.

17

I SPRINT FOR THE WOODS, RAGE RUNNING UNDER my skin like a herd of bison, trampling my good sense into dust. Brother Stockham's hands, his eyes, Brother Jameson's sneer—it all swims before me, mixing with my tears, blurring my sight. I don't know why I'm crying and it fills me with new fury. Brittle undergrowth claws and slaps at my legs, pulls at my bad foot, but I just run and run. The hem of my dress catches on a branch. I pull hard at the skirt and keep going.

Panting, I get to the grove and fall to my knees on the cold earth. When I catch my breath and raise my head, the forest looms, dwarfing me.

I sit quiet for a minute, but it's just the familiar noises of the woods around me—creaking poplars, rustling leaves. The Lost People are whispering in the tops of the branches, looking on. Out here, far from Brother Stockham, far from the hope in my pa's eyes, I can breathe. I feel better tucked away in here, in these trees.

As my heart slows and my skin cools, I realize I'm not dressed proper; it's a bright autumn afternoon but crisp, and inside the trees it's right chill. I should have brought at least my cloak. My dress is also torn something awful—up one side to above my knee. I smooth the fabric, feeling a pang of regret. This dress is the only thing I have that was my ma's. Inside my moccasin, the ring digs into the side of my bad foot and snuffs out the thought. I don't have time for regrets. I have just enough time to get to that cabin, get inside. Unless . . .

I try to shove the thought from my mind, but it barrels in: unless Brother Stockham really can be in two places at once. Or two moments in time, because what did he mean, speaking on my grandma'am like that? How would he know what she was like? And why did I feel like I could tell him about the woods after he lied to me about being out here? Was he trying to trick me?

Stop it.

My head aches, echoing the throb in my leg. I'm bone tired, but there's only one thing that matters and I don't have much time. I climb to my feet and head toward the center of the grove to get my bearings. I rub my hands over my arms for warmth and turn to the northwest. A branch snaps behind me.

"What are you doing out here?"

I spin.

Kane is standing at the edge of the clearing, his arms folded over his chest. He's wearing a sensible winter cloak, but his head is bare.

Relief washes me as I let out my breath. A spark of joy

bursts in my heart. I want to run to him. But I draw back. What am *I* doing out here?

"Could ask you the same thing."

"Came after you."

"Why?" I can feel the cabin—hidden in the trees behind me—signaling like a torch.

"Saw you leave. All upset-like. Wanted to make sure you were all right."

"You shouldn't be out here," I say.

"Neither should you."

I look him over careful. "Well, I am."

"Me too."

I move toward a fallen log on the edge of the clearing and sit.

He crosses and settles beside me. "Aren't you cold?"

"A mite," I admit. He removes his cloak and drapes it over my shoulders. I think to protest, but I'm too grateful for the warmth. "Thank you."

"It's all right."

There's a pause and I'm suddenly aware of how close he sits. I can feel the heat of his body through our clothes. My own skin feels on fire.

"I'm good at this." He rubs at the back of his neck.

"What?"

"Running after you."

The false attack. He's admitting it. My feelings about that, lodged inside my secret heart, burst up into my throat. I speak before I lose my nerve. "I know what you did at Harvest, coming after Edith and me—"

He cuts me off. "It's fine, Em. Truly."

"But you didn't have to do that."

"Yes, I did." A silence. Then he smiles. "Just stop running off, all right?"

"I'll try." I smile back.

"So"—he looks around the grove—"what *are* you doing out here?"

I hesitate. Should I tell him?

"Gathering."

"This far?"

I shrug.

He rubs a hand over his shaved head. "Without a cloak or satchel?"

I don't answer.

"You're not thinking of going back to the Crossroads, are you?" His eyes are so worried I want to laugh. I *wish* the Crossroads were my concern.

"I'm not going back to the Crossroads."

"You sure?"

"I'm sure." And then, just like in the Kitchens, I want to tell him—I want to show him the cabin, tell him about Brother Stockham in the woods the other day. I want to confide in him.

"Good. I don't want you to do anything unthinking. I know Affirmation's coming up."

I freeze. "Yes . . ."

"I mean, I . . . I heard about Brother Stockham's proposal."

Word travels fast. My face flames and I cross my arms over my chest. "Don't want to speak on it." I stare at the ground.

"Don't have to."

Then, my tongue running along ahead of my mind like a runaway cart, I'm speaking on it. "Course Pa thinks this is the best thing that could happen to us. Finally! A chance to clear our Stain." I close my eyes and shake my head. "Pa's so hopeful—he's walking about with his head high for the first time in I don't know how long. He doesn't want to hear that I don't want to bind to Brother Stockham. He doesn't want to know that Brother Stockham skitters me—proper skitters me—'cause it's always like he's seeing into my head, seeing my thoughts!"

Oh, for the grace! I snap my mouth shut.

Kane stares at me with wide eyes.

"I shouldn't have said that." I turn away from him.

"Em, it's all right." His tone is so gentle it makes my insides weak.

I clench the edges of the cloak tighter, keeping my hands tucked around me, keeping them from wandering where they have a mind to go. This is addled; I'm addled. My temper boils up again, but now I can't figure at who exactly—Pa? Brother Stockham? Myself?

"Why'd you come after me?" I turn back and stare at him hard. "Truly? Why?"

"I told you—"

"Sure, you were worried. Worried about the Stained girl. The cripple." I stare at my bad foot, feeling shameful tears throbbing behind my eyes. I can't cry. I won't.

It's silent for a few horrible moments. I half expect him to pick himself up and ask for his cloak back.

When he speaks, though, his voice is soft. "Why does it bother you?" He's looking at my foot.

I bite my lip. Surely he knows why it bothers me. Even so, the words come. Halting and unsure. "It . . . marks me. Can't—can't do things proper."

"Don't see it holding you back too much," he says, looking around the grove. "You're out further than anyone I know would dare."

"You say that like it's a good thing."

"Good or not, takes courage."

We sit in silence a moment.

He speaks again. "There was a story in one of my ma's books I read once, about a town overrun with mice. The townspeople called a piper to come and take the mice away. He could do it magic-like; he'd play music on his flute that the mice would follow, so the townspeople promised him a huge reward to drive the mice from the town."

I look at him from the corner of my eye. I can't figure what he's speaking on, but the gentle currents of his voice are tugging at me again. He's leaning forward, forearms resting on his knees.

"So he played his pipe and headed for the river, and the mice followed him and were washed away and drowned. But when he came for his reward, the townspeople wouldn't pay.

"The piper warned them if they didn't pay, something terrible would happen. And still they wouldn't pay. So he wandered through the town at night, playing a soft, magic tune on his pipe, and all of the children in the town left their beds while their parents slept, and they followed him."

I lean forward. Never heard a story like this.

"They followed him clear up a mountainside to a cave. The piper played his music and the children followed. But there was one young girl with a bad leg; she couldn't walk fast like the others, and though she wanted to follow the children, follow the music, she couldn't keep up.

"The piper went on ahead into the mountain, the children followed, and she came in time to see them get sealed inside that cave forever."

I stare at Kane.

He chews on the side of his lip, eyes on the ground. "When I read that story, I think, *I'd rather be that girl than any of those children who could follow the piper.*"

He looks sideways at me. "That story's about paying what's due, that's plain, but I've always thought it's also about curses being secret blessings."

I can't speak. I can't see how my foot could ever be a blessing. But that he thinks it—that he'd tell me that story, that way . . .

"I came after you because I wanted to. And to tell you I wish things were different." He turns me gentle to face him, tugging me forward. I let go of my crossed-arms wall and let him pull me.

He runs a hand up my arm to my neck, my jaw, and holds me like that, his thumb brushing my lower lip. His hands are warm and rough. Then he dips forward and our foreheads touch. I can smell warm woodsmoke, and something that shoots desire straight through me.

I can't breathe.

We shouldn't be out here, he shouldn't be touching me this way, but right now all I want is to be out here with him. Only him.

And then, outside the clearing, branches snap. And snap

again. And again. The brush is being parted violent-like: something or someone is coming toward the clearing at a real determined pace.

Kane grabs me by the shoulders and pulls me to him, toppling us off the log to the forest floor behind us. He puts out a hand to catch our fall, but I hit the ground hard and gasp. I am squeezed between the hard earth and the length of his body. My dress has torn further, and the rough bark of the fallen tree scratches my bare leg and digs into my elbow.

I shift under him and bite back a cry as my thigh catches on a sharp bit of bark.

He clamps a hand over my mouth. We are nose to nose and he's slowing his breathing with some trouble. My heart is beating a violent rhythm, threatening to burst through my chest. His forearm is heavy on my collarbone and his dark eyes plead with me: *Quiet.*

It's dead still. No birds sing, no squirrels chatter. The shafts of sunlight that glimmer through the overhead boughs are weak. Even the wind has fled. I search his eyes for—what? Courage? The look he had in his eyes a moment ago—just to see it one last time?

But he turns his head, resting his cheek on the hand covering my mouth and putting an ear to the air. His body is warm on mine, but my blood runs cold.

Several seconds tick by.

And then I hear it.

It sweeps through the low scrub, its body brushing through dry whispering leaves. It enters the clearing, and the twigs snapping under its steps suggest it's sizeable; my weight at least, mayhap bigger. The footfall is regular, plodding.

But the way it is breathing—oh, the *breathing* makes the skin on the back of my neck prickle, every hair on my body rise. It's a low and guttural snuffling, as though following a trail. As though it is . . .

Searching.

Fear clutches at my heart, my throat. I have to draw air in short, silent sips.

It's crossed the clearing, sounds real near to us now. Just on the other side of the fallen log. If I could reach through the tree, I could touch its bulbous eyes, its hideous snout . . .

And then the footfalls stop and the snuffling quiets. There is a ragged panting. It is *right there.* Kane's body tenses on top of mine and a wave of panic crosses his face and I know, oh Almighty's grace above, I *know* . . .

It's found us.

And then Kane's leaping over the log, metal flashing in his left hand.

A knife. Where did he get a knife?

I hear a loud half-bark, half-squeal. I'm caught in the cloak a moment before I can scramble to my knees. I grasp at the fallen tree to pull myself up, afraid to look . . .

Kane is doubled over, hands on his knees, breathing hard. A flash of black-and-white hindquarters is disappearing into the brush on the far side of the clearing.

Kane straightens and throws his knife halfheartedly into a tree, then turns to me. He's grinning. Has he lost his senses?

He lets out a full breath of air. "A badger," he says. "A bleeding *badger.*"

"A badger?" It's Watch on the fortification wall with Andre all over again.

"A badger." He shakes his head, looks to the brush, then back at me. "Do you think we overreacted?"

I climb over the fallen tree and the tightness in my chest eases. And then I bust out laughing. Kane's smile widens and he begins laughing too. We drop onto the fallen tree, cackling with relief, hooting at our panic.

"At least you had your knife," I say, gasping for breath.

"You should have seen the look on its face!"

This sets us laughing harder, laughing until we are crying. It feels so good to laugh—or to cry—that when we finally get calm I feel reckless, giddy. I wipe at my teary eyes and breathe slow. The moment from before is gone, but I feel so close to Kane. I want to tell him as much.

"Can I trust you with something?"

He stops smiling. His eyes grow serious. "You can trust me."

"I need to show you."

Kane crouches beside me, staring at the cabin with disbelief. "What is it?"

"Don't know."

"You been in?"

I shake my head. "Just found it yesterday."

"Who else knows about this?"

"I've only told you. But Brother Stockham knows it's here."

Kane turns wide eyes on me. "How do you know that?"

"Saw him here yesterday."

"You saw him here yesterday."

I nod.

"When yesterday?"

"I came in my free time—just after noontime."

Kane looks at me strange. "Couldn't have."

"Why?" My heart sinks because I know what he's about to say.

"Because he was with Council all afternoon."

"I know." I look at Kane, helpless.

We are quiet a moment.

"Why would he need a cabin here, this far from the fortification?" Kane sits back on his heels. I sit quiet. He jerks his head at the cabin. "Are we going in?"

We've been out here awhile. My pa might figure I'm still with Brother Stockham, or gone to Soeur Manon's. Kane, though—someone might be wondering about him. I glance about. The wind trickles through the spruce behind us: Lost People whispering secrets. Secrets I need.

And that decides it. "We're going in. But Kane"—I grab at his arm as he moves to get up—"someone might be inside."

Kane stares back a long while. Then he nods. "We'll be real careful."

18

WE START DOWN THE SLOPE, MOVING FROM TREE to tree as quick as we dare. The loose carpet of leaves crunches as I move—my bleeding bad foot!—but Kane is far quieter. A lifetime later we reach the last of the trees that will shield us. We stand with our backs to the trunks, about two strides apart.

I risk a look around the tree. We're twenty strides from the cabin; a small clearing of low scrub separates the trees from the front door. There's no way we can cross without being in full view for a good few seconds.

Kane crouches low and grabs a chunk of branch from the forest floor. Then he takes a quick half step around the tree, draws back, and hurls it at the front door. As he darts back to his cover, it hits the door with a thud. I hold my breath.

Nothing.

When I look over to Kane, he's gesturing with his head. We creep out from behind our cover and move quick across the little clearing.

My heart is beating fast, blood thrumming in my ears as we approach. My head aches something fierce, but I can't worry after that now.

There's no light in the cabin and the sun in the forest is waning. Kane pushes on the latch, beckoning for me to stand back. He gives a gentle push and the door swings wide with a soft creak.

Again, nothing.

He tilts his head toward the door. We step inside.

It's one small room, no furnishings. There's a wooden crate in one corner and a half circle of candles, stuck by wax onto the wooden floor, around one side. "Doesn't look like much," Kane says in my ear, making me jump. When did I latch on to his arm?

I pull my hand away, staring at that box. I have a bad feeling in the pit of my stomach. This room feels too . . . hot. I'm too hot.

"I'll stay on lookout." Kane swings the door shut save a couple inches and turns, his eyes trained on the woods beyond.

I make my way to the box and settle on my knees. The candles are halfway burned, but not warm. The lid comes off easy enough. Inside are more candles and a small book, covered in brown leather.

The book's pages are yellowed and dog-eared—like Soeur Manon's books—but instead of drawings and neat lettering, it's full of scrawling handwriting. The charcoal is smudged on the page in places, making parts unreadable.

"Kane," I whisper, holding the book up.

His eyes leave the woods outside the cabin. When he

sees what I'm holding, he abandons his post and crosses the room. He trips halfway through, and when he rights himself he turns to examine the piece of floorboard that caught his toe. He kneels and runs a hand over it.

"Kane," I say, impatient.

But he digs into the board with his finger and flips up a large brass ring. It's fastened to the floor. He gives a violent jerk upward and a large portion of the floor lifts and folds back.

I tuck the book under my arm and scurry forward on my knees to get a look.

There is a cavernous hole below. It's too dark to see more than a few feet in, but the air that rushes out is damp and stale.

Kane whistles low and sinks to his knees. "A hideaway of some sort?" There's the seed of an idea in his eyes.

"We don't have a flint," I remind him. I don't want to admit that I'm scared: the cool air feels like death, and I don't want to go down there, don't want that darkness around me.

Kane chews on his lip and looks around the cabin. The candles are useless without a flint. He nods at my book. "What is that?"

"Somebody's writings."

He takes it from me and flips to the first page. "It's a letter. It says 'Dear son.' That's how letters start—'Dear.'"

"You can read it?"

He frowns as he flips through the pages. "I'm used to the printing in my ma's books—not someone's scribblings. But my ma taught me how to make some letters. Wouldn't be fast, but I could figure it."

"Who wrote it?"

He flips until he finds the page where the writing stops. "It's signed"—he reads the words slow—"'Your father, H. J. Stockham.'"

H. J. Stockham.

Brother Stockham's grandpa.

Kane glances at me, his eyes unsure—like he knows what I'm thinking but isn't certain I should think it.

But I have to ask. "Will you read it to me?"

He studies me a moment.

"Kane, please. I need to know what Brother Stockham does out here. If I have to bind to him this Ice Up, I need to know . . ." I can't finish.

Kane's eyes go soft. "Course, Em."

He flips back to the first page and starts.

"'Dear son, it is the eve of your sixteenth year. You will take over the settlement soon, and I am certain there can be no better leader for these people. I am proud of the man you . . .'" Kane shrugs. "Smudged," he says.

This is a letter to Brother Stockham's pa. The first bit is H. J. Stockham speaking on his son's virtues and what it takes to "be a leader." It *is* slow going, and some words are missing. Often Kane has to pause to sound the word out, but I'm full amazed he can do it at all.

"'My father founded this settlement. He taught me that our position rests upon the safety of everyone. To that end, Council has been'"—Kane shakes his head; he can't read that word—"'and often ruthless. We do what must be done; I have always believed this. But I am old and my heart grows heavy. I find myself reflecting on my actions. Praying on it does not fill me with ease. I seek'"—Kane shakes his head again—"'and I wish to repent. To that end, I must disclose the matter of . . .'" He stops, frowning at the writing.

"What?"

He looks up. "'Clara Smithson.'"

My grandma'am. I don't know if I want to hear it—if I want Kane to hear it. Her Waywardness, propositioning the man who wrote this book, being sent off to the Crossroads—it's all right here, in this book.

Kane studies me.

No. I have to know. I swallow the lump that rises in my throat—feels like a knife blade—and nod for him to continue.

"'You have been told that Sister Clara was an adulteress; that sending her to the Crossroads all those years ago was due her Waywardness. But I know the truth. I know that her death was a sin against the Almighty. My confess'"—Kane frowns—"'confession will right that wrong. The truth, my son, is something I entrust to your keeping and it is this: I loved her.'"

My mind whirls. Kane and I exchange a glance. He continues, "'And her death amounts to the worst betrayal. You see, Clara found something in these woods I had not the Honesty or Bravery to re'"—Kane sounds it out slowly—"'con-cile. She had no chance to speak of her finding to anyone—her death saw to that—but I must share it here, for I cannot allow you to make the same mistake.'"

Kane pauses and looks at me again. My head spins. There is a fluttering in my heart—it wants to burst from my chest and fly from this room. My grandma'am's death wasn't on account of her Waywardness . . . My grandma'am wasn't Wayward. I'm not truly Stained.

"Read on," I whisper.

But then, a sound off in the woods—like a herd of sheep being driven across the Watch flats.

Kane and I freeze, staring at one another.

"What is it?"

He shakes his head, his eyes wide. It's coming closer, louder and louder.

A coldness settles in my throat. Bison don't group together in the woods, so it can't be a herd—doesn't sound to be that many, anyhow. Whatever it is, it's laboring up the rise on the far side of the gully, about to crest the hill behind the cabin.

No windows on that side to see what it is and no time to hide in the woods; we'd be halfway to the trees and in full view when it got here. But suppose whatever it is finds us here?

Kane drops the book, jumps up, and pushes the cabin door closed.

We look at the trapdoor.

The noise is getting faster and louder as it comes toward the cabin.

Un homme comme l'elephant. Andre's voice whispers in my ears, mixing with the noise outside and conjuring bulbous eyes, a long trunk, hoofed feet . . .

We scramble for the opening in the floor. There's a decrepit ladder that empties into a small cavern of hollowed earth. I grab the book and go down into the darkness blind,

Kane follows, his body sealing out the cabin's light and the trapdoor banging after him.

In a heartbeat we are encased in the black damp and that tightness in my throat is back. Kane's hand finds mine and he pulls me to him, wrapping his arms around me. We huddle in the dark, slowing our breath. In a few short moments I can make out the ladder in front of us. Tiny cracks of light seep through the cabin floor above us. It's cool and dank in this cellar, but my skin is red hot.

The noise outside the cabin stops. Then: a breath letting go, like a rush of wind. Any shred of hope this is another common forest animal dies right then and there.

There's a thick silence.

The door creaks. I wait for footsteps, but none come.

And then! Then the floor whines directly above us and I can tell the thing is crossing the floor where the trapdoor lies. Mayhap it doesn't know there's a cellar. I hold my breath and pray to the Almighty that the ring in the floor fell flat so it doesn't discover it. There's a whistle above us, soft but familiar. I can't figure why; it's not a birdcall . . . And then I know. It's that sound I heard in the woods the other day, the one Brother Stockham followed. There's a soft rustling above and the trapdoor creaks again. Things are entering the cabin, but they're not moving like anything I know. They're ghosting across the floor, barely touching the surface.

I feel dizzy and press into Kane, feel his heart beat wild against mine.

I am Honesty. I am Bravery. I am Discovery.

And then sounds, low and muffled. Voices? I can't figure the words. The language is clipped, has sounds in it I've never heard.

It stops.

There's a soft rustling and the door creaks shut. I strain to hear outside the little shack. After a moment comes the same rush across the forest floor. It fades. We stay frozen together for a long while. My head pounds, my skin burns and feels cold at once.

"Let's go." Kane's voice is so loud in the silence I near cry out. He pulls me toward the ladder and goes up first, pushing the trapdoor back to climb through. It makes a horrid loud noise and then blessed light shows the way out. Kane reaches for me, and I'm about to head up the ladder when the look on his face stops me cold.

His mouth hangs open, eyes wide with alarm. He's looking over my shoulder, looking at something behind me.

I turn. The bones are dirty, yellowed; they near blend into the shadows.

They're jumbled in a row on the far wall of the cellar. Skulls stare at me, slack jawed. There are shackles on the floor. Some bones remain in the irons, detached from the rest of the skeletons.

A hot flush courses through me. And then . . . then those bones are reaching out, talking to me in garbled whispers. *Find us,* they say.

I lose my senses, spin about, and dive for the ladder. Scrambling up, I find Kane's hands and grab tight, and then he's pulling me up into the cabin, away from the brittle bones and poison air.

I want to collapse on the floorboards, but Kane keeps me on my feet and kicks the trapdoor shut with his foot. I'm gasping, trying to form words as Kane pulls me toward the door.

We stumble from the cabin and up the hill. Kane's eyes are wide, his jaw working like he's thinking hard. I trip twice. The light is fading fast and I'm starting to misjudge my steps. It's near dusk; surely my pa will be wondering where I am. He'll have to make dinner himself. He's a terrible cook.

Someone laughs out loud. I look at my hands: they're shaking. I'm so hot, but it's so cold out here—something's wrong. I want to tell Kane, but I can't get a breath to do it.

I swipe with my right hand, find Kane's arm and clutch at it.

"Em?"

Les trembles are dancing before my eyes, swaying in a waltz rhythm. I open my mouth.

"Em?" I can hear panic in Kane's voice. I imagine his dark, beautiful eyes full of worry. Beautiful Kane.

His arms are around me now. Are we going to dance?

I want to tell him there's no music, but the forest floor lurches up at me and the trees shatter into a thousand pieces.

And then everything is black.

19

THE RIVER CHURNS BELOW MY FEET. I SHIFT THE cold bundle to one hand and tie the cloth tight around it so it won't unravel when I toss it in. My grandma'am's ring flashes on my hand. Brother Stockham stands beside me.

"Our salvation lies in Discovery," I say, and throw the baby at the frothing waters below.

As it leaves my hands the bundle shifts, comes alive. *No!* My fingers scramble for it back, but it is beyond reach, plummeting to the river below. It falls, writhing, its cry echoing along the riverbank . . .

I'm in the grove, staring at the trail. My grandma'am's ring is hot now, burning bright on my finger. The sun sinks double-time and the black night rushes in around me. The sound of hoofbeats floods the woods. My eyes can't leave the trail, but I feel the beasts circling near, hoofed feet stamping, dusty fingers reaching for me—

Kane is standing over me, brow creased with worry. He's saying something about the woods, but it's like I'm listening underwater. Then Kane becomes Tom, who becomes my pa with his hunched, sad shoulders. They shift and change into one another and shift again, looming at me in turn, speaking words I can't figure. And then they're gone and Brother Stockham stares down. He doesn't speak, just watches me with his gray hawk eyes. I can't feel the ring on my finger— did he take it from me?

I move to feel for it, to search my hand with my other, but I can't move. I'm pinned, my arms at my sides.

My eyes fly open.

I'm staring at a smoke-stained ceiling. A grass mattress is against my back, heavy blankets on top of me. The smell is familiar, strong and earthy. Sage smoke. I take a breath and cough.

Soeur Manon appears above me. She puts a thin hand to my forehead and looks close at my face. I cough again. She grunts and then straightens. "You eat." She moves away to a pot over the hearth.

I push the blankets back and struggle up on the bed. The scratchy nightshirt I'm wearing isn't mine. I glance about her dingy one-room cottage and find my moccasins under a chair nearby. My stomach is more empty than it's felt in a long while.

"What—why . . ." My voice is a croak.

"*Ce garçon—du sud,*" Soeur Manon says over her shoulder as she ladles something from the pot. "He find you by the river and bring you here." She approaches with a small bowl and spoon. "*Tu etais trés malade,* Emmeline. God's will you are alive."

My head feels wooly. "Sick with what?"

She forces the bowl into one of my hands, the spoon into the other. *"Le fievre."* She steps back, her arms folded, and waits for me to start eating.

I take a mouthful of broth and think on her words. I had the fever. Kane brought me here. From the river? No, from the woods. From the—

Cabin.

Broth catches in my throat and sets me to coughing until tears spring to my eyes. I take a deep breath and wipe at them with the sleeve of the nightdress. Force myself to look at Soeur Manon.

"How many nights ago?"

Her eyes are grave. *"Deux."*

I've been here two days. My dreams—Brother Stockham, the grove, the faces staring down . . .

"Did—did anyone visit?"

She clucks her tongue. "Too many men here."

"My pa?"

"Oui. Ton pere, Frère Stockham, Tom . . . mais"—she raises an eyebrow—"you ask only for that one."

"Which one?"

"The boy that bring you here."

Oh, for the grace! "When? Was anyone else nearby when I was asking . . ." I can't finish.

Soeur Manon raises her eyebrows. *"Non."*

What else did I say in my fevered state? I switch to French, hoping Soeur Manon thinks my struggle to find words is because of the language. *"Et quand . . . quand je dormais, est que . . . j'ai parlé des . . . des autres choses?"*

"Je pense que tu as rêvé de les fantomes."

I was dreaming on ghosts? A prickle dances up my neck and into my hair. That cellar, those bones . . . "Why do you say that?"

"Because in your sleep you speak of"—she pauses—"*les personnes qui sont parties longtemps.*"

I frown, trying to unravel her words. I was speaking on the people who left long ago. People she thinks are ghosts . . . the people who were taken by the *malmaci?*

I was dreaming on the *malmaci,* that's certain, but I feel like something happened at the cabin that was important. Something I'm forgetting . . .

The book. I dropped it in the cellar. My heart sinks. I'll have to go back to get it, back to that pit of death. Who were those people that died there? Are they what my grandma'am found?

Joy sparks through my fear. My grandma'am wasn't Wayward—not like everyone thinks. And if I can get that book, I'll know why she was put to death and why it was a betrayal. I can wash my Stain clean *without* binding to—

My thoughts stop there. Brother Stockham's been in that cabin. Surely he's seen the journal, and surely he knows I'm not truly Stained.

He wants me for a life mate when Council disapproves. So why hide that? First he lies about being in the woods, now he hides this. An ice-cold feeling grabs hold of me.

Soeur Manon takes the bowl from me. "You must clean up. Go home."

My blackened foot hurts something fierce. I can't help but limp as I walk to the washbowl near the hearth. I risk a glance at Soeur Manon, who shakes her head, looking grim.

"*Le fievre n'etait pas bon pour ton pied.*"

"Can't figure how I got sick," I mutter.

"Work too hard," Soeur Manon states.

I raise my eyebrows. Don't think anyone could accuse me of that.

"Think too hard," she amends.

That might be closer to the truth.

"I think what trouble you here"—she touches her brow—"burn under your skin." Her hand makes a tinkling motion over her arm.

I turn and wash quick near the fire, pulling on some clothes my pa brought over. I'm tying my *ceinture fléchée* when she puts a hand on my shoulder.

"*Ta robe.*" She holds up my ma's dress. She mended it—you can't notice the tear unless you're looking hard for it. But . . . Kane brought me here from the riverbank, with my dress torn—what must she think we were doing out there?

I fight a blush and meet her eyes. If she thinks we were up to something Wayward, her face doesn't say it. I take the dress from her. "*Merci, Soeur Manon.*"

She nods her snowy head and turns back to the hearth. Usual. Never says much. But as I watch her hobble away, it occurs to me she's also never asked accusing questions, never fussed when my gatherings were meager. She's never glanced at me wrong, even knowing what I do to myself on purpose, even knowing I'm Stained. She's only ever taken care of me. A small part of my secret heart swells, watching her small frame bend to gather something from the table.

I want to thank her somehow. Want to tell her I feel safe

in the Healing House. But she turns around and speaks again. "Also, I find this."

I look at her outstretched hand. My grandma'am's ring is a bright circle on her creased palm.

My breath stops.

"I think the ghosts give you a gift."

My pa's so relieved to see me well, he doesn't even ask what I was doing by the riverbank, where Kane supposedly found me.

"My girl," he says. He looks older somehow—his brow more lined, his beard more gray. He clasps me in his thin arms. Hugging his frail chest, I feel a pang of remorse.

"You stay inside today. Soeur Manon said to rest another day." He draws back, holding my arms in his bony hands. "I'll make tea before I go."

All the secrets I'm keeping from him are suddenly heavy on my chest. I watch him bend to the stove to stoke it, get the water on. He nods at a chair and I sit, grateful.

I watch him fumble with the tea pouch, my thoughts chasing one another around. I know he wants a better life for me. Would he ever see that I'm after that too? If I tell him about what I've found now, without the book to prove it, will he believe me? Or would he forbid me to go back to that cabin? Would he tell Brother Stockham?

He sets a cup of hot bergamot tea before me, his hands trembling as always.

"You just rest up."

I nod, bringing the cup to my lips.

"Affirmation's in three days," he adds.

I stiffen, the bergamot smell filling my nostrils. I know why he's so concerned with me resting. He's worried about me being presentable when I accept Brother Stockham.

He'll never understand about me needing to get that journal. Won't believe there must be a reason Brother Stockham didn't tell me about his grandfather's confession. I push the thought of confiding in him into a tiny corner of my secret heart.

When he's gone, I stay in our quarters, mending winter wear and cleaning, my thoughts chasing one another around and around until I'm half addled. The cabin, the book, the trapdoor, the bones . . . *I must disclose the matter of Clara Smithson.*

I pull the ring from my *ceinture* and study it in the firelight. Soeur Manon thinks it's an unearthly gift, and I'm not about to set her straight. But her words have skittered me. Nobody gave me this ring; I took it. Then I got the fever and dreamt of "the people who left long ago." That rush of breath we heard outside the shack fills my ears.

I took my grandma'am's ring.

Mayhap she's coming to get it back.

20

THE NEXT DAY PA TELLS ME SOEUR MANON doesn't need me. I go to Sister Ann for chores instead. Her face is pinched and thin.

"Stay close today, Emmeline," she says, packing candles into a crate.

"Course, Sister Ann."

"I mean it truly." She frowns. "No one is permitted outside the fortification unless it's on Brother Stockham's say-so."

My heart sinks. "Why?"

When she looks up, her eyes are scared. "There was a Taking last night."

The words send a cold shock through me. I've never lived through a Taking. The last one happened before I was born.

The sounds from the cabin fill my ears. Enormous rush of poison breath. Soft creaking on the floor. "Who?" *Not Kane. Not Kane.* I send a silent prayer to the Almighty.

"One of the Watchers."

"Frère Andre?" Did he go after his Elephant Man again?

Should I have told someone? I thought it better not to, thought it was safer for him.

"No. Pellier. I think his first name was Bertrand." She shakes her head like we shouldn't speak on it further. "Just stay close. Tom's wintering up the wastewater ditch. The beams around the trench are rotted; help him replace the wood before securing the gate for *La Prise*. Tomorrow you'll need to help with preparations for Affirmation. Come to the hall when you're done at Soeur Manon's."

I dress warm and head out, a sickness in my stomach. As I'm crossing the courtyard I see a group of five Councilmen, their cloaks sweeping the stairs of the Council building. And then my heart leaps: he's on the outskirts of the group, but his bare head gives him away.

I misstep—turn the ankle on my bad foot—and feel a burst of pain as I stumble. My eyes water, and I right myself, blinking back tears. The group's still there, but now Kane is gone.

They turn to watch me as I head for the south wall.

That's when I notice that they're everywhere: the other seven Councilmen are on the tops of the walls. And though it's day, the Watchers are out. All at once I feel a dozen pairs of eyes on me, sizing me up, watching as I take a deep breath. I limp for the south side of the courtyard as fast as I'm able.

"Emmeline!" Tom calls to me from the wastewater ditch. He's dressed in a winter cloak, holding a shovel.

I make my way to his side, foot aching.

"Foot bothering you?" He holds out a hand and helps me step across the trench.

"Just tired of pretending." I don't tell him I couldn't push through the pain if I tried. Not anymore.

We look at one another, quiet.

"I'm so glad you're all right," he says.

"Me too."

"We visited—me and my ma—but you were asleep the whole time."

"Soeur Manon told me. Appreciate that."

He smiles. In this moment he's my Tom: easygoing, easy-speaking.

I jerk my head toward the expanse of the fortification behind us. "Everyone's skittered on account of the Taking."

His face shifts to a worried frown. "I know."

"You hear anything about it?" I ask.

"No. I'm just real grateful you weren't on Watch when it happened."

There's a question in his eyes. He wants to know what I was doing when the fever struck me. I could tell him now. I want to tell him . . . but all I say is "Me too."

He's trying not to look hurt, but I know him too well; he knows I'm keeping something from him. He clears his throat and gestures at the gate. The ditch is half a stride wide and passes under the fortification wall. The gate, held in place by the posts we're meant to replace, slides down into the trench, closing off a sodden space just big enough to crawl through on your belly. There's a hole dug for a new gatepost on the near side of the ditch. "Best to get on with it."

He digs a second hole on the opposite side and I wait to help him hoist the new post in. We use his *ceinture* to haul the beam into place and pull it upright. The silence stretches between us until it hangs in the air. I want him to say something easy-like. I want him to say something. Anything.

I hold tight to the *ceinture* while he fills the dirt around the post. When we're finished with the second one, he looks to the gate where it hangs, high up against the fortification wall. He unties its lashings and lets it fall heavy into the trench. Then he slides a thick pole across the top, between the wall and the new posts, so the gate is impossible to open from the outside.

He dusts off his hands. "All done." He starts collecting his things.

I can't take it anymore. "Tom, can we speak plain?"

He turns. "I'd appreciate that."

I take a deep breath, trying to figure where to begin. "I—I want you to know that everything's all right."

He looks down, retying his *ceinture,* silent.

"Tom?"

When he raises his head, it's plain on his face he doesn't believe me.

"Look," I say, "we both know I'm not telling you everything, but I need you to believe I'm doing the right thing."

"Chasing off into the woods is the right thing?"

"I don't chase off into the woods."

"Sure you do. You ran off just the other day. And returned in Kane's arms, out of your head with fever."

I shake my head, staring at the ground, but I don't have words to contradict him.

He sighs real heavy. "It was a harsh thing to say the other day, that you're Wayward on purpose—but Almighty! What am I supposed to think?"

"I've got reasons."

"You're above this, Em."

And then I'm angry. I'm fed up with him judging my virtues, fussing over my whereabouts. I haven't done anything that hurts anyone. In fact, it's been the opposite. "Mayhap there are worse things."

"Than what?"

"Being Wayward."

Tom pauses. "You don't mean that," he says.

"Don't I? I'm sure you'd rather have Edith safe than me upholding my virtues."

"What are you speaking on?"

"Harvest, Tom. Edith wasn't with me when the alarm rang. She was all alone. The hall was closing and I ran back to get her. We hid in the well until the fortification was cleared."

Tom's mouth drops open. "But Ma said—"

"Your ma told you what she told everyone else—what *I* told everyone else."

His face goes white. "B-b-but surely someone saw you do it?"

"Andre won't tell." Bleed it! Why did I say his name? I hurry to cover. "The point is, your ma covered her mistake. And I was Wayward because I couldn't bear to leave Edith to the *malmaci*."

He's quiet a moment, studying the ground. When he looks up, his eyes are full. "Thank you," he says quiet.

"Don't thank me. It's not why I did it."

"I know that. I know you did it because . . . because you care for her. But this Wayward business . . ." His chest hitches. "I just don't want anything to happen to you."

My anger softens. "Nothing will."

"You aren't yourself anymore."

I bite back a reply. I want to tell him I'm exactly myself—more myself than I've ever been.

"You're always thinking on something I can't figure."

"Do you really want to know what I'm thinking on?"

He pushes his blond hair back from his brow. "I know about the proposal."

I throw up my hands. "Everyone knows!"

"So?"

"So I don't want to bind to him."

"Why not?"

"Just . . . I don't. I can't."

"Because of Kane?"

"No! I mean—I . . ."

"Em, if this has something to do with that trail . . ." He doesn't finish.

There's that look again. That longing. Like he wants to know, but he can't bring himself to admit it. I make a decision. "I need to tell you something. Something you can't tell anyone."

He nods.

"It's about my grandma'am. She wasn't Wayward—not the way everyone thinks."

His eyes widen. "What makes you say that?"

"I found a letter. Out in the woods."

"A letter."

"Yes! I can't explain everything right now, but please believe me when I say it's there. It proves I'm not Stained."

He doesn't blink.

"And I need to go get it."

This breaks his staring spell. He closes his eyes, scrubs his hands through his hair. I can see his virtue lecture oncoming and I need to cut it off at the pass. "Em—"

"I just need to go back one more time. It's going to be troublesome, what with everyone on high alert on account of the Taking, so I'll need your help."

He looks at me, his prairie-sky eyes heavy with rain-clouds. "But why does it matter? You're binding to Brother Stockham."

"Don't you see? I can set my family's name clear. Wipe the Stain clean." *I can Discover what my grandma'am found in those woods.*

"I've never cared you were Stained, Em. I only want you to be safe."

The rainclouds in his eyes are threatening to burst. I realize I can't tell him about the rest—about the cabin and the bones and my dreams, about Brother Stockham and Kane. Tom's so used to being scared, it's all he knows. That means he'll forever just put that wheat-haired head down and live his life inside this fort. But if he can't look up, can't see past these walls, then I need to do it for him. And I'll need that book to do it.

"I know. I know you want me safe." I touch his arm. "And I will be." My fingers squeeze into his shirt. "Don't tell anyone about the woods? We've always kept one another's secrets—"

He gapes. "One for the other, is that right? I'm supposed to let you put yourself in danger in exchange for keeping *my* dangerous secret? Your Waywardness is the same as mine?"

"Course not. Tom—"

"I can't help my secret! What you're doing . . ." His shoulders sag. "I'm worried."

My stomach clenches tight. "You've been my friend despite everyone eyeballing me since I was young. I'm telling you I'm doing what I have to." I say it slow and measured because I'm afraid I'll cry. I bite my lip to stop it from quivering.

His eyes brim with tears.

I squeeze his arm. "I won't do anything that could end me at the Crossroads."

"Promise?" His face is so trusting, it near breaks me in two.

"Promise."

But I'm lying. Again. Affirmation is in two days—after that, *La Prise* will be upon us and we'll be locked inside the fortification until the Thaw. And I'll be Brother Stockham's life mate. Promise or no, I have to get back to that cabin. And I think I know a way.

I push the guilt down deep. Then I give Tom a smile I don't feel, and go to find Kane.

21

I STOP BY SOEUR MANON'S, HOPING SHE HAS something—anything—for me to run to the Kitchens. She frowns when she sees me, but when I ask, her eyes light up like she's figured something. She smiles. Then she rummages around and finds a bundle of herbs. *"Ils sont des 'herbes d'amour.'"* Oh, for the grace! I flush to my scalp, take the bundle of love herbs and flee.

When I push into the Kitchens, Sister Lucy is hanging onions to dry. She nods her head toward Storages when she sees my bundle.

He's near the entrance, sleeves rolled up as always, head bare, eyes like dark pools. Relief washes his face when he sees me. He pushes off the wall, unfolding his arms, his mouth pulling into that funny smile. I can't smile back. Blood is rushing in my ears. I'm dragging my foot something terrible too, but I don't care about that right now.

As I approach, his smile falters, his brow crinkles. He looks, for the first time I've ever seen, uncertain. And it's so unguarded, so honest, that the cabbage moths already flitting in my stomach start thrumming so hard I can barely think.

And I know I'm about to do something foolish.

I glance behind me. Sister Lucy is turned toward the ovens, her back to us. I toss the herb bundle at a crate on the floor. Then, before I can change my mind, I step forward and bury my face in Kane's chest.

He draws me tight to him, his grip iron-strong, chest hard under his shirt. My face is in his neck now: warm skin and woodsmoke. The million cabbage moths soar up and close off the air in my chest.

He pulls me around the corner into the first pantry, closing the door with a free hand. Then he grabs me by the shoulders and draws back. "Em." His voice is husky and soft: wind whispering through the spruce. "You're all right."

I manage a nod.

"I was worried. You . . . well, you were so bleeding sick." He looks at me so long I have to drop my eyes.

I find my voice. "Did—did anyone ask what you were doing? When you found me, I mean."

"No." He lets go of my shoulders and steps back.

I miss his hands straightaway, but my head clears a bit. "I'm sorry. For taking you to that cabin, I should have never—"

"Better than you being there alone."

I swallow. "Bertrand Pellier, from the north—"

"I heard." Kane's face is troubled.

"Do you think us going out there . . . Did . . . I mean, did we make it angry? Is it our fault?"

"It was a Taking, Em. It wasn't our fault."

"Was that the *malmaci?* Out there?"

"I don't know for certain. But"—he rubs a hand over his shaved head—"well, at first I thought I was imagining it, but the more I think on it, the more I'm sure."

"Sure of what?"

"Those voices above us, in the cabin. They were speaking words that sounded like ones my *kokum* used to speak."

Kokum. The First Peoples part of his blood. "Your grand-ma'am."

He nods.

I stare at his face, trying to figure his meaning. The voices sounded like his *kokum.* Like First Peoples' speech. The First Peoples who used to live on this land? The rush of sound through the woods . . . The creak of the floorboards above us . . . My stomach drops as the pieces fit together.

You see, Clara found something in these woods.

The hair on my neck stands up. Ghosts of the First Peoples—my Lost People. Is that what my grandma'am found out there?

"But what about Brother Stockham? What about those bones?"

"Don't know," he admits. "But I could read some more of that book for the answers."

"I dropped it in the cellar." My voice breaks. Tears well up and spill out.

"Hey, it's all right." Kane reaches forward, takes my face in his hands and brushes at my cheeks with his thumbs. "We'll get it back."

I swallow. I'm going to have to tell him my plan for that.

"Should we tell someone?" Kane asks. "Your pa or—"

"No!" I say. "It's just . . . we don't know what's going on yet. And my pa's so hopeful over this proposal—no." I don't tell Kane about Tom, and I can't admit that even after our scare at the cabin, even knowing how much we're risking, I can't bear to give this up. I want to wash my Stain clean on my own; I want to prove Discovery my own way.

Kane chews on his bottom lip, his eyes searching my face.

Is he having second thoughts? It's not fair of me to expect him to do something he doesn't want to do. "You don't have to . . . to come with me . . ."

"I'm not leaving you on your own." He frowns. "We do this together."

I choke back my relief. It takes everything in me not to throw my arms around him again.

"But we'll need to get back to the woods unseen," he says.

"Won't be easy."

"Not with Watch and the Councilmen watching everyone." He blows out a breath. "Almighty."

Tell him. "I've figured a way." I take a breath. "I'm going to tell Brother Stockham yes."

He pulls back like I've burned him.

I speak quick. "Just for now. I—I think I can convince him to let me go back to the river. Just once more before Affirmation. If I can get to the river, I can get back to the cabin. But Kane—" I grab at his shirt to keep him near. "It's not real. Once I get the journal back . . ." I trail off.

Kane's eyes are unhappy, uncertain again. "Em—"

"It's not real," I repeat. The rough wool of his shirt between my fingers burns my skin. "You said you wished things were different. I wish that too—I mean . . . I want . . ." I can't finish. I tug at his shirt.

He lets me pull him closer. "What do you want?" His voice is so soft. It's unbearable.

I can't say it. My heart is beating so fast it's going to jump from my chest. But he's here, he's so close, and he doesn't want me to be alone.

"You."

He sucks in a breath and closes his eyes. When he opens them, they aren't uncertain: they're dead sure. He places both hands on the sides of my neck, under my jaw, and pulls my head gentle toward him.

My heart stops.

His mouth is close, closer . . . and then . . . then we are kissing.

Feather-soft, his lips brush mine. Brush them again. I let go of his shirt, place my hands on his bare forearms. At the feel of his skin, something boils up under mine.

I lose my thoughts, push forward, bite down on his lip. He makes a sound that weakens my knees. Then his hand is running into my hair. He grasps my plait in one fist, slides the other hand to the small of my back and pulls me closer, kissing me like I'm air and he's drowning. Heat simmers and rushes through me, making my head spin. We press together, a bonfire searing through our clothes, everything wrong and impossibly right at once.

He breaks away with a ragged breath. "We can't."

"I know." I lean forward again.

He grabs my arms and holds me back. "You don't have to tell him yes. I can get back to the cabin—"

Footsteps echo through the Storages hall. We break apart as the door swings open. I lean down and start examining the dry stores, and Kane reaches up to a shelf above him.

"You two find what you need?" Sister Lucy peers into the dim pantry, wiping her hands on her apron. She steps in and heads for a barrel on the far side.

"Got it." Kane grabs an empty crate from the shelf. "I can finish up, Sister Emmeline." His eyes are wide, and he jerks his head at the door.

"Good." I keep my voice low to control the shake and push to my feet. "I'm needed at Soeur Manon's." I head for the door but have to brush past him. My shoulder bursts into flame where we touch.

I risk one last glance back at his face. That look in his eyes . . . I put a hand on the doorjamb to steady my legs before I leave.

22

IN MY DREAM, I'M STANDING AT THE BASE OF the tree-dotted hill. A group of Watchers is standing at the crest. The hawk circles high above.

The trees around me shift and lose their leaves, become gleaming white bones, reaching for the twilight sky. A rush of breath whistles through their skeleton fingers.

Find us.

I turn my head and see her. Running through the trees toward me, a blur of blue among the bones, long dark hair whipping behind her.

And then I see the Watchers raising their hands to their shoulders, grabbing for their weapons. I try to tell her to go back, to hide, but my tongue is frozen and I can't move.

Gunshot shatters the woods, and the shriek of the hawk echoes my silent scream.

In the morning I prepare for my visit to Brother Stockham. Kane said I didn't have to tell him yes, but he's wrong. No one's going to be let outside the gates without Brother Stockham's say-so, and my dreams are telling me I don't have much time.

I watch my pa over our porridge bowls, focusing on that tremble in his hands as he scrapes his bowl. I don't want to tell him. Can't bear to see him full to bursting at the news when it's not the truth. It makes me angry and sad, his joy over this thing I don't want. This thing I'll never accept.

But it won't look natural if he doesn't know first.

"Pa."

He sets down his bowl, wiping at his whiskers with the tail of his *ceinture*.

"Going to see Brother Stockham."

His eyebrows raise.

"Going to accept." I have to look at my hands when I say it. Don't want to see his happiness—his relief.

There's a silence.

I glance up. He's studying me. And the look in his eyes isn't what I figured. It's not relief—it's . . . concern.

"You sure?" he asks.

Am I sure? He's been coaxing me this way for weeks, he's been guilting me into accepting Stockham, and *now* he wants to know my heart? Anger surges through me.

"Course," I say, sharp.

He nods. "Just want to be certain it's what you want."

"You said yourself it's for the best."

"I did."

"You said sometimes it's hard to see what's best."

He nods.

"So why are you asking now?"

"I just—" He scrubs a hand through his beard. "I said those things because I didn't want you to think you weren't good enough for our leader."

My wrath dies, like a candle being snuffed. "Beg pardon?"

"Because you are, Em. You're good enough for anyone. Didn't want you thinking you couldn't accept on account of"—his eyes go to the table, to my foot beneath it—"anything that worries you." He looks me in the eye. "You're worthy, my girl."

My heart drops into my stomach.

"But I'm real glad, if you're sure."

I can't get any words out. I just nod.

He clears his throat. "I'd best get to the smoke house." He stands and sets his bowl in the dish bucket. When he passes the table, he stops and puts a hand on my shoulder. He squeezes it real gentle, and disappears out the door.

I stand, shaky, and head to my room. My eyes are hot with tears and my thoughts are muddied. Can it be true? Was my pa just worried I wouldn't accept even if I wanted to? All those times he was looking on me with that worried frown . . . I push it all from my mind—don't have time for all of that now. Now, accepting Brother Stockham's proposal is the only way back to the truth. I swallow hard, brush and rebraid my hair, put on a clean tunic and my winter cloak. I hide my grandma'am's ring inside my *ceinture*. It's strange, but I feel like having it will give me strength today.

As I approach the Council building, though, I feel a panicky sickness.

I stop a minute and think on the courting visit.

We can change things.

Brother Stockham has been hiding that journal, hiding the fact I'm not Stained, yet he practically urges me into the woods. I know agreeing to our binding will get me what I want. But that alone makes me feel like I'm missing something. Something right in front of my face. And now, with my pa telling me he doesn't mind if I don't accept . . .

Brother Jameson appears at the top of the steps to the Council building. I pick up my pace. Can't be caught standing here like I don't know my own mind.

His arms are folded over his chest, his face stony. "Sister Emmeline."

I offer him the Peace and try to keep my voice steady. "Morning, Brother Jameson. I'm—I'm here to speak with Brother Stockham."

"Ah, yes. The proposal."

I nod and move to climb the stairs, but he grabs me by the arm. He pulls me close and bends low. "I suppose you believe binding to the good Brother will make people forget about your Stain?"

I swallow hard and tear my arm away. "I suppose you'll do your best to keep reminding them."

His voice gets deadly. "It is my duty to keep this settlement safe."

I raise my chin and meet his ice-blue eyes.

"Brother Stockham cannot see you for what you are, Emmeline. But I do. And when you repeat the mistakes of those Waywards who have gone before, I will be here. And I will set things right."

I climb the stairs, feeling his eyes branding my back as I go.

Inside, the wooden building is quiet. But the silence here isn't comforting like the quiet of the riverbank. Here, it feels sickly.

"Emmeline."

I near jump from my skin at Brother Stockham's voice. He appears in the doorway to my right. His long, dark hair gleams in the light, sharp points against his cheekbones.

"I was relieved to hear you are well."

I swallow the fear that rises in my throat.

"I visited."

I nod, hoping I don't look as owl-eyed as I feel.

"At first I was very worried. But then I realized that everything is happening as it should."

"Beg pardon?"

He smiles. "You can't be lost to me."

That strange look in his eyes is back, just like when we were at the ceremonial hall. I need to say my piece before I lose my nerve. I force my tongue to work.

"Brother Stockham, I'm here to discuss the proposal."

He sweeps an arm toward the room behind him. "Come in."

I follow him into a room that has a big table sitting before two windows. The windows have shutters but no scraped-thin rawhide to cover them, like in our quarters. I venture closer to peer out. This room overlooks the courtyard. I can see the Kitchens beyond the weapons shack.

"How is it possible you have had the fever for days, yet look just as beautiful as ever?" His speaks from behind me.

I put my fingers to my lips. They feel swollen from yesterday. From Kane. I turn, find him watching me careful. My tongue gets wooly in my mouth. I need to get this over with. But the way he's looking on me—Almighty!

I train my eyes on the floor, hoping it looks modest, and say, "Brother Stockham—your proposal. I'm . . . I'm real glad to accept."

The silence that follows is not what I was figuring on. When I look up, his head is tilted. My heart thuds in my throat. Twice. Three times.

"Emmeline, I—" His voice sounds caught.

I feel a wash of panic. Mayhap he doesn't believe me. I force a slow smile at him.

His face lights, mirroring my smile. "This is very good news."

I can't bear to linger in this moment. "You'll talk to my pa about the arrangements, I suppose?"

"At once. We will be the first to bind, after Affirmation."

I look at the desk, trace a finger along it, preparing to ask my favor without seeming suspicious.

He speaks again. "You don't know how much this means to me." The honesty in his voice throws me. He hid the truth about my grandma'am.

I swallow.

Didn't he? Is it possible he hasn't been out to the woods, hasn't seen the journal? Is it possible it was someone else out there?

I force the words out: "And me."

He smiles. "I knew we would overcome our family burdens." My eyes fly to his shoulder, to his clean white shirt that hides the mess of scars beneath. His father's teachings. My insides twist.

214

What have I done?

He clears his throat. "I will spread word."

A flash of movement on the steps catches my eye. I force another smile and turn to look out the window. Kane is standing on the steps, speaking with Brother Jameson.

I've seen this before. Yesterday, before I joined Tom at the ditch, Kane was with Council. And before that, when I was with Andre in the weapons shack, he was with Council then too. I was so skittered by finding the cabin I didn't think too long on it.

I'm thinking on it now.

Why would a common south-quarter boy have Council's ear? And Jameson's, no less.

With effort, I force myself to turn to Brother Stockham. "Brother Stockham—"

"Please call me Gabriel."

"Gabriel," I say. The name feels strange on my tongue. "I'm needed at the hall for preparations."

"Of course." He steps back, smoothing his tunic. "I will escort you out."

His hand is hot on the small of my back as I pass through the doorway, but my thoughts whirl. Kane on the steps, with Jameson. Brother Stockham in the woods. *I don't go to the woods.* A thought bursts through the chatter in my head: the reason I'm here. "Broth—Gabriel, I have a request."

"Of course."

"I was wondering if I might go back to the riverbank once more, before *La Prise* sets in." He stops dead. I speak quick. "I know I'll need to be real careful, but it'll just be the once. Just one time before I can't see it again until the Thaw."

When he turns to face me, that strange look is in his eyes again. "I thought you would ask," he says.

Ice crawls up my spine. And now I know that look: it's exhilaration. The hair on the back of my neck rises.

He presses a kiss onto the back of my hand. "Of course you may. I will alert Council."

I am about to turn away when he takes my arm. "Emmeline, this will change everything." He holds my gaze. "Thank you."

I nod, my breath tight. Then I turn and hobble down the steps. Brother Jameson is gone; Kane is disappearing around the side of the weapons shack.

I risk a glance behind me, but Brother Stockham has shut the doors.

Walking as brisk as my leg allows, I head for the shack. I don't want to be in view from the Council building windows. I let out a near shout when I get round the corner. "Kane!"

He's halfway across the courtyard already, but when he turns, his eyes go wide. He crosses back toward me.

"The barns," I say, when he gets near. "Make an excuse to leave chores."

I don't hear Kane approach, but his shadow stretches onto the wall in front of me. My heart thuds in my throat.

I turn. He approaches with a sure stride, but I hold up a hand to stop him. "You're with Council an awful lot."

He looks around the courtyard quick, then he grabs me by the arm and pulls me into the barn. It's empty; the sheep are out for tick grooming before *La Prise*.

In the dim light, Kane turns to me. He rubs a hand over his head. "Em—"

"Just tell me why."

"I was trying to tell you in Storages. But Sister Lucy came in."

I wait. The barn creaks.

He takes a deep breath. "He . . . They're—they're watching you."

"Who?"

"Brother Stockham. Council."

I stare at Kane. Watching me? How would he know they're watching—

"Been watching you for near a month. Ever since you tied those threads to the trees."

I frown. "I never told you about the threads."

"I know." Kane holds my gaze.

My insides freeze over.

"That's what I'm trying to tell you. Council has been watching you for the past month . . . through"—he closes his eyes a moment—"through me."

My mouth opens. Closes. When I find my voice, it's hoarse. "What exactly are you speaking on?"

"Weeks ago, Brother Stockham paid a visit. He had a task for me. He . . . he wanted me to watch you."

"For what?"

"Wayward acts."

My thoughts are numb. I stare at him.

"It was the only way I could keep you safe."

"By *watching me for Wayward acts?*"

"They were going to anyway. I thought this way . . ." He

fumbles for the words. "I thought this way at least they'd wait for me to report. And if I didn't, they'd have nothing on you."

I back up a step, catching my bad foot on a board and sending searing pain into my leg.

His eyes widen. "Em—"

But my mind is whirling. The threads. The day in the woods I heard footsteps following me. Kane's been watching me—listening to me—for weeks.

"What have you told them?"

"Nothing!"

I stare into his wide eyes. Images come like a flood: Kane finding me in the grove, looking at me strange during Jameson's talks, that day he happened on me at the river.

Oh, bleeding Almighty.

"Why should I believe you?"

He steps back like I've slapped him, but my thoughts are running now. All that talk about finding new things, going out where I shouldn't be; was he just trying to find out what I'd been up to?

You can trust me.

And I did. I did because he—

My stomach hollows out.

Because he saved me during the false attack.

I came after you because I wanted to.

What if Brother Stockham rang the alarm and told Kane to come after me to win my trust? What if . . . what if standing up for me against Charlie Jameson, telling me that story about the crippled girl and the piper—what if it was *all* to win my trust?

218

His eyes are searching my face. His shoulders slump. "I'd never do anything to hurt you," he says soft. "You have to know that."

But it's not an answer, not truly. "Why didn't you tell me straightaway?"

"Because I—I thought you were just being your day-dreaming self, running off to the riverbank and woods. But there's something bigger than all that—I see that now." His voice has a note of hysteria in it.

I look away from his tortured face.

"Em, *please*. It wasn't worth telling at first. But now . . . now with things the way they are . . ." He reaches for my arm.

Now. Now I'm on the verge of proving Discovery, now I'm not just some daydreamer with a bad leg. I'm worth the truth *now*. Hurt and rage fuel my tongue. I want to hurt him back. "Did Council promise a reward for watching the Stained cripple?" I tear away from his grasp.

"Em—"

"Or did you just like pretending to be one of them for a few sorry weeks?"

"Course not!"

"Because you sure looked comfortable consorting—"

"What choice did I have?" he shouts.

I lunge forward and shove at his chest with both hands. Hard. He stumbles away, doesn't fight back. My voice is hoarse, accusing. "Don't talk to me about *choices*."

We stare at one another. The eyes that were verging on panic are now so lost I want to die.

"Em," he says. "I made a mistake. I thought I was protecting you."

My tears blur his perfect face.

"And I want to protect you because . . . because I love you."

A hot wind blows through my head, muddying my thoughts. I look down. We stand there a long while, me staring at the dirt floor, Kane staring at me. The boy with the eyes that drink me in and drown me, the boy whose skin lights mine on fire.

When he speaks, his voice is broken. "I'm going to get the book back. Tomorrow you can head for the riverbank; Council will think I'm following you to watch you. You stay in sight of the Watchtower and I'll head for the cabin. Will you let me do that? Get the book back for you?"

My secret heart is tearing at the edges. I don't know up from down anymore.

Brother Stockham knows I'm not Stained but hid the proof. He proposed and watched me for Wayward acts. And when I accepted, he acted like I was the Almighty Himself bestowing a blessing.

Kane kept this from me. And now he says he . . . loves me?

I want it to be true. I want to be back in Storages pressed tight to him, kissing his mouth raw. But . . . who knows what Kane loves? The thrill of breaking rules and Discovering things? Me? I don't know, and I don't have time to figure it. So I do what I'm getting real good at. I lie.

"All right."

The look on his face is sunlight glimmering through tree boughs, tearing my heart to bits.

"I'll get it, Em."

I can't look at him as he turns and leaves the barn. I let my head fill up with pounding feet and winter death winds.

A bunch of women are bustling around the hall setting tables when I arrive that afternoon. Tomorrow, the first day of Affirmation, there'll be a meal to give thanks. The second day, Brother Stockham will lead a ritual where everyone affirms their commitment to their virtues. The third day, bindings are declared. *My* binding to Brother Stockham.

Two Councilmen hover in a corner of the hall, overseeing the women. I see Kane enter from a side door and clasp arms with one of them.

My stomach churns.

I bow my head and help Sister Ann lay wreaths of sage. Then I tell her I'm needed back at Soeur Manon's for something, and hurry out.

At our quarters I bundle up real warm, tuck my grandma'am's ring in my *ceinture* and draw my cloak tight to my chin. I head across the courtyard for the east gates. Each step, I have to force myself not to run—it takes an excruciating long time to get there.

People are shuttering their windows tight, bringing in loads of wood from their woodsheds. They've got a worry to their brow; they can feel *La Prise* coming in.

Brother Jameson is standing at the gates with his arms folded. He raises a hand to stop me. "No one leaves the fortification," he says firm.

I draw back my hood.

"Ah. Sister Emmeline."

"I have Brother Stockham's say-so to go to the river a short while."

"I heard." I expect him to look upset, but he looks smug.

It's his usual look, sure, but today it sets a chill to my spine. He jerks his head to the high walls of the fortification. There are four Watchers patrolling this side of the wall. "Don't go far now."

It's starting to snow, tiny flecks of silver. I walk calm as I can manage across the Watch flats and down the incline to the river. I find a rock and sit in full sight of the Watchtower. The chunks of ice are giant snowflakes on the water, spiraling lazy as they drift downstream. Soon the whole surface will freeze and a solid ribbon will remain—glinting in the winter sun. It will look serene, but it will be deadly, with unpredictable ice and water beneath so cold it could stop your heart.

I risk a look back at the silent walls of the fortification. After a few moments, I get up and venture close to the water. I stay there awhile, my heart pounding. Then I wander a few steps downstream.

When I get to the bend in the river where the bank gets high, I dart in close to the wall. There's no space here to walk along the river, but I'm out of sight of the Watchtower. With any amount of grace, Watch will think I'm at the water's edge.

I scramble along the steep bank, grasping at roots and clumps of sage, praying to the Almighty I don't slip. Frozen chunks of river drift past silent behind me. It's slow going, but I only have to make it a little ways—until the willows above me along the bank get thick. There's going to be a heartbeat in time when Watch can see me if they're looking this far along the bank; I pray they're looking elsewhere.

I go up, my leg screaming in protest as I push against the

crumbling soil, digging at the bank with my hands. I grasp the willow stems at the top and scramble, hauling my bad leg, pulling myself over the side and rolling into the brush.

I draw my hood and crawl forward, worming along the deadfall on my belly, tugging my cloak from the underbrush every now and again. When I get far enough into the woods where I'm sure Watch can't see, I clamber to my feet. Then I head west for the grove.

I am not Honesty. I am not Bravery.

Please let me be Discovery.

23

IN THE GROVE, THE FROZEN WOODS ARE QUIET. The rows of stark poplars have a sheen from the silvery frost. They glisten like dew on a spiderweb.

I stop in the middle of the grove and think on being here with Kane. He'd said he wished things were different.

Well, things *are* different.

I pull my grandma'am's ring from my *ceinture* and put it on my finger. I was always so sure of her guilt, hated her for it. I think on how I got this ring and feel a rush of shame.

You are very much like her.

If that's true, then I'm courting my own death. I could well end up at the Crossroads for this. But what's left for me in the settlement if I don't prove I'm not Stained?

A breeze groans the poplars around me. It's a bitter wind—the air is heavy with the promise of snow. I need to get on with it before the very idea of dusk and all that comes with it freezes me to the spot.

I look around to get my bearings.

There is a girl standing on the far side of the grove, star-ing at me. She moves. Lifts her hand in a greeting.

No.

That can't be. My eyes are playing tricks—

But I can see her plain. She's my age, with long dark hair, big eyes. She's wearing strange clothes—blue, like the sky.

She smiles, shy. Then she turns and disappears.

"Wait!" My voice echoes in the forest. I push hard for the far side of the grove. When I get inside the trees, I see a flash of dark hair behind a far tree.

I crash through the brush after her, my foot screaming, my mind churning.

Who is she? Where did she come from?

Catch her. Find her.

Branches whip at my face, grab my cloak. The trees stream past, blur in my sight as I fix my eyes on her head. She's much faster than me, but it seems she's hanging back a bit. Mayhap she *wants* me to follow?

I lose her and stop, breathing hard. The trees all look the same. I paid no attention to which direction she headed from the grove. I look about, trying to find the sun through the bare branches.

There's movement at the corner of my eye. She's twenty strides ahead, peeking around the trunk of a tree. Then her dark head disappears again. Silent.

Too silent.

She's making no noise as she goes; I'm crashing through the forest like an oversize bison.

I pause.

Mayhap I'm dreaming; mayhap I'm imagining her.

My mind feels fuzzy. I'm hot—is the fever back or am I hot from running? I pinch the inside of my wrist, stamp my foot hard on the frozen forest floor. Both parts of me sing with pain. It feels real, but the girl . . . It's like she stepped out of my dreams.

My dreams. Yes. She's exactly the girl I've been dreaming on—the one who's been calling to me, asking me to find her.

I spin about. I have no idea where I am. Seems I'm west of the grove, but I can't be sure.

A small trail empties out ahead of me. I push ahead, watching the trees for the girl to reappear. When I brush aside the branch hanging over the end of the path, I draw up short. The pole with the red cloth bends in a frost-filled breeze.

I'm back at the Crossroads.

I close my eyes and breathe deep so my mind doesn't splinter into pieces. *Easy.* It's day. I've been here before and lived to tell the tale. There's no way she's a Wayward ghost looking for some sort of revenge.

Is there?

My grandma'am's ring feels hot and bright on my finger.

The girl appears at the top of the hill that leads to the gibbets. She smiles again—that same shy smile. Then she beckons and disappears down the other side.

My chest is tight and my hands shake as I pull my cloak tight around me. Should I follow? I try to think on what waits for me back at the fortification, but all I feel is a nothingness that wants to swallow me whole.

I am Discovery.

The wind gusts at me something fierce as I climb; I have

to bend my head against its force. When I crest the hill and raise my eyes, my heart stops. I'm a good hundred strides from the gibbets at the bottom, but it's plain from this distance: the cages are empty.

Empty.

I try to catch my breath back in the rushing wind. The girl is moving sure among the gibbets, heading for the far side.

My feet move, slipping down the cliff. By the time I reach the bottom, my skin is slick beneath my winter clothes. Sweat beads on my upper lip and I breathe hard, staring at the rusted cages. The doors hang open, like the skeletons inside them pushed them out and flew away. Or . . .

Like they were never there to begin with.

This can't be. I bend, put my hands on my knees and hang my head, trying to slow my breath. My grandma'am's ring glares at me.

Have I plain lost my senses?

A thin, fluting whistle echoes through the Crossroads. This time I know it straightaway: it's the sound I heard when Kane and I hid in the cabin's cellar—the same sound Brother Stockham followed that day I saw him in the woods.

My eyes search for the sound.

It's the girl, waiting outside a line of trees on the far side, her fingers to her lips. She makes the sound once more, then gestures for me to follow. She's not smiling anymore, she's beckoning urgent-like.

My voice comes out a croak. "Wait!"

She doesn't.

I lurch after her. I can't be left alone in this place.

The wind rushes over the hills and sends the gibbets

twisting as I stumble through. There are hot tears on my face—when did I start crying?

Back in the woods we're sheltered from the wind. She's ahead, not stopping, leading me with little backward glances. The stark-white poplars are sun-blasted bones now and white flakes are falling around us like ash.

When I stumble over fallen brush and fall to my knees, she pulls up short and waits for me to get to my feet. Then she's off again. We come to a tree-dotted hill. She stops and whistles again. It echoes through the woods.

And then, a whistle answers back.

She smiles and starts up the hill before us.

My leg is on fire and every bone in my body feels boulder heavy. I scramble through the slick dead leaves, pull my heavy body up the incline. When I get to the top, I recognize the hill we've climbed. We came from a different direction and are looking at it from the side.

It sits at the bottom of the gully, flickering with light like a tiny candle: the cabin. She's led me to the cabin.

I hobble down the slope as fast as I'm able, but she's far faster. She gets to the cabin and darts round the side, up the steps, and in through the door.

My breath is coming fast and jagged, the pain a white-hot blaze searing into my hip. I am dragging, dragging my body with me, my mind drifting slow like the ice in the river.

I cross the clearing. The bright taste of blood is hot in my throat. I half crawl, half stumble up the steps, reach for the door with clammy hands. I'm about to push it open when it swings wide and a backlit shape blocks my path.

Hands seize the front of my cloak and drag me across the threshold. The light is so bright, spots dance in my eyes. The door slams behind me and I'm pushed to the wall and held firm.

A muffled voice reaches my ears, speaking words I can't figure. The shape before the light shifts like it's reaching for something.

More light illuminates the space, bringing the shape before me clear.

I want to scream, but my voice is gone.

I'm staring at the Elephant Man.

24

I JERK BACKWARD, TRY TO SCRAMBLE AWAY, BUT there's nowhere to go. I'm caught, my back pressed against the wall, my cloak held tight in one leathery fist. Behind the Elephant Man looms another. There are two, leering with bulbous eyes, raspy breath.

The ghost girl led me to my death—led me to the *malmaci*.

I lunge forward, clawing and raking at the Elephant Man. It loses its grip on my cloak and falls back. Putting my head down, I draw back and then push off the wall, charging straight through the center of them. I knock both off balance and burst through, but I'm brought up short by a painful choking feeling. My cloak is tight around my throat—one of them has a corner of it. With a swipe I tear it free and lunge forward again. My eyes are blurry with tears, but I can see two walls facing me. That crate with candles sits on the floor. Where is the door? I've lost it. I'm cornered.

I whirl. They're both shouting strange words, advancing on me with their hands up, like they're cornering a wild animal. I won't be able to surprise them this time, and there's no way I'm strong enough to get through them again. I shrink back against a wall, sink to the floor, and throw my arms over my face. I can't die here. Not like this.

A girl's voice rings out: *"Nakana!"*

There's a silence. I brace myself for their hands on me, but nothing comes. Peeking out over my forearm, I see the Elephant Men draw back. They look at one another, shifting their weight. Then the ghost girl appears, pushing her way between the creatures. She points at their faces, points at me. *"Mâkwêyihtam."*

The one before me cocks his head. He speaks to her—it's muffled. They're half human, half . . . I can't figure. Their nightmare faces are shiny and smooth and the sounds they're making . . .

She kneels in front of me and her hands flutter up to touch me. I flinch and duck my head.

"We won't hurt you."

She's speaking English. I risk another look over my arm. She's smiling at me. But then I look to the Elephant Men, standing there, hulking and rasping. She looks over her shoulder, points again to their faces.

There's a sound of protest from one of the Elephant Men.

"It's *her*," the girl says.

There's a pause while the Elephant Men look at one another, their heavy breathing filling the cabin. Then the Elephant Man closest to me reaches a leather-clad hand to his neck. There is a popping sound as he touches something under his chin, and then he pulls at his face. His bulbous eyes and long nose strip away, and in their place is a dark-haired young man with a sharp face and deep brown eyes. He holds his elephant face in his hands, staring at me.

The other does the same—making the popping noise, pulling at the face. He has a rounder face, and the same beautiful eyes. Somewhere in the back of my mind I take in that both boys are dark-haired, have slightly dark skin—like the girl—and wear blue clothing.

"Akohp," the girl says to them.

The sharp-faced boy springs to a corner of the cabin and returns with a wool throw. He passes it to the girl and steps back again.

She reaches forward with the blanket. My mind is going every which way. I let her wrap it around my shoulders. My fingers are wooden as I grasp the blanket and try to get a breath.

"We won't hurt you," she says again.

I want to speak, but my tongue is sluggish, my thoughts are splintered. Is she . . . Are these my Lost People?

"You understand? *Tu comprends?*" She puts a hand on my knee. Her hand is warm.

I draw a breath.

She peers at me. *"Parlez-vous francais ou anglais*? English or French?"

I force my voice out. "Eng-English."

She sits back and says, "We've been looking for you a long time."

I frown. There is a long pause where we do nothing but look at one another. Her eyes are shiny.

I force out the only thing I can think to say: "W-w-why?"

She smiles. "Because you're the Lost People."

They wrap me in another blanket and pour me a drink that the girl—Matisa—says will bring warmth to my insides. I can't figure how: it's cold on my tongue, but sure enough, when I swallow, a real pleasant warmth spreads in my chest.

I watch them move sure but quiet about the cabin, shifting silent to a pack in the corner, over to the strange glowing torch that sits on the floor, back to one another. They speak their language here and there, and speak English to me in words that sound both drawn out and clipped.

Matisa settles beside me. She gestures to the boys. "My brother, Nishwa"—she points to the round-faced boy—"and my cousin, Isi"—the boy who had me by the cloak. Nishwa inclines his head, his eyes curious. Isi looks at me with a wariness I'm well used to.

They're wearing the strangest clothes I've ever seen. Tight-fitting pants and shirts, jackets similar to a kind I've seen in storybooks—and moccasins.

They're real enough, surely not some fearful imagining, and they don't look like they want to hurt me. There's something about their dark eyes and straight hair that tugs at my thoughts. They don't look like anyone I know. No, that's not true. They look something like the south-quarter people. Like the First Peoples part of them.

They remind me of Kane.

"I'm Emmeline," I say.

Matisa nods. "I know." She smiles. "I dreamt you, Emmeline. I've been dreaming you a long time."

"I've been dreaming you too." Never saw her face in my dreams, but I know it's her; I can feel it. We study one another, like it's the most natural thing in the world. "Why did you call me that? 'The Lost People'?"

Matisa looks at the boys. They sink to their haunches on the floor and she swings around so she's facing me. Her brown eyes are warm, her face open. "The answer is long."

But I have so many questions I don't wait: "Where did you come from?"

She cuts the air with her palm. "Far away. Farther than you can hope to walk in a week."

"How did you survive?"

"I dreamt we would survive this place." Matisa lifts her chin and throws a look at the boys. "If we follow our dream paths, we know these things." Nishwa fiddles with his elephant mask.

She looks back at me like she's explained everything.

"Your dreams told you how to survive the *malmaci?*"

Matisa frowns like she doesn't understand.

"The bad spirit that lives in these woods," I explain.

Matisa exchanges a glance with the boys.

"How did you survive out here?" I ask again.

Three pairs of soft brown eyes measure me. The wind outside the cabin howls.

Isi crawls forward and speaks to Matisa in their language. His eyes have barely left my face since taking off his mask. Matisa nods and waves her hand, dismissing his words. Then she pours me more of the warming drink as he sits back.

"Our people left this place long ago. I know nothing of this *malmaci,*" she says.

I study her face. She's telling the truth. Is it possible they just didn't encounter it in these woods yet?

"When did your people leave?"

"Generations ago."

My heart leaps. The left-behinds. "Why did they leave?"

"Many years ago the animals we shared the land with began to die from a sickness we could not explain. Some of our people died too. And when our peacetime leaders began to dream that visitors would arrive and more death would follow, we left. Took our people and fled to the mountains."

She's speaking on my people's arrival. A thrill rushes through me. She *is* the Lost People; *this* is what happened to them.

"Years passed and our elders began to dream that the visitors had died. All but one group of people." She smiles. "Your people, Emmeline. We sent scouts to learn more about you, but when our scouts didn't return, these woods became a forbidden place."

My thoughts are running with her words. The *malmaci* appeared as a sickness at first, then it started the Takings. I stare at her. It's by Almighty's grace alone she and these two boys have survived this long.

"Your scouts were Taken by the *malmaci,*" I say. "It was dangerous for you to come."

Isi mutters something in their tongue. Matisa looks at her hands. "I listen to my dreams," she says. "When I began dreaming about a Lost People—and about one girl who was dreaming of me—I knew we had to find you."

"You came for me?"

She looks up and nods.

"But . . . why?"

"That answer is even longer, but I believe your dreams

have been telling you what mine have been telling me. We were meant to find one another."

My dreams. They brought me here, to this cabin, to the journal. To the truth about my grandma'am. They urged me to prove my Discovery virtue.

I've done that. I've Discovered the Lost People. I stare at the three. The drink is heating me through, clearing my head. They have the strangest clothes and objects—nothing like the left-behinds Tom and I have found. They're so clean, and none of their clothes have rips or stains. All at once I feel ashamed of my shabby clothes and tangled plait. But one thought washes that away:

They've survived out here.

I pull the blanket off of my shoulders. "You need to come with me to the settlement."

Matisa shakes her head. "No. My dreams told me to find you. Only you. We have been waiting in these woods, trying to make contact with you." She looks at the boys. "Nishwa and Isi ventured a bit too close some days." She points at the mask in Nishwa's hands.

He looks down, sheepish, but Isi frowns. "Scared away that old man, at least."

Andre. "But why did you need to scare him away?" I ask.

Matisa holds my gaze. "If the wrong person finds us, all is lost. This I know."

"But they need to know that you're here. You can help us."

Matisa says nothing, just watches me with her patient brown eyes.

"We've been trapped here five generations! People need to know we can get out, find others."

They exchange glances. Isi talks to Matisa in their language.

She looks at me. "Our *moshum*—our grandfather—commands our warriors back home. He studies the war habits of other peoples. He told Isi the Lost People would be warlike."

"We aren't!" I insist. But I think on my dream, with all the Watchers firing on Matisa just as I finally find her, and a spike of fear pierces me. She's right. Her heading back to the settlement with me isn't a good idea. People are too afraid.

"I came to find you," Matisa says. "My dreams told me you will know who to trust."

I stare at her hard, figuring her meaning. "You're saying I can't trust just anyone."

"I dreamt time and again of a hawk circling its prey." She looks at me careful. "Emmeline, *you* were the prey."

Isi crawls forward and passes me a hunk of dried meat. The meat is a mite tough, but it's something to occupy my mouth while my thoughts run ahead.

I found the Lost People. I can prove my Discovery virtue, prove my grandma'am wasn't Wayward how everyone thought. I don't have to bind to Brother Stockham . . .

I don't have to bind to Brother Stockham.

The thought makes my head light with relief. But I push it aside. I have to think this through. Matisa won't come back to the settlement now, and nobody's going to take the word of a Stained girl, are they?

A hawk circling its prey.

Just like in *my* dreams. Brother Stockham? Whatever is written in the journal is something he doesn't want people to see. Why he never burned it, I can't figure. Unless . . .

Unless he didn't see it, unless someone else was in this cabin. That day I thought I saw him in two places at once. Was it Matisa or one of the boys? Or was it someone else?

If the wrong person finds us, all is lost.

My thoughts flash back to Kane on the Council steps. I shove the thought of his dark eyes, the feeling of his thumb on my lower lip, down deep. Can't let my heart make the decision. Not this time.

The circling hawk in my dreams was always watching me. I think of Jameson's sneer.

When you repeat the mistakes of those Waywards who have gone before, I will be here. And I will set things right.

Grace! As I rub at my eyes, I realize I'm tired, deep in my bones. I have no idea how long I've been outside the fort.

Think.

I need someone who's real virtuous to help me; someone people will take serious.

Soeur Manon is frail; people might think her mind was getting old. And she doesn't read English. Frère Andre? My pa? Sister Ann can read. But first I need someone to help me talk to people . . .

I need Tom. He's virtuous, well respected. His parents would help him figure out the journal, and he could tell me.

And we've always kept one another's secrets. My throat gets tight. Mayhap we won't need to keep those secrets after this. Mayhap there's something better for both of us, out there. We just need to convince the right people to take that chance.

I need to hurry. If Watch has started a search for me, I won't get the chance to tell Tom anything. But my dreams have led me here, like Matisa's dreams led her to me. Surely bringing the truth back to the settlement is what I'm meant to do.

It occurs to me I don't yet have that longer answer she was speaking on, but that'll have to wait. I need to get back.

"All right. The three of you need to wait for me here."

"You're going back?" Matisa asks.

I nod. "But I need to get something first."

The cellar is cold but less fearful when lit by the strange, bright lamp that Nishwa holds. The light bounces off the walls, revealing a space four strides by five strides. The boys crowd in behind me. The book lies where I dropped it, right in front of the pile of dingy bones.

Nishwa clucks his tongue as Isi pushes past me. I watch Isi kneel next to the skeletons, muttering. He runs his hands over the bones, pulls them from the iron shackles. Nishwa holds the light high.

I step forward, grab the book, and turn to Matisa, fighting the urge to push past her and scramble back up the ladder. "What's he doing?"

"He wants to bury them, like he did the others."

The others. I frown into Matisa's face, and then the meaning of her words hits me. The Crossroads. I turn. "You took the bones from the gibbets."

He looks back at me, his eyes guarded. He nods.

"Why?"

"They deserved rest." He clenches his jaw and looks away.

Rest. He buried my grandma'am, and what was left of the others. We don't bury our dead—haven't in generations.

There's not enough land near the settlement for that, so the Cleansing Waters have been our way. It skitters me, thinking about their bones under the earth like that. But knowing Isi wanted them to be at rest, even though he didn't even know who they were . . .

I swallow a lump in my throat.

He busies himself, collecting all of the bones into a pile while the light from Nishwa's lamp casts long shadows on the dirt wall behind.

Matisa and I leave the frozen cellar.

"What is this place?" Matisa asks, sorting through her pack and retrieving another hunk of dried meat. She hands it to me.

"I don't know. But I think this book will tell me." I wish I had enough time for Matisa to read it to me. I tuck it inside my *ceinture fléchée*, tying the knot so it hides the bulge, and then I tie my cloak tighter around me. The light in the cabin is bright from the strange lamp whining away on the floor, but I know the light outside is waning and I need to get back. I stare around the shack, at the small pack in the corner. There's no way they can wait a night for me here, not with the few blankets they have.

"Matisa, how have you survived out here?"

"We have our supplies in a cave, a short ride from here."

"Ride?"

"We came by horse. They are tied outside."

Horse. My heart leaps. I've never seen one before, only seen pictures in Soeur Manon's books. Always wanted to see one. They're tall, with large nostrils and big hooves—the moment hiding with Kane in the cellar of this cabin rushes back. The noise through the woods was hoofbeats, sure, but it was no hell-beast making it. And the sound—well, now that fear isn't addling my mind—it must've been their breath, like sheep huffing out air. Matisa and the boys were looking for me that day, and I disappeared under the shack. I want to burst out laughing.

Matisa is watching me, waiting for me to speak.

"I'll be back," I say. "Meet me here tomorrow afternoon."

25

WHEN I CLIMB UP FROM THE RIVERBANK, I FEEL
like I'm looking on the fortification for the first time. I mean,
really looking. After being with Matisa and the boys, the
weathered posts look sad and tired, not strong and fierce.
The bodies shifting around the tops of the walls look that
way too. But then I see the glint of a spyglass in one Watcher's hand and the thought of being caught makes my insides
turn. I pray to the Almighty no one was spying me with that
glass when I slipped away.

The doors on the north side of the river are open, though,
which makes me think I'm safe. Surely if someone checked
the riverbank and found me gone, they'd assume a Taking
and fortify. Likely none of the Watchers have paid my whereabouts much mind since I left the gates. Being the Stained
cripple does have its uses. It's a bittersweet thought, consid-
ering Kane gave me the idea in the first place.

I cross the Watch flats and duck inside the gates. Brother
Jameson is a few strides away, talking with a thin woman—a

gatherer. My stomach clenches hard, but I slip past with a respectful-like nod and limp toward our quarters. He doesn't call after me. I cross the courtyard without anyone so much as glancing my way.

Inside, I close the door behind me and breathe deep. As I cross through the kitchen, I pull the journal from inside my *ceinture,* intending to hide it in my room, but a knock at the door from the common room stops me dead.

Tucking the book back inside the folds of my belt, I tell my insides to stop racing, tell my mind to stay calm. I open the door and find Sister Ann standing there, her mouth in an unhappy line.

"Emmeline, where have you been to? You weren't at the Healing House when I checked. You're meant to be helping with the Affirmation preparations."

A hot flush rushes through me. "Brother Stockham allowed me to the riverbank this afternoon."

She frowns. "Whatever for?"

I open my mouth and close it again. What can I tell her? She's looking at me with those tired eyes, waiting on my reply, so I say the only true thing I can. "I accepted his proposal. We're to be bound during *La Prise.*"

I expect her to huff, ask me what that's got to do with anything. But her eyes go soft, the line on her brow smoothes, and her tight shoulders slump. "I heard," she says.

We look at one another. And there's something in Sister Ann's eyes I've never seen, a . . . sadness. Like she's looking on herself at my age.

"You went for a think."

"Something like that." I can't imagine Sister Ann viewing "going for a think" as useful, but here she is, looking as though she understands.

"I remember the autumn before I was to bind to my husband." She says it quiet, like she's thinking hard on that memory. "I wanted that autumn to last forever."

My mouth near drops open at this. I think of Tom's pa. He smiles easy, but he's got a serious manner; Tom's quite a bit like him. There's nothing awful about him, least not to my eyes, but mayhap that's not the point. Mayhap just being expected to bind—to anyone—is burden enough.

I look at Sister Ann. Never figured we had too much in common, her and me. She's so virtuous and I'm so . . . But now that she's standing here, with that understanding look, I can see we are something alike. And that day two years ago, when she would've headed out of the settlement to find Edith—*that's* the kind of Wayward I am. Isn't it?

She shakes her shoulders, like she's remembering herself. "Enough lollygagging. I need help taking candles to the hall."

The book is branding my skin through my tunic, under my *ceinture*. I can't keep carrying it about—suppose someone expects me to use my *ceinture* for something and I have to take it off? It isn't likely, but it would fit my luck.

"Where's Tom?" I ask.

"Barns." She gestures for me to follow her. "I've got two crates in our kitchen." I stay in the doorway, throwing a frantic look around for a hiding place for the book. I spy Pa's trapping satchel by the outside door. With the settlement closing up for *La Prise*, he's not using it these days. Won't for months.

"Just going to grab my scarf," I say.

"Hurry it along," she says.

I limp across our kitchen quick, out of her sight, and dig into my belt to pull out the book. As I drop it into Pa's satchel, she calls again. "They're waiting on these!"

I catch up to her in her kitchen, where she points to a crate on the floor.

Outside, the air is cold and the sun is low in the sky. I need to find Tom before we're all locked away for the night. Sister Ann pushes into the hall ahead of me and makes her way to a table. There are all kinds of women milling about, fixing the cloth on the head table and so on. The Councilmen have disappeared.

As I walk across the threshold, Kane steps into my path, arms crossed over his chest. My pulse jumps into my throat at the sight of him. A part of me wants to grab him aside, tell him what I've found. But Matisa's words come back.

You will know who to trust.

"Sister Emmeline," he says, loud enough for Sister Ann to hear. "Sister Lucy needs a runner." Sister Ann looks back over her shoulder and nods, continuing on to the far side of the hall. Kane takes the opposite end of the crate and leans close. "Meet me at my quarters," he says real low. His cheeks have two bright spots in them. His eyes flash with something. Fear? Is he afraid for me or for himself?

"Obliged," I say, and hand him the crate. Then I duck out of the hall.

I push all thoughts of him from my head, focus on the task I need to do—quick, and secret. I need to find Tom.

I limp fast for the barns, watching for Councilmen. But even Brother Jameson has disappeared from the north gates;

just the Watchers on the tops of the walls remain. The sun is just atop the hills—it'll be dusk real soon. Inside the barns the earthy warmth of the sheep tickles my nose. It takes a moment for my eyes to fix themselves so they can see. I move in, listening for voices.

I find Tom. He's alone, thanks be, cleaning out the feeding troughs. When he sees me, relief crosses his face. "Em, I was worried. Ma said you weren't at Soeur Manon's—"

"Can we talk?"

He puts down his shovel and wades out of the mass of dingy sheep.

I take his arm and draw him toward the far side of the stable. The words want to burst in a rush.

"Tom." I take a deep breath. "I found them."

"Found who?"

"The Lost People."

His eyes are wide and white in the dark.

"I went back to that trail, back to where I said I needed to go, and I found them. They aren't ghosts, Tom—they're real people. First Peoples who used to live on this land."

Tom grabs my arm and draws me close. "Em, that's addled."

"I know it is. But I'm telling you the truth. The Lost People weren't Taken—they fled. And they're back to help us."

Tom just stares at me.

"Tom? We're not alone out here."

He blinks. "How did they survive the *malmaci?*"

"Don't know yet, mayhap they can teach us how." I touch his arm. "Tom, they're real."

He responds slow. "They're real people."

"Yes."

"Here, in these woods."

I nod and hold my breath.

The sky in his eyes changes from clouded to bright blue. "What are they like?"

I grab his hands. "Incredible. They know lots of things—they *have* lots of things we don't. A torch that lights up just—just like that"—I snap my fingers in front of his eyes, making them go wider—"with no flint at all. And these—these masks and all kinds of—of things . . . " I'm tripping on my words. "And they're here to help us, Tom. Finally."

He smiles wide, squeezing my hands back. "Can't believe it."

"I know."

"You've been wondering so long about those bones and left-behinds. And now . . . Almighty, Em! You found them!"

A little laugh bursts from my mouth.

Tom's eyes shine and his breath comes fast. "What did Council say?"

I pause. The sheep rustle soft beside us.

"Em? When you told them, what did they say?"

I swallow. "I can't tell them. The Lost People—the girl—told me I can't trust them."

The smile leaves Tom's face. He stares at me hard a long while. Then he looks at the dirt floor, scuffs his feet in it.

"Tom, I'm telling the truth. The Lost People are out there."

"I believe you," he says real soft. But when he glances back, he's looking at me like the day I told him about finding something to clear my Stain. He looks plain fearful. "But how do you know it isn't a trick?"

"It isn't."

"They told you not to tell *Council* about them. Mayhap they want to get into the settlement because they're planning something awful against us."

"There's three of them. They aren't planning something awful."

"You sure there's just three?"

That stalls my thoughts. I don't actually know that for certain. But if they wanted to harm us, why lurk around, waiting for me to find them? A little voice in my head wonders if they need me to get past Watch. No. I might not know much right now, but I do know what I feel deep down.

"They're here to help us."

"But how do you know?"

"Because I've been dreaming on this girl, on these people. My dreams have been telling me to find them."

The fear in Tom's eyes shifts to doubt. "Your dreams."

"That's right."

Tom frowns.

"Tom. Please. They can help us."

He stares at me. Then he runs his hands through his blond hair, impatient-like. "Help us do what?"

"L-l-live. Get out of this wasteland, find a better life. Do something more than just survive."

"You're telling me Council wouldn't let us do that?"

"I don't know! But I know something strange happened that Brother Stockham is keeping secret. And it's something my grandma'am found out. And they killed her for it."

"How do you know all this? The Lost People tell you?"

"I found a journal that says as much."

Tom's frown deepens. "A journal."

"A confession. From H. J. Stockham to his son."

"And where is this journal?"

"I left it in Pa's trapping satchel."

Tom's eyes grow wide. "Why did you do that?"

"Because I didn't want anyone else to get hold of it!" My voice has got a desperate edge to it. Didn't expect Tom to kick up this much of a fuss. "We need to go find out what it says."

"We?"

"Course! Tom, I'm telling you all this because I need your help." I grab his arm. "I'm going to bring the Lost People so everyone can see for themselves. You need to talk to people you can trust—let them know what I've found. There's a Watcher who'll help me. Tomorrow, before the ceremony starts, I'll get him to let me out of the fortification. You unbolt the wastewater-ditch gate. The Watcher will leave the ditch unguarded. We'll come round the riverbank way. Once we're inside, people can see the truth for themselves. They can see they're here to help us, not harm us." It comes out of my mouth in a rush: my foolproof plan. My great idea.

Tom just stares at me.

"Tom?" I squeeze his arm. "I need your help. Please. You need to unbolt the gate."

Silence. There's nothing but the rustling of the sheep in the dark corners. I take a deep breath and try again. "You're the only one I can trust with this."

But his eyes are glassy and when he speaks, his voice is strange. "I said you should stop, Em. I told you that."

"Stop?"

"All of this."

I frown. "I found the *Lost People*—"

"You don't know anything about them! You have no idea the danger you might be putting us all in!" He pulls his arm from my grasp. "I can't help you."

The words strike a blow to me so strong I near lose my breath. I stare at him, at his mess of blond hair and prairie-sky eyes—so dark now it's like the sun has never shone in them once. His jaw is set and his hands shake at his sides. I can see now he's afraid—he's so afraid he's barely Tom anymore.

"Can't or won't?"

"Won't. And if your pa doesn't turn that book over to Council, I'll . . ."

My voice is just a whisper. "You'll what?"

He doesn't answer. Just stares at me, his lower lip trembling, eyes red-rimmed.

You will know who to trust. The dirt floor of the barn surges up at me. I throw a hand out to the wall to steady myself.

And then rage washes me. I'm going to lash out at him, shake him, shout. I'm going to scream that he's sentencing us to another *La Prise*. He's sentencing me to a binding I can't endure. All because he's scared.

A gust of wind hits my back as the barn door swings open behind me. I don't turn—I'm too rapt, staring at Tom's face. It's pale. Terrified.

And then a hand clamps down on my shoulder.

26

THE HAND SPINS ME ABOUT, DIGGING INTO MY skin. Brother Jameson looms over me, flanked by another Councilman. Behind him, Brother Stockham stands in his cloak, arms crossed, one thumb grazing his bottom lip.

"Sister Emmeline, we have some things to speak on," Brother Jameson says. His face is smug, satisfied. And full of hate.

Brother Stockham makes an inviting sweep of his arm toward the door. He doesn't look angry, but he's watching me close.

I swallow hard and move forward into the men. When I cast a quick glance behind, Tom is standing in the dim light, arms at his sides, eyes wide with fear. And anguish.

Brother Jameson forces me outside the barns and into the glare of the setting sun. I'm blind a moment and miss the step, turning my ankle on the earth. I bite back a cry.

There's a woman spreading seed for chickens outside the coops. She looks up curious-like, then back at her work just as quick. A man hauling skins passes by, his eyes low. Brother Jameson keeps his large hand on my shoulder as we walk, and Brother Stockham falls into step beside me.

He glances at my hand. "That is an unusual ring, Emmeline. Where did you get it?"

Bleed it! I'd forgotten to hide it when I left the shack. I was so concerned with getting back to the fort with the journal . . .

I swallow hard and force myself to meet his eyes. "It . . . was my grandma'am's."

Brother Stockham raises his eyebrows.

I look between the men, my chest tight, my thoughts skittering every which way. As we're heading through the courtyard, something flashes in the corner of my eye. I glance to the side. Shaved head, arms crossed, watching from a corner of the weapons shack: Kane. A wave of dizziness washes me and I have to grab at Brother Stockham's arm so I don't stumble. I hide my face in my hood, my eyes blurring with tears.

We climb the stairs to the Council building, Brother Jameson leading the way, Brother Stockham and the other Councilman at my back. Inside the doors, Brother Stockham turns to face me.

"Emmeline, Council has learned you left the riverbank today. Both a Watcher and a gatherer saw you return from the woods."

I can't speak, can't move. His quarters are still. No sound. No life.

"You betrayed my trust," Brother Stockham says. "And

you have committed a serious offense. It pains me greatly, but justice must be done, for the continued safety of the settlement."

My stomach drops through the floor. Jacob Brigston swims into my mind—tied up, thrashing in Council's grip.

My voice comes out a rasp. "What kind of justice?"

"Council has advised the most severe of punishments." He presses his lips together and the weight of his words sinks in. He means the Crossroads.

Panic shoots through me. "But surely heading out to the woods isn't an offense that warrants—"

"If it were just the once, no." Brother Jameson cuts me off. "But we know about your wanderings. You are dangerous, Emmeline. You don't believe your Wayward actions risk the settlement." He looks to Brother Stockham. "That Cariou boy did well."

My blood turns to ice.

Brother Stockham speaks. "I have asked Council for one day's reprieve, so that I might pray on this matter before meting your punishment." I try to draw a breath. "Council warned me of this possibility. I am devastated that I could not see how shortsighted my proposal was."

But he doesn't look devastated; not one bit. There's something glimmering in his eyes. Admiration? Excitement?

The Councilmen shift, impatient-like. Brother Stockham inclines his head down the hall, and the men turn and herd me along the passageway. A large door stands open at the end. It looks heavy, like a cellar door, and has a bolt on the outer side.

"You will remain here for the night."

Brother Jameson pushes me hard from behind. I stumble forward into the small space, my leg on fire.

"Brother Jameson will alert your father that you have been detained," Brother Stockham says.

Brother Jameson speaks in a low growl. "Your Waywardness will not be the demise of this settlement, Emmeline. We will not allow it."

The door slams shut with a heavy clang behind me. The bolt slides across the lock.

Their footsteps fade. There is no window in this room, only a husk mattress in one corner. The entire space is three strides by three strides. The air feels close, like there's not enough of it. I turn around and press at the door, knowing it's useless; it's bolted from the outside. There's no way out.

I stand, listening to the quiet. Then Tom's scared face and Matisa's trusting eyes swim before me.

If the wrong person finds us, all is lost. This I know.

A wail builds in my chest like a gale-force wind.

I think of the book tucked inside Pa's satchel, his sad eyes . . . when they tell him . . .

My secret heart shatters. My knees give out and I drop to the floor, curling in, my face to the floorboards, the wail bursting out in a desperate keen. Tears stream down my neck in a scalding river.

I've failed outright.

I don't know who knows about the journal, who was hiding it. I don't know what it says. If Tom turns it in, they'll think Pa was hiding it for me. I need to set them straight. Except . . .

If I save Pa, there's still Matisa. If I don't speak on her, no one will ever know the truth. They'll gag me and bind me and drag me to the Crossroads. I'll forever be the Stained girl who followed a Wayward legacy. But if I turn Matisa over to the wrong person . . .

All is lost.

What does that mean? That I'm not just sentencing myself, I'm sentencing everyone?

That Cariou boy did well.

I think about Kane standing in the courtyard, looking on. Sobs wrack me. I was lying to myself. Deep down, underneath all of my hurt and rage, I believed him. I believed he loved me. My entire body aches with the memory of him pressed close in that storeroom. The story he told me . . .

I cry for what must be hours, cry until I have no tears left—until my whole body is weak, useless. Then I pull myself along the rough floor, onto the husk mattress, and fall into a deep, dreamless sleep.

The whine of the bolt wakes me. Someone is opening the door. It's too dark yet for it to be day. For an addled moment, I see Kane stepping over the threshold.

Then Brother Stockham's face appears sharp in the shadows, lit by a single candle.

He holds a dipper of water toward me.

I climb to my feet, my body stiff, the front of my tunic still wet with tears. My foot screams with my deadweight as I stumble toward him. I take the dipper and gulp the cold water. I'm used to the dull ache of hunger in my belly, but I've never been so thirsty.

I hand him back the dipper. He smiles.

Brother Jameson appears behind him, twisting a bit of twine in his hands.

I stumble back toward the wall, my heart springing into my throat. "Please . . ."

"Emmeline, everything will be all right. Please don't fight while Brother Jameson binds your hands," Brother Stockham says.

Brother Jameson crosses toward me. In my mind's eye I can see the Wayward shearer thrashing about on the ground, reflecting in Jameson's bright-blue eyes. Brother Jameson's knuckles going white on the leather twine . . .

I near spill every thought then and there. But I look to Brother Stockham and freeze. He has a finger to his lips in a shushing motion. And there's something in his eyes, something reassuring. Like it *is* going to be all right.

Jameson grabs my wrists behind my back. He wraps them, and as he tightens the knot, the twine bites into my skin. I don't cry out. I'm filling my mind with thoughts of the golden poplars, the shining river, the heady smell of sage.

Jameson forces a strip of cloth into my mouth and ties it behind my head, ripping stray wisps from my messy plait. I can feel a note of panic creeping into my thoughts. I squeeze my eyes shut and picture:

Swallows swooping along the banks, humming insects, sweet clover.

They lead me from the Council building into the cool blue of early morning; the sun isn't up. Everything seems real peaceful, the way the river does when it freezes. There are Councilmen standing on the tops of the walls—no Watchers. Brother Stockham blows out the candle and hands it and the empty dipper to Brother Jameson. Then he takes my arm and steers me toward the east. Are we going to see my pa? Are they going to let him say goodbye before they take me? Should I tell Brother Stockham about the journal—that I put it in Pa's satchel?

Les trembles moving in the wind, showers of gold snowflakes.

We don't go to the quarters. We head toward the gates, where another Councilman stands. He opens it as we approach. Brother Stockham nods back to Brother Jameson, who falls behind. Then Brother Stockham picks up his pace as we pass through the gates.

It's just us on the Watch flats. He's pulling me along and I have to quicken my pace, dragging my leg as we go. Why are we heading east? What did Brother Stockham decide last night? The twine cuts into my wrists and I nearly choke at the spit gathering in the back of my mouth.

Shining river, diving swallows.

The cliff walls have a light dust of snow coating their tear stains; the wind is bitter cold. He takes me past the bend in the river and starts along the trail to the Cleansing Waters.

When we get to the boulder gate, where the river speeds up to press through the gap in a roar, all my calming thoughts vanish in the wind. Chunks of ice swirl toward the opening. When they hit the gate, they splinter and rush through or are forced under and lodge in place. I remember that bundle I threw into the waters just weeks ago, remember my dream. It was alive when I threw it . . .

There's a soft bleating sound on the wind, like a lamb looking for its ewe. I look about, searching for the beast, but then realize it's coming from me. I'm crying again. My tears are drying in cold rivers on my cheeks.

Brother Stockham turns to me. He frowns.

"Emmeline," he says, reproachful. He pulls the gag away from my mouth and wipes his thumb across my cheek. "I told you everything would be all right."

27

MY VOICE, RAW FROM CRYING, COMES OUT A croak. "Why—why are we out here?"

"Best to speak where the wrong ears can't hear."

My tears stop flowing. I stare at him.

"Council. They assume we've come out here so I may mete your punishment. They wouldn't understand."

I blink my puffy eyes. "Understand what?"

"You and I. The woods."

Answering him, the trees bow in the wind. I glance about. Tiny flecks of snow swirl around us. The sun is creeping over the high bank of the river, a thin slice of orange against the blue dawn.

"I want no more secrets between us." He steps forward and puts his arms around me. For half an addled moment I think he's embracing me, but then his fingers are working at the twine on my wrists. He's—letting me go? He undoes the twine but lingers a moment, holding me. When he steps back, I near collapse in relief. I rub at my raw wrists, staring at him wide-eyed.

He points to my hand and asks, "Where did you get it?"

I look down at the ring. My mouth is bone dry. I force my tongue to work. "It was my grandma'am's."

"So you said. I was hoping you could be honest with me about how it came to be on your hand."

My breath is coming in short sips. I close my eyes, trying to clear my mind, but all that surfaces is Jacob, terror-stricken, thrashing about on the ground.

When I open them, Brother Stockham's studying me. I shake my head.

"You are afraid," he says. "Afraid of being dragged back to the Crossroads, back to where you got that ring. Afraid you will die, hanging there?" When I don't speak, his face softens. "We are to be *bound*, Emmeline. Do you think I would let that happen to you?" He takes my face in his hands. "I will right the wrongs of the past." Then he dips his head and puts his lips to mine, kisses me soft. His chin-length hair falls forward, brushing the sides of my face.

I break the kiss and pull back. "Why . . . why are we out here?" I ask again.

"I told you. So we may speak plain."

There's something in his voice that shoots a sliver of fear through my insides. I pull my cloak tight around me.

He steps away and spreads his arms wide, gesturing to the frozen trees, the rushing river. "What you said the other day, about listening to the land? Your instinct was correct: the woods have secrets they are trying to tell us. But no one since your grandmother has bothered to listen." He drops his arms and tilts his head. "Tell me what you've heard in these woods."

A crow calls from a treetop, a strangled, ugly cry. I glance about. The Lost People aren't watching from the woods anymore. There's nothing out here. Just me and him.

"Emmeline," he says. My eyes snap back to his face. "I have already told you I won't send you to the Crossroads. What are you afraid of?"

I dreamt time and again of a hawk circling its prey. Emmeline, you *were the prey.*

"Do you not trust me?"

I swallow hard. "It's just that it's not yet day . . . and we're near the woods, and there was a Taking—"

"We are in no danger."

I glance about once more. If I make a run for it, he'll catch me in a heartbeat. "How can you be sure?"

He steps close. "There can be no Taking without my say-so."

My heart stutters. "Beg pardon?"

"We both live with family burdens, Emmeline." He turns to gaze at the ice chunks washing past. "But our togetherness will overcome."

"I don't understand." My mind flies to a picture of him in the woods, the strange half circle of candles on the cabin floor. No Taking without his say-so. He . . . controls the *malmaci*'s Takings?

"My father burdened me with a position that was built upon the advice of his father and secured upon people's terror of the unknown."

He takes the edges of my cloak in both hands and pulls

me near. "But I will not make the same mistakes they made."
He's so close I can smell the bergamot soap on his skin.
He sighs. "My grandfather couldn't risk the unknown. He
regretted that, needed to repent. He wanted salvation."

"For what?"

"Murder."

The wind whistles straight through my bones. I swallow.
"My grandma'am's."

He pushes a stray hair back away from my face, tucking it
into my hood. His eyes shine. "You see? You know the history, the answers, deep down." A sad smile crosses his face.
"They were in love."

"They—they were?"

"As we are."

I squirm, stumble on my words. "But she—she . . . "

"Was a widow, he a married man."

"She didn't proposition him?"

"No."

He's gripping my cloak tighter with every word I speak,
but I have to keep talking. I have to know. "But he was afraid
of the settlement finding out about them? That's why she
was sent to the Crossroads?"

"Certainly their illicit love would have destroyed his
position."

"But . . . but everyone thinks she acted alone. That she—"

"Your grandmother's actions were unsanctioned, Emmeline," he replies in a mild tone, "and my position—my family's
legacy—depends upon that history being kept secret. Why
ruin two families over one sin?"

My mouth opens and closes, but no sound comes out. I stare at him, my thoughts whirling, my head awash with confusion and rage and hurt.

"I don't believe he meant for it to end the way it did. I believe they might have kept their love a secret, might have kept it contained to the cabin he built, far into the woods where few would dare to venture. They might have lived the rest of their days with their secret life in the woods, had it not been for your grandmother's curiosity, her fearlessness toward what lurks beyond."

"What are you speaking on?"

"Her Discovery, Emmeline. Her curiosity was her undoing."

"My grandma'am was sent to death by your grandpa's hand."

He nods. "Your grandmother chose the unknown over my grandfather. He chose his position as leader over her. But *we* will do things differently. When I wandered those woods and found his confession, I realized you and I are two halves of a whole; two people carrying the burdens of our ancestors."

I try to take a breath in the icy wind, but I'm breathing so shallow it's like I'm gulping down water. I'm missing something; some piece of this puzzle.

Clara found something in these woods I had not the Honesty or Bravery to reconcile . . .

"I want no more secrets between us," he says again.

I think again of the cabin, the candles.

"Do you control the *malmaci?*" I ask.

For a moment I think he's going to laugh, but then his eyes turn serious.

"I live with a family burden, like you."

"You keep saying that. But I'm the only one here who's Stained."

He sighs and gestures at the boulder gate. "The Cleansing Waters are for more than just disposing of our natural dead."

Our natural dead. I frown.

He watches the river careful. "My father started the Takings."

The wind screams through the trees, clear through my head.

He continues, "I've often wondered if he believed in the *malmaci* at all. He never said. I know my grandfather didn't, he wrote as much in his journal. He guarded the borders against ordinary dangers: large predators, unwanted visitors. But the lore of the evil that was here when we arrived was strong in people's minds. For some, it has just grown stronger over the years."

The wind blows fierce inside me, jumbling my thoughts. "You don't believe in the *malmaci?*"

"I know that I have never seen it." He turns and looks at me keen. "Have you?"

I shake my head, mute.

"I cannot answer with certainty whether or not the *malmaci* exists. What is more important here, Emmeline, is that fearful people are easily led."

My thoughts are all muddy. It can't be true. But the look on his face is so honest, so open . . .

"My father understood that well, and he found a way to keep the fear fresh." Brother Stockham looks again at the water rushing through the boulder gate.

My heart is beating out of my chest. "He—he killed his own people?"

A flash of pain crosses Brother Stockham's face. He nods, his jaw tight.

"Why?"

"To lead."

I stare at his tortured face.

"He was . . . an ambitious man. He believed the people needed a leader who wasn't afraid to sacrifice the occasional lamb for the good of the flock."

"The good?"

"Order, Emmeline—something the people are desperate for. We need only look at Council to understand this community's willingness to be led. Our Councilmen don't even need weapons to enforce their control."

The wind gusts around us. I think of the crowd watching Jacob struggle as Council strangled him. Some of them lauded it. Said it was the Almighty's will.

"My father brought the threat of the *malmaci* close to dissuade risk takers, people who would rather chance the unknown, the terror of the great beyond, than contribute to the settlement." He looks at me, admiration replacing the pain in his eyes. "But not you."

"But—but the Takings have been happening for years; ever since our people arrived."

"Perhaps," he says. "Or perhaps those Takings were simply accidents. People who wandered too far and were set upon by wild animals, people who froze on the prairies or fell to their deaths in the ravines. Regardless, people will believe what they will. And fear is powerful."

Could it be true? Who would remember those Takings long ago? There are just a handful of people who lived through his father's rule. Soeur Manon and Frère Andre are two such. I think about Soeur Manon telling me to *ask the woods,* and Frère Andre forming a kinship with me over our wanderings. Was it because there was some truth they'd stored away in their hearts and forgotten?

Like they believed, somewhere deep down, the *malmaci* might not exist?

I breathe deep, trying to slow my racing heart. "The first settlers were near destroyed by the *malmaci,* years ago."

"Certainly they were set upon by something. But was it a monster, or has that history taken on a life of its own in the people's imaginations?"

The river roars.

How did you survive out here? I asked Matisa. Her frown, like she couldn't figure what I was thinking on, swims before my eyes.

A chunk of ice smashes on the boulder gate. I picture someone being thrown into that water, their body splintering into shards on the rock . . .

"That Pellier man . . . " I say. He's my proof Brother Stockham is mistaken. But as I say his name, I realize it's no proof at all—and I don't want him to answer.

"I want no more secrets between us." There's a right skittering sheen to his eyes.

I can't think what to do. I nod.

"My father insisted that love—that desire—was the path to ruin."

My father taught me many lessons.

I think on those scars under his cloak, under his shirt. Sharp crystals of snow sting my bare cheeks.

"But everything has happened as it should to prove him wrong. We have replayed a history that was bound to recur." He looks like he's weighing a thought. He scrubs a hand over his face. "Brother Bertrand was an unfortunate sacrifice. I needed to distract Council from watching you too close, needed to reignite their fear. They were starting to become suspicious of that Cariou boy's reliability."

He notices my bewilderment and smiles. "An ordinary man would be quite jealous. The way he looks at you—like you're the summer rains after a drought. But his love for you is nothing compared to what you and I are fated for. When he went after you that night of Harvest, I knew I'd found an ally, whether he knew what he was doing or not."

I take a painful breath. Kane *did* come after me during the attack. His scared eyes at the hall flash through my mind. *Meet me at my quarters.* He knew what Council had planned for me; he was trying to warn me.

"I know you have been out in the woods because I too have been out there. I have been reading, praying, trying to determine my path. It has been unbearable at times." He touches the scar on his neck. "Pain can help remind us what is important. But I think you understand. I know how you punish yourself too when you are uncertain." He looks to my foot.

His back. The crisscrossed flesh, branded by lashings. "But I thought your pa . . ."

"My father would've thrown me to the Cleansing Waters, if necessary. I never gave him reason."

"But . . ."

But I should've known that. His welts were angry, red—like Tom's hands. Not scars that were old cuts, long healed. Blood rushes through my head. I thought our worries about our fathers somehow marked us the same—I thought that, though I knew my pa would never do what I thought his pa had done. Knowing what truly marks us the same . . .

I wipe clammy hands on my cloak and my grandma'am's ring catches the sun coming over the cliffs.

His eyes snap to it. "I understand your curiosity, your determination to prove yourself. I've been watching you to see if you could pursue the Discovery that lives in my heart." His words aren't making any kind of sense. I focus on what I know to be true.

"You turned me over to Council," I say. "*You* told them about my wanderings, pretended Kane reported me to you." Relief sparks through my confusion and fear.

"I was playing the role they expected. Do you think my position is so secure? If I were to defy Jameson outright today, I would be hanging tomorrow. Jameson is a zealot and they are sheep. They are comfortable in their stunted idea of Discovery. As my father was."

He's saying it like it's obvious, and I realize one thing is true: Fear can account for all kinds of horrors. All kinds of betrayals.

He steps close again, parts my cloak and takes both of my shoulders in his hands, pressing hard. "But our love will help me forge a new path."

My throat's closing off. *Our love.*

"Tell me our path," he says.

You will know who to trust.

I don't want to guess wrong again.

Think. He's waiting.

Our salvation lies in Discovery . . .

"We need to"—I fumble for the words—"prove Discovery. A new way."

He closes his eyes a moment. Then drops my arms and steps back. When he looks at me again, he is relieved. "You're certain?"

"I've dreamt it."

He tilts his head, tracing a thumb over his cheek to his chin. "I think you've *seen* it."

A flush races up my chest and into my cheeks. He sees the truth on my face. I nod, my throat tight.

"Tell me," he says.

I hesitate.

"Emmeline, this is important. I need to know what you've seen out there."

"The Lost People. They're—they're here."

28

AS SOON AS THE WORDS ARE OUT, I FEEL SICK.

But he smiles. "He said they 'appeared like ghosts from the woods, strange tongue, stranger effects.' He said, 'If they return, Clara's kind will find them.'"

Appeared like ghosts . . . If they return . . . My grandma'am found people like Matisa?

"It's all in my grandfather's journal. The one you took from the cabin."

"I—"

"I know you can't read."

Her curiosity was her undoing.

Dread seeps into my chest. Was Tom right? Is Matisa here to harm us? No. It can't be true.

His eyes pierce mine. "Where are they now?"

"The cabin." Brother Stockham looks off into the woods, to the west. "They're too scared to come to the settlement," I add quick.

"They were seeking you."

"Yes."

My heart is thrumming something fierce, my stomach is knotted.

"You are so like your grandmother, Emmeline. It's why this has happened exactly as it did before." He stares at the woods. "We have come full circle."

Full circle. The journal. My grandma'am.

Her death was a sin against the Almighty. The worst betrayal.

My voice is a whisper. "What happened back then?"

He turns to me. And now, *now* it's like he can see how confused and scared I am. His eyes soften. "All I truly know is what my grandfather confessed. I've spent many hours trying to imagine it: his conflict, his confusion." He frowns. "He was afraid. The people your grandmother found were mysterious. Were they benevolent, or had he been wrong all along in his unwillingness to believe in the *malmaci?* Were they its agents? Or something equally dangerous? Your grandmother believed they were here to help them; she wanted him to tell the community about her Discovery."

"He asked for time to decide, but your grandmother's curiosity was too great, her desire to share her Discovery too strong. Desperate, he found a way to keep her quiet without dirtying his hands with her blood."

And the picture comes clear. "He put lies in Council's ear, rumors about her adultery, her Waywardness," I think aloud. "She was already feared and disliked for her forest wandering, her daydreamings." I know this. I know it because I've lived it.

"Propositioning a married man—the leader, no less—was all Council needed to send her to the Crossroads."

"But why didn't she speak?" I ask, my heart heavy. "Tell them what she'd found?"

He raises his eyebrows. "Perhaps for the same reason you didn't tell Council what you found? She was waiting for my grandfather to speak the truth, to choose her over his position."

He thinks I *wanted* him to save me. I push the thought aside as something worse starts to sprout in my mind. "What happened to the people?"

"He acted impulsively; on the pretense of sharing food, he drugged them with bittersweet and imprisoned them. He was afraid to release them, and afraid to reveal their prison: how to explain the cabin? How to explain Clara? They died in their shackles."

The sick feeling in my gut deepens.

Our scouts didn't return.

The bones in the cellar of that cabin are the lost scouts. Brother Stockham knew it, and he waited for me to follow in my grandma'am's footsteps.

We have come full circle.

But why does that matter? A spike of fear pierces me.

"What will happen to the Lost People I've found?"

"My father shut out the world beyond, did ruthless things, to maintain his position. I have a choice. I can choose that path, or I can choose the path my grandfather wished he had: opening his heart and mind to the unknown. Opening his heart to desire." In a sweeping motion he draws me close, drowning me in his cloak. His mouth is inches away. "My path is clear."

He presses his mouth to mine. Hard. He moves forward, forcing me back toward the willows. I stumble and he catches me, pulls me into his arms, lowers me into a thatch of branches. I am pinned between the ground and his insistent mouth.

Images scream through my mind: the churning Cleansing Waters, Jacob's bulging eyes, that dusty book, hidden for years. He's been waiting for me to become eligible, waiting for me to prove his father wrong . . .

My father had no use for decisions made from love.

Realization knifes through me and with it, cold fear: all of this hinges on his belief that I love him back. I bite back a cry of panic.

He's breathing fast and his hands are inside my cloak now, running all over me. "I could have kept my family's secret," he says against my neck. "But I chose us." He kisses me again. All I can smell is the bergamot on his skin. I want to pull away so bad my teeth ache. I try to put my mind to something that takes me away from this moment, but the golden poplars have vanished, so I am reaching, reaching for anything . . .

He breaks the kiss and draws back, eyes raking over my face. "We have proven my father wrong." He smiles. "Haven't we?"

I nod, every inch of my body crying out. I try to smile, try to match the hope, the excitement on his face.

"I knew that Cariou boy meant nothing to you."

And now my secret heart betrays me. I feel a pang, so deep, so true, that it near takes my breath. At once, I can tell something in my eyes has spoken plain. The elation in his is snuffed out. He draws his head back further.

"You accepted my proposal."

The blood drains from my face. "I did."

"And yet?" There is a dangerous undercurrent in his voice.

"We are to be bound. When—when *La Prise* comes, Gabriel, we . . ." I can't say it and make it sound truthful, so I raise my head and press my mouth to his, fighting my every instinct to push him aside and scramble away. My skin crawls away from his body, heavy, so heavy, on top of me.

He lets me kiss him a moment more. Then he puts his forearm on my collarbone and shoves me back to the earth.

I try to take a breath, but his weight is closing off the air. I try to speak. "Gabr—" I can't finish. I cough, trying to find my voice. But it wouldn't matter if I could speak, because I can tell by the look in his eyes that he knows. He *knows*.

Pain twists his features as he pushes me aside and jumps to his feet. He spins away from me, his head bowed, hands on his hips.

I gulp air and stumble up onto my bad foot.

The wind blows hard, bending the bare willows like blades of grass. I glance to the woods, then back to him.

His torso heaves with a deep breath as he runs his hands through his hair, smoothing it onto the nape of his neck. When he turns back, his face is calm, but his eyes are stricken.

"You don't love me." His words are a poison arrow piercing me straight through.

I can't move. Can't deny his words; can't say I do and make it sound anywhere close to the truth.

274

His next words are so soft I can hardly hear him. "He was right."

His father. "No. Gabriel, he wasn't right—" But I don't know what to say. He's been waiting all this time, harboring this strange notion that our love is the answer.

"I waited for you to help me prove him wrong." His voice grows louder. "I took that chance. If you had denied me, if you had never risked the woods or found those people, I would have known to stay the course. To lead." His face changes, his mouth pulling into a mean line. "But you lied. And you will ruin me."

He advances on me, his body taut.

"I won't, I—"

"You'll betray me, like your grandmother." He stalks forward. "You will tell the settlement about the Takings, and I will end up neither leader nor your lover."

"No!" I stumble backward. I'm right next to the bank, the river is roaring loud at my back. My hands flutter up in front of me. "Gabriel, please! The people I found—they can still be *our* Discovery."

He stops. His eyes go dull. "The people you found do not exist."

I stare at him, fear creeping through my hairline. "What do you mean?"

"I will make sure of it. Like my grandfather did."

I bite back a cry of despair. "But you can still—"

"No!" He stares at me like he's staring down *La Prise* itself. "My father was right."

I can't get a breath in the wind. His hawk eyes are full of a pain so deep—

He lunges, grabbing me by the cloak and dragging me hard toward him. His grip is strong. I struggle backward, but he spins me around, pins my arms to my sides. Turns so we are facing the river. Huge chunks of ice are catching at the edges of the boulder gate. Some slip through and are dashed to bits as they drop over the shelf. He shoves me forward, moving me closer to the edge of the bank. My moccasins slip as I try to scramble backward.

"This was not the path I hoped for."

He stops pushing and lifts me. My arms sing with pain as he crushes me to his chest; my feet dangle useless in the air. "But you have shown me the way, Emmeline," he breathes in my ear. "I will lead. Without you."

And then he casts me over the bank to the water below.

29

THE FREEZING WATER SLAPS THE BREATH FROM me as I plunge below the surface. Everything is black, spinning, squeezing at me from all sides. My feet touch something solid, but then I'm rolled by the force of the water and I can't figure which way is up. Currents grab me with their greedy fingers, chunks of ice bash at my back, my legs. Everything is ringing with a hollow, deafening scream.

I'm back at the surface, bursting through. I have one moment of clear thinking to take a big breath of air, and then the boulder gate is rushing toward me. I claw at the water as I'm spun about. I hit the shelf at the gate, something knocks into me, and then I'm back under in the roaring whirl of water. It blinds me, fills my ears with its howl, grabs at my chest and squeezes tight.

I'm dying. I can feel it.

Kane, my pa, Soeur Manon, Tom—they're here. Their faces loom in the churning waters, eyes so sad and lost.

Kane! I shout in my mind. *I'm sorry.*

But they're spinning away down a dark hole, and new images wash toward and over me: Matisa and her family in chains, starving to death. My grandma'am's gaping skull, her skeletal hand holding the ring.

Death screams toward me in an icy, black cloud.

But now . . . now the battering of the waters calms and it feels real peaceful. Feels like I'm back in the cool of the woods, where I belong. Feels like the Lost People are here, fluttering down from the branches of *les trembles*. They're opening their arms to me, cradling me, telling me it's all right. They're talking to me from far off, but I can hear their voices like music, feel their shadowy fingers grasping at my clothes and skin. They brush my hair from my forehead.

The spinning stops. My mouth is full of water. I gag and spit. And feel blessed hard ground against my back.

"Emmeline!" Matisa is over top of me, shouting. She takes my face in her hands. "Emmeline, stay awake!" A whirl of faces swims before me: Matisa, Nishwa, Isi, Kane . . .

Kane?

They're hollering, moving around me in a blur. And then someone hoists me up, throws me over their shoulder. Moves me through the air. I'm tossed higher again, across something broad and earthy-smelling. I cough a painful cough and then we are moving through the woods. Branches blur and deadfall whips by, fast, like in my dreams. It sounds like the thunder of a great herd of bison all around me. Hoofbeats pound hard on the earth, filling my senses.

Every inch of my body has been wrung with ice-cold hands; little pinpricks bite at me everywhere. The forest screams by. It goes on forever, it goes on a heartbeat.

And then I am back on the forest floor, my feet crumbling beneath me.

"Hold her!" I'm grabbed under the arms, held upright.

I stumble forward, let those arms guide me. There's a bright space in the coulee ahead of us—a cave, lit from within. My eyes can't focus proper, but as we push inside I see a yellow glow. "Emmeline!" Matisa's shouting again. "Hey!"

What does she want? I want to tell her to stop shouting, but my tongue's gone numb. I can't get any sound out.

There's a ruckus beside me: people moving about and talking a language I can't figure. And then Kane's face is before my eyes. I'm real glad to see him. I need to tell him something.

"Em, can you hear me?"

I try to nod my head, but I'm shaking hard, trembling like birch in a windstorm. I want to clench my hands together to try to make it stop, but they won't move, neither.

"Trust me?"

I trust him. I trust him now. But that's not what I wanted to say. I've forgotten what I want to tell him . . .

He's taking off his cloak, his shirt, his leggings . . .

Hands pull at my wet cloak, strip it from me. I'm grateful; I want it off. The weight is so heavy it's hard to breathe. More of my clothes are stripped away and then hands are pushing me toward a mound of blankets. I'm shoved inside, my head spinning, everything awash in that yellow glow.

Kane is next to me, wrapping me in his arms. Everything is soft, like a bison calf's velvet skin. And suddenly I remember. I want to tell him *I'm sorry*. But I'm heavy now, so heavy I can't move. I let my eyes seal shut. Let a cloud of dark swallow me whole.

My dream self is moving though the woods. Soft leaves brush at me from all sides. My feet are my own—not perfect—but though I limp, I move steady and sure. The smell of woodsmoke wraps me in warmth. I find a poplar tree and put my head against its trunk, close my eyes tight and breathe in the smoky air.

I'm staring at someone's legging-clad thigh. I rub at my eyes, raise my wooly head, and find Kane. He's sitting beside me, his hand on my brow, gazing down. I put out a hand to touch his smooth forearm to make sure he's real.

I raise my head to look about. I'm wrapped in blankets in a corner of a cave. The glow of a smokeless fire bounces off the smooth walls. Matisa and the boys sit on the other side of the flames, talking quiet. A wave of relief surges through me. I go to push the blankets aside but stop dead.

I haven't got a stitch on.

I grab the blankets tight, my eyes flying to Kane's face.

"Afternoon, Em."

My throat feels full of ice shards; I can't speak around them. I look wide-eyed to the blankets and then back at him.

His brow creases. "You were so cold. We were worried you'd fall asleep and wouldn't wake up."

It comes back in a rush: The river, Brother Stockham throwing me to the icy darkness, Matisa and Kane appearing. They brought me here, to this cave. I remember them stripping off my clothes. But before that . . .

Before that, Kane took off *his* clothes.

My face flames red hot.

Kane rubs his jaw and looks away.

He must've seen my foot, probably felt it against his . . . I squeeze my eyes tight, feeling a wash of shame. But the truth of his words hits, and a rush of gratitude floods in. He saved my life.

I am here, with him, and my bad foot is nothing.

I sit up, wincing with the effort. Tucking the blankets around myself, I notice a large purple bruise along my left arm. I'm too shy to look with Kane so near, but it feels like it goes a long way down my body. My hair is a tangled mess and damp, but the cave is as warm as Soeur Manon's kitchen, lit by the fire and a lamp that stands on the floor, whining quiet. There are large packs in the corners of the cave.

Matisa and Nishwa are drying clothes over the fire. Isi looks over and measures me with his hard eyes, but there's a smile tugging at his lips, like he's relieved I'm all right.

Kane reaches forward and touches my face, trails his hand to my bruised shoulder. And then I remember him standing in the courtyard before I was locked away.

My voice is raw, like I haven't used it in weeks. "How—?"

He puts his hand on my brow again and smoothes back my hair. "I figured something wasn't right when Stockham told me not to follow you to the river. Said he didn't 'need' me watching you anymore. Then I saw you with the Councilmen. Came straight to the cabin for that book." He nods at Matisa and the boys. "Got way more than I bargained for." He smiles. "There was a bit of a scuffle before I figured they weren't interested in harming me."

I remember how scared I was when I found them, when

they found me . . . I look at Kane. He's got a dark ring under one of his eyes I didn't notice before, and his bottom lip is bruised. But he doesn't look scared or confused. He looks like himself: beautiful, brave.

"We headed back to the fort at first light. Took a while to sort ourselves out. Thanks be, they wanted to skirt the fortification riverside. We spotted you and Brother Stockham at the Cleansing Waters. Got there just in time to see him throw you . . ." Kane's jaw clenches and he looks away, back at the group. "Matisa here can swim something fierce."

I look over at the three and notice she's drying two sets of clothes over the fire: hers and mine. "Matisa," I say, "I don't—I . . ." My voice catches. "Thank you."

She shrugs. "Your boy has good aim. Once I caught hold of you in the water, he hit me with the rope like we were standing still."

The boys nod, looking with admiration at Kane.

Your boy. I glance at him and he rubs his head. "Guess the knife-throwing practice was good for something," he says.

My mind spins. "How—how did you get past Watch without Stockham's say-so? To get to the cabin, I mean."

"Told Jameson I'd found something out in the woods while I was watching you. Something he'd be interested in."

I raise my eyebrows.

"He didn't ask what. Think he was too wound about you and Brother Stockham."

The horror of those moments at the river floods back. Brother Stockham was calling it love, but he's wrong: he doesn't love me. I watch Kane sitting so calm.

"You"—I swallow hard—"went out at dusk. After a Taking."

He shrugs. "If the *malmaci* got me, it got me. Wouldn't be much inside the settlement for me if you were at the Crossroads."

I close my eyes against the tears that spring up. He did it for me. After I turned from him. My voice is so tight I have to force the words. "Kane, I'm sorry. I should've believed you—"

He cuts me off. "And I should've told you." He brushes my hair back. "And it doesn't matter anymore."

A bone-tired wave washes me. I lie back.

Kane frowns. "You should rest." He moves to tuck the blankets around me, but I grab his arm.

"Stay with me?"

"Course." He goes to pull the blankets up again, but I squeeze his arm, stopping him.

"No. Kane—*stay* with me." I nod at the blankets. I can picture my bad foot beneath, but it doesn't fill me with shame anymore. I look at him.

His dark eyes go wide. Then he rubs the back of his neck, blows out a breath, and looks around.

Matisa and the boys are looking everywhere but at us.

His voice is so soft I strain to hear him. "Course." He lies next to me and moves in under the blankets. When he puts his arms around me, I can feel his heart beating fast. His body is trembling just the littlest bit, and it's red hot, burning through his clothes into my skin. I press my face into the hollow of his neck, breathing in his woodsmoke warmth. I draw my head back. "Tell me that piper story?"

His eyes drink me in, shining a warm, perfect light on my bare shoulders. He smiles. "Course, Em."

30

"HE'LL BE LOOKING FOR YOU," I SAY.

We're gathered round the smokeless fire watching Nishwa portion out hot broth into metal cups.

"Eat first," Matisa says, like we've got all the time in the world.

I can tell Matisa's the sort who's never in a rush for things to happen, just like her brother Nishwa. Isi's a different story; he's pacing while Nishwa moves snail slow, measuring out the broth like it's the most important thing on Almighty's green earth. And the broth might *be* the most important thing. They have supplies, but not near enough to last five of us very long. It's plain they need to make a run for it.

Kane sits beside me, forearms on his bent knees, his thigh pressing into mine. He's sticking close, like he doesn't want me out of his sight ever again.

I slept hours—the whole day and into the night—wrapped in his warmth. When we woke, the wind was whistling soft outside the cave and a thin dusting of snow coated the ground. The clothes that Matisa brought me were warm and dry, but I wanted to stay inside the blankets with Kane forever.

He insisted on Matisa coming with me when I went to relieve myself in the woods, though I'd told him about the lie of the Takings before I drifted off.

I stumbled from the cave out into the starry night and was met by a soft rush of breath—just like the one I'd heard in the cabin the other day. They'd brought me to the cave on the back of one of their horses, and the beasts were wandering quiet nearby as I stepped out into the trees. I stopped to watch them shift about—so calm, their breath steaming in the cold. I imagined how they'd be when I looked at them in Soeur Manon's books, but they're so much more beautiful than I figured.

I'd never been out in the woods in the full dark before. Instead of it feeling skittering, though, it felt like a shadowy embrace. *Les trembles* shifted and sighed, like they'd been holding their breath for years, waiting to welcome me. Skeleton branches danced shadows on the walls of the coulees.

Matisa trailed behind, talking soft to the horses. I tucked behind a tree, skin flushed, feeling alive finger to toe. The moon was a thin sliver of light, but the stars were so brilliant the whole sky was drinking me up. I thought about Soeur Manon speaking on being a child and looking at that night sky, and I understood.

When I returned, Kane was waiting with his funny smile. And even though everything was upside-down and still is, I've never felt so whole, so full.

I take the broth from Nishwa and drink it quick. I can't

help but make a small sound of pleasure when I'm done. Isi watches me across the fire.

"He'll be coming for you now, Matisa," I try again. "Mayhap he told Council he's seen the *malmaci*. They'll shoot first, that's their way."

Her eyes are calm. She wipes at her mouth with a cloth and speaks. "We always knew we were taking a risk."

"But you should go—get out of here before he finds you, before they—" I don't finish. When I told them about the bones in the cellar—their scouts—Isi's eyes went real dark, then he jumped up and left the cave, but Matisa and Nishwa just sat there, silent and calm, thinking. When Isi returned, his face was blank, but he started pacing the cave end to end. He's still pacing.

"I'm sorry." I'll never say it enough. "This is all my fault. You need to go."

Matisa frowns. "My dreams told me not to leave without you. Can you leave your people?"

I look into the coals. What exactly would I be staying for? If I left with these new friends, I'd be running from a settlement that had never wanted me, from Brother Stockham, who'd wanted me for all the wrong reasons.

And going back to the settlement is courting our death. No doubt Brother Stockham's told everyone I've been sent to the Crossroads, and he'll be wondering where Kane is and how much he truly knows. Everyone's already half addled with the *malmaci* seeming to circle ever closer. We walk out of the woods like ghosts—Lost People at our sides or no—there's no guarantee they won't shoot us on sight. Almighty knows Brother Stockham would give the order himself; he's probably scouring for Kane's whereabouts right now. And at first light Council will hunt for Matisa and the boys, if they aren't hunting already.

Brother Stockham knows I took that Almighty-loving journal; he'll look for it. And Tom knows it's in Pa's trapping satchel. What if Tom goes to Brother Stockham with it?

What would he do to my pa?

To Tom?

My heart clenches tight.

Isi nods at the wind outside. "The winterkill comes."

Takes me a minute to realize he means *La Prise*. It's a strange word for it, but it's also exactly the right one. Affirmation has already started and the settlement is closing up until the Thaw. The thought of *La Prise*—the winterkill— barreling down on us sends an arrow of fear to my heart.

I look at Matisa's calm eyes. She's risked so much. But for what? "Why did you come?" I ask.

Isi stops his pacing a moment and looks to Matisa.

"I told you the answer was long," she says.

"We don't have much time," adds Isi.

"Then you'll have to talk fast," I say.

Isi crosses his arms, his brow like thunder, but Matisa waves him off. "Emmeline is right to ask." She studies me. "The quick answer is this: death is coming again for our people. Our elders have seen it, just as they saw it years ago."

"What kind of death?"

"A war. The Dominion is coming."

The Dominion: the people of the east. "And they are coming to fight?"

"Some of them, yes."

"Why?"

"We have things they need."

"What kinds of things?"

"Matisa," Isi's voice rasps from the corner. "Hurry up."

"The important thing is that the war will be bloody. It will not end well." She swallows and looks at her hands. Again I wonder about her home, her family. She says her people used to war with nearby tribes for food and people, but they banded together years ago in the face of the threat of newcomers—people like us. Over the years they learned the Dominion's languages to better understand what they were up against. "For years we have known this, but for years our elders have also been telling an old tale of our people. It is about two dreamers from different times who have the answer to keeping death at bay."

I frown. Different times. "You think you and I are those dreamers?"

She nods.

"But what's the answer?"

She shrugs. "It will become clear, if we listen to our dreams."

I study her. I see for the first time that beyond her gentle eyes and easy manner there's a heaviness, like she's carrying something she shouldn't. It's the kind of weight brought on by knowing too much. By having to make decisions that aren't easy.

Like leaving your home.

I look at Kane. He meets my eyes, silent. I push to my feet. "Need to go for a think."

"Em!" Kane calls as I leave the cave. The wind takes his voice and whisks it into the trees.

I tuck myself in under a sweeping spruce. The boughs make a roof and walls around me, sealing out the icy wind and the moonlight.

Kane ducks his head inside. "You can't think in the cave?"

I give him a half smile. "Not used to so many people watching me when I do it." I sink to the needle-covered ground and draw my knees to my chest.

He stands there a moment, looking at me. "You need to think alone."

I fight back tears and nod. "That all right?"

"Course. I'll be waiting outside the cave." His eyes are gentle. "Em?" he says. "I'm following your lead. No matter what." He gives me a smile that's meant to be reassuring, and disappears.

And then the tears come. Not desperate, painful tears; mixed-up tears. Tears of sadness and anger and guilt, tears of thankfulness and relief. I let them stream down my cheeks and sit quiet, listening to the wind in the top of the spruce. It's a big, soft voice shushing me, telling me it's all right.

But I don't know what to do.

Matisa trusted herself, trusted that leaving her family was the right path. And her people were imprisoned here, starved to death or Almighty knows what else, because our leader was afraid. Yet she tells me she's not leaving without me.

I scrub at the tears with my sleeve.

We should go now, before *La Prise* is howling down around us. Leave those stifling walls, the suspicious stares, the people who never understood or cared for me . . .

Except it's not that easy.

I'd be asking Kane to leave his family: his ma who taught him to read, who raised him kind and brave.

Worse, I'd be leaving my pa to Brother Stockham. Tom won't realize his mistake until it's too late.

My chest aches. Tom was always trying to get me to believe my Stain didn't matter, to stop being so afraid of what people thought, and now his own fear will be his undoing—

My thoughts stop.

Tom was always trying to get me to believe . . .

I care more about my Stain than anyone else.

My pa. All this time I thought he was disappointed in me. Thought he was just tired of me being a burden. But each moment he looked at me that hopeful way, each time he was begging me to take his meaning, it wasn't Stockham he was asking me to accept . . .

I take a deep, shaky breath and hug my knees close. Images swim through my head: Edith's blue eyes drinking in my words, Andre showing me that arrow, Soeur Manon mending my dress, Sister Ann's understanding face . . .

Been so afraid of how I look to others, I was unable to see a truth that was right in front of me. There are people in the settlement who look at me less kind, sure, but they're afraid. And if fear has blinded me, can I fault the people around me for the same thing?

I can't just up and leave.

I press the palms of my hands to my wet eyes, trying to think.

Tomorrow afternoon, the second day of Affirmation will be in full ceremony. What might happen if we try to get back into the settlement? Watch might have orders to shoot anything that isn't Council, but . . .

But mayhap I can get to Andre first. Like that night I was out at the Crossroads; I know where he patrols. And if I can get to Andre, I can get in and then—

Then what?

Get my pa? Tell the settlement about Brother Stockham?

Will anyone hear what I have to say? Will they urge Council to listen to my Discovery, to accept the Lost People I've found?

I don't know. All I know is that I can't leave, and I don't have much time. Andre will help me get back inside. After that—well, we'll just have to see.

My dream comes flooding back. Watch standing on that hill, between me and the cabin, shooting Matisa down.

I shiver.

I think about Kane, standing outside the cave in the howling wind waiting for me. What has Stockham told Watch about him? Probably to shoot him on sight; Kane knows too much. And he defied Council and headed into the woods for me, so I'm not letting him risk his life again. No. I have to do this on my own. It's just . . .

There's no way he'll let me go back alone.

I close my eyes again, thinking.

Honesty, Bravery, Discovery.

I want to be Honesty. But I need to lie just one more time.

Long minutes later I stand and push out of the spruce boughs, then I take Kane's waiting hand and lead him inside the cave.

Around the fire, I stare into the coals so I don't have to look at anyone. "I have to go back," I say. "My pa's in danger and I can't leave him."

Four pairs of eyes alight on me. "I have a plan." I keep my voice steady to feign truthfulness. "I got someone to unbolt the wastewater ditch yesterday. Today when the Watch shift changes, I can get inside."

Kane's voice is perplexed. "I thought you said Tom hung you to dry."

"It's not Tom," I say quick, "it's a Watcher." I will away the flush creeping up my neck. I continue, "We'll need to get past the Councilmen in the woods, but I can get to that ditch unseen."

"This is what you must do?" Matisa asks.

I nod. "I have to." I stare at the coals and wait with my breath held. I can feel the four of them shifting, looking at one another.

"Leave the Councilmen to us," Isi says.

Relief and gratitude fill me. "You have guns?"

He and Nishwa exchange a glance. "Not exactly."

"What's that mean?"

Matisa smiles. "It means all Isi could steal from our *moshum* were a few gas masks. He has the weapons under lock and key, but we decided he wouldn't notice a few masks. The boys were worried about poison gas—the Dominion has been using it."

Poison gas? Kane and I look at one another, confused. But the first part of Matisa's answer registers. *Masks.* The seed of an idea springs up, emboldening me.

"Never mind," Matisa says. "We have Nishwa's twenty-two—a rifle. But it is mostly to scare away wolves."

I look around at them. "I don't want you to get hurt."

"We don't need guns, Emmeline," Isi says. Matisa nods in agreement.

"All right," I say.

Kane reaches over and squeezes my arm. "I'm coming with you."

I force a smile.

That's what you think, beautiful Kane.

31

"YOU SURE IT'S A GOOD IDEA TO HEAD STRAIGHT *for* them?" Kane whispers to Nishwa.

Isi shoots him a look.

We're looking at the cabin from the top of the north hill. There's a Councilman standing outside it with a rifle—looks uneasy. I wonder how Stockham explained this cabin. A device of the *malmaci?* Built by people plotting to harm us? Another Councilman paces the ridge of the hill on the far side. He's being none too secretive, but I guess Councilmen aren't exactly trained in tracking and hunting. They've only ever had to tie up people for the Crossroads. My stomach lurches.

"We need to draw them as far from the settlement as we can," Nishwa says.

"I know. It just seems a mite . . . dangerous." Kane rubs his bare head and draws his hood.

"Isi checked the woods from here south to the fortification. The Councilmen are here or farther out," Matisa says.

spirit
airlines

BOARDING PASS

Issued 03-19-2017 06:02AM

Customer Name
LUSERO/LAURA

From
DENVER

To
LOS ANGELES

Flight #
NK947

Seq #
012

Depart
7:05AM

Arrive
8:42AM

Date
19MAR17

Conf #
UC1P3T

Gate
A52

Boarding
6:20AM

Zone
3

Seat Number
22A

SUBJECT TO CHANGE **NO CARRY-ON BAG**

DOORS CLOSE 15' MINUTES BEFORE DEPARTURE

Carry-On   Checked
0   0

spirit
airlines

BOARDING PASS

Customer Name
LUSERO/LAURA

From
DENVER

To
LOS ANGELES

Flight #
NK947

Date
19MAR17

Seat #
22A

ZONE
3

"What if they find the horses?" I ask. The beasts are tied to poplar trees a half-mile back.

"We hope they do," Isi says.

I frown.

"It is part of the plan," Matisa explains. "We left the horses in a perfect spot to ambush your Council."

I don't know exactly what she's speaking on, but I decide I don't want to. They said they wouldn't kill the Councilmen, just restrain them. But what they'll do to get to that part . . .

"You should go," Isi says. He's been looking at me different ever since we made a plan to get back to the fort. I can feel a blush on my cheeks. I clear my throat and nod.

Matisa steps forward and presses her forehead to Nishwa's and Isi's in turn. Then she turns to Kane and me. "Come on."

"Wait. You're coming with?"

"Yes," Matisa says.

A spike of fear pierces me. "That's not a good idea."

"Why?"

"It's just not. I had a dream—"

"I had one too. And it told me to come with you." She looks at me, not angry but impatient.

"Matisa—"

"I'm going." She starts ahead of us, then pauses and looks back. "Are you?"

I swallow. I can tell by the look in her eye she won't be talked out of it. I think quick. It's not how I planned it, but mayhap her coming along is a good thing. At least if things go bad, she can get Kane back here safe. I turn to Isi and Nishwa. "The Councilmen have guns."

Nishwa nods. "They will not see us to shoot us."

I don't know how to thank them, so I put a hand to my chest in the Peace. Kane clasps their hands, each in turn. Then we start down the hill after Matisa.

When we get near the bottom of the hill, I hear that fluting whistle. It's the boys, talking to one another as they move into position. I send a quick prayer to the Almighty to keep them safe. We reach the bottom of the hill, skirt the gully, and head southwest through the rows of bare poplars. It starts to snow: tiny flecks dancing on the cold wind. Matisa and Kane set a steady pace, crossing through the ravine and up the other side. They're far quieter than me. I know Matisa would be even if I could walk normal. When we near the grove, I start to favor my bad foot and fall several strides behind them. They're out the opposite side before I enter it.

Kane turns back and watches me a moment. "You all right?"

"Fine," I say, then make a show of biting back a cry of pain.

"Your foot's troubling you."

"The river swim didn't help, but I'll be fine," I say.

Matisa frowns at me, saying nothing.

We press on until we get to the dead scrub. Snow coats the top of the brush in a fine powder and the wind is quieter here. I take the lead but go excruciating slow on purpose, pushing aside bare branches careful-like and wincing with every other step. I'm heading east, toward the river. Finally we reach the willows just south of the Cleansing Waters. I labor onto my stomach on the cold forest floor. Matisa and Kane sink beside me, looking at my leg.

"If we head straight east in these willows, we'll come to

a part of the riverbank that's hidden from the Watchtower. Get over the edge and hug close to the bank until we can see the fortification. We'll wait for Watch to start their shift change. When they do, we make a break for the wastewater ditch. We'll have to move fast."

Kane chews on his lip. His eyes are worried. "Emmeline, hate to say it, but you might be too slow, with your foot and all."

My blood thrums in my ears and I bite my lip, pretending I'm thinking hard.

"How's about you wait here in the willows? We'll do exactly as you say—over the ridge, along the bank, and head for the wastewater ditch when Watch starts to change. Once we get inside, we'll come back for you." His eyes are so sincere it near undoes me.

I look at Matisa.

She nods. "It is a good plan."

I feel a wash of relief that she doesn't offer to stay with me. I pretend to think on it some more. "All right."

Kane and Matisa raise themselves on their elbows to peer at the fortification. Then they flatten to the earth. He jerks his head forward. She crawls off through the willows.

"Kane," I say suddenly. He turns back with a questioning look. Tears are springing up and I wipe my eyes quick, hoping he thinks it's the cold wind biting at them. "I love you." I crawl forward and push my face into the space between his shoulder and neck. Breathe him in one more time. Woodsmoke, warmth.

He puts a hand on the nape of my neck and presses a kiss to my forehead.

"And I love you, Em."

Then he's gone, disappearing through the willows on his belly, and I'm alone, listening to the whistling wind. I roll onto my back and watch the flat sky crying little flakes of snow.

But there was one young girl with a bad leg; she couldn't walk fast like the others.

The snow drifts and brushes my face—soft feathers that hint at the blistering ice coming on the wind.

That story's about paying what's due, that's plain, but I've always thought it's also about curses being secret blessings.

I swallow the guilt that threatens to choke me right there. I didn't want to lie, but I need to pay what's due and my secret blessing will make sure of that. Mayhap it was always meant to.

I tell myself I'm not afraid. My hands are shaking, so I tuck them under my arms. The snow whispers down onto my face.

I count a few beats in my head. Kane and Matisa are surely at the edge of the willows by now. In a few moments they'll be along the riverbank and waiting for Watch to change shifts. I roll over, crawl back toward the trees and stand. Listen to the woods a moment.

Silence.

I draw my cloak aside and put a hand to my *ceinture,* feeling the bulge of the Elephant Man mask beneath. If this plan goes bad, if I'm detained once I get inside the fort, at least I have the mask: people will start asking questions. Andre, surely. And if Tom hasn't turned in my pa yet, he can get help reading the book.

And if I'm shot on sight . . . well, same thing.

My throat gets tight. Regardless, they'll need to open the fortification to come out for me. There'll be a ruckus and Kane will be able to get away. Go with Matisa and the others, mayhap come back when it's safe—

I stop my thoughts there. That's only if it goes bad. And it won't. I got back inside the fortification once; I'll do it again.

I limp as fast as I can, pushing through the brush and heading for the west side of the fortification. By the time I've skirted the Watch flats the snow is swirling heavier, goose down landing on my eyelashes. I blink. The sun is hidden behind the great blanket of gray sky and I'm too far inside the trees to see the fortification, but I know I'm nearing the corner Andre patrols.

I told Kane and Matisa there was a Watch shift change in the afternoon. I said Frère Andre had told me that—said it was the best time to break for the wastewater ditch. But they'll be watching for that shift change forever, because it's not coming.

The wind whistles in my ears, the air is bitter cold; *La Prise* is showing her hand. And if I don't make it inside now, I might never have to take shelter again.

I crouch at the edge of the woods, inside the first line of trees.

There are two Watchers on this side of the fort. One of them looks like Andre, but I'm not certain. The glint of a spyglass flashes and I shrink back against the trees.

Fear riddles my chest.

I close my eyes, listen to my heart beating wild, the wind

whistling through the stripped trees. I hear a new sound. Faint. A *thump, thump, thump* coming from inside the fortification. Part of the virtues commitment ceremony.

Need to move.

I stand and push aside brambles, moving for the Watch flats.

I stop when I'm hidden by the last screen of scrub. The second Watcher has turned, and the first—Andre, I'm sure of it now—has the spyglass out again. It's my chance.

I push off my good foot to pop up above the brush but am stopped dead. A strong hand hauls me back down into the bramble. I land on my knees and scramble around.

A Watcher looms over me.

I shrink back, my eyes raking over him, over the long scar cutting down one cheek. It's the Watcher always hanging around Andre, around the weapons shack.

"Je ne peux y croire! Il a dit que tu étais ici!" He launches into a stream of French, speaking so fast I can't understand. He's breathing hard, his eyes wild. *"Viens!"* He lurches forward and grabs me by the wrist. I jerk backward, but his grasp is a steel trap.

"Wait!" I say. "There are people. *Les Perdus.* They're here!"

He's not listening; he presses through the scrub, hauling me behind him as I scramble to my feet. *"Viens!"* he repeats.

"S'il vous plait—please!"

He stops for a heartbeat and wraps one meaty fist around both of my wrists. Then he turns and continues, pulling me like a man possessed by the Almighty Himself.

He's dragging me back to the flats. Back to Council.

My dream floods in. All of those Watchers, standing on the wall, just as I find Matisa . . . *Almighty.*

I tug backward, but I'm held fast. I try to calm myself so I can remember some French—so I can stop him, explain. But we emerge from the line of scrub out onto the flats and the fort comes into view.

They're up there, standing at attention. And now that my dream is bursting hot and bright in my mind, I realize something that makes my knees go weak.

That instant, in my dream, it's not Matisa they're staring down as they reach for their weapons.

It's me.

The wind is keening. Sounds like the song my mother used to sing. My mind is going to shatter from fear, and all I can hear is that tune.

Sleep, little one, with your secret heart,

We're well out on the flats; just us and the wind and the snow.

Take to the night like the swallow.

Two of the Watchers have gone dead still on the wall.

When morning time brings what your secret heart sings,
Set your feet to the same path and follow.

The Watcher is dragging me now; my legs are locked stiff with terror. It's too late. Can't get my tongue to work and I can't break free. The Elephant Man mask burns into my side, under my *ceinture*. I have a fleeting thought for Kane's warm hands—

Three Watchers are still.

Thump, thump, thump. The drums from the ceremony beat louder. In my head, in my heart. Four, five, six; they're all facing us.

We're close now—can see their faces. None of them is Andre.

One of them puts his hand to his opposite shoulder. Grabbing for his weapon. The rest do the same, raising their hands to their shoulders. Just like in my dream.

We stop. The Watcher releases my hands and steps away.

I could run, but I'd never make it. We're too far out onto the flats and I'm too slow. My mind blanks and my body turns to syrup—slow, slow. I drop my eyes to the snow-crusted prairie grass at my feet and wait for the shots. Wait for the buckshot to pierce my heart through.

Thump, thump, thump.

Silence.

I look up, blinking away snowflakes.

All six are standing at attention on the top of the wall, looking down at me. But they don't have their rifles trained on me.

They have their hands across their chests in the Peace of the Almighty.

My heart stutters.

And then the west gates swing open and Frère Andre is standing there, wide-eyed. We stare at one another through the blowing snow. He's holding the journal.

32

"VITE!" HE SNAPS AND WAVES ME INSIDE.

I force my legs to move. What—?

He hurries me inside the gates. As they bang shut I'm surrounded by a dozen Watchers. They're looking at one another, at me, back at one another. Some of them are muttering and crossing themselves. The other walls are bare of sentries; everyone but the west-side Watchers have left their posts.

Andre reaches forward and claps my captor on the shoulder. *"Bien,"* he says.

The Watcher nods back at him. My legs are weak. I look around at the crowd again, back to Andre. My eyes are so wide they're drying up in the wind.

"I think I see you in the woods," Andre says, looking pleased. "And I send Luc down the wall to find you."

Luc takes a deep breath and smiles. At me.

I stare at him. Then I blink and point to the journal in Andre's hands. "Where—where did you get that?"

"Your friend from the east—*le blond*."

Tom.

"I keep it safe for him today. Yesterday he find me, say if you return from the woods today, I let you in. That you bring a gift from the Almighty. I tell my Watch." He frowns. "But this morning Frère Stockham tell us you are gone. Crossroads."

"Then why—" I look around at the Watchers. Afraid as the settlement is right now, how is it possible at least one of them didn't shoot at me?

"Your *mémère. Elle est une gentille dame.*" It takes me a minute to realize he's saying that my grandma'am was a good woman. "I think the Almighty does not allow the same death two times." He points to the key ring on his *ceinture*. "I keep the weapons locked." He nods to the Watchers. "*Parce qu'ils sont effrayés*—they are afraid. Councilmen go to *le bois,* but nobody know why."

My knees give out in relief and I sink to the ground. I take a deep breath. Tom went and got the journal after I was taken away. Even though it was no sure thing I was coming back, he did it.

"Do you know what's written in there?" I point to the journal.

Andre shakes his head. "*Non. Mais*"—he leans close—"Tom say it tell of your family innocent. And people whisper *des les Perdus.*"

The Lost People. Tom shared it, then. He shared my find with someone. He's starting to spread the truth. I want to laugh and shout with happiness. But fear cuts through my joy. Suppose Council's heard people talking? Wouldn't they do whatever they could to retain control? Make an example of someone, some show of force to keep people in line—like they did with Jacob? Thank Almighty the weapons are locked up; no one here can do anything rash in their fear. I just pray Isi and Nishwa managed to disarm the Councilmen in the woods.

"Emmeline!" A shout comes from across the courtyard. I scramble to my feet as the Watchers turn. "Emmeline!" It's Kane's voice.

I push through the line of people and find Kane and Matisa hurrying through the courtyard. How did they get inside?

I feel the Watchers around me—tense, shifting. They're murmuring to one another in French. I glance about and see them looking to Frère Andre.

He fingers the key, gaze locked on Matisa. He nods. The Watchers push past me, moving for Kane and Matisa.

"Don't hurt her!" I choke out as I limp after them. *"Ne la blessez-pas!"*

Kane pulls Matisa behind him and stands his ground, one hand out—asking them to stay back. The Watchers surge toward them, form a circle around them, but they don't advance on Matisa. I reach the ring of Watchers and push through.

"Le don de Dieu," Frère Andre mutters, walking into the circle. Then he crosses himself. The rest of the Watchers do the same, and sink to their knees.

I stumble into the middle and Kane grabs me to him, crushing me against his chest. I press my face into his neck, near crying with relief. He runs a hand down my hair, stroking my plait.

"How did you get in?" I pull back.

"Like you said. Watch changed and the wastewater-ditch gate was unlatched."

Tom. He must've done it after all, before hearing I was sent to the Crossroads this morning. Watch didn't change, though; they came to see who Andre was letting in the gates. My lie became truth.

"Why are you here?" His face is so perplexed and relieved. I owe him the truth, but I don't have time to explain.

"Tom helped me after all." I point to Frère Andre. "And Andre."

The Watchers are on their knees, looking on Matisa like she's the Thaw.

"Emmeline," Frère Andre says, his eyes fixed on Matisa, "you bring this gift to us. From the woods. It is a sign of good things." He repeats himself in French and the Watchers murmur in agreement.

I look around the ring of faces—these brave men and women who have guarded our settlement from an unseen enemy night after night—and see that they are not a bit afraid. They're full of hope and purpose.

You will know who to trust.

I thought I was looking for one person, but I was wrong.

I speak so the group can hear. "We need to share our gift."

The drums *thump* as we push into the ceremonial hall. Brother Stockham's head is bowed at the pulpit as he prepares the Affirmation rites. Brother Jameson stands at his side, holding the cloth. Nearly the entire settlement, dressed

306

in their ceremony best, is packed into the space, so we have to force our way through the back row of people. Frère Andre goes first, flanked by two Watchers. I follow close behind, my cloak drawn tight around me, hood hiding me from the crowd. The rest of the Watchers follow. Kane and Matisa wait around the side of the hall; they won't come in until we're sure it's safe.

We are our own solemn procession. My gaze stays on the feet shuffling before us. My heart is in my throat, beating loud as the drums. I am a mishmash of nerves and elation.

For an instant I wonder if I've acted too hasty, if surprising Stockham is the way to do this. I wanted the settlement to see the truth on his face, but now I wonder if he won't find a way to twist my words, turn the settlement against me before I have a chance to explain. Then I remember the Watchers' reactions to Matisa. No. People have been kept in fear for a long time, but they won't choose it over hope. They'll choose the promise of something better.

I want to risk a quick look around for Tom and my pa, but I keep my eyes to the wooden floorboards. By the time we get to the front of the crowd, the hall is buzzing with hushed whispers. The drums stop.

Brother Stockham's voice rings out. "Frère Andre, *que fais tu?* What is this?"

Frère Andre and the Watchers part and I step forward, pulling back my hood and raising my head.

There is a low gasp from the crowd. I hear my name whispered. Brother Stockham freezes, the blood draining from his handsome face.

I force my voice out loud and clear. "I brought the settlement a gift."

He stares at me. Brother Jameson stands at his side, his face the same mask of disbelief.

"I brought the unknown," I say.

The air goes still. I match Stockham's stare, but I can feel the crowd around me shift in bewilderment, look to him for an answer.

"Did you." His voice is quiet, but it drops like a stone in the hall.

"I did."

He waits.

I breathe deep. The presence of the Watchers gives me strength.

Honesty, Bravery, Discovery.

"I've proved Discovery a new way. On my own." My voice gains volume as I speak. "And you can no longer lead us." I'm as calm as a windless prairie. No fury in my words, just cold determination.

There are a few gasps. I break Stockham's gaze and look around. A handful of Councilmen stand at the sides of the hall, mouths agape, looking as shocked as the rest. "I found the First Peoples who once lived on this land; I found the Lost People."

A murmur starts in the crowd. They gesture toward me and whisper behind their hands and shake their heads. I see my pa. He's staring at me like I'm a ghost.

"And I can show you," I say, meeting his gaze.

Frère Andre repeats my words in French, telling people not to be afraid. I look about, find Tom in the crowd. His eyes are wide, hands at his side. But for the first time in forever, those prairie-sky eyes aren't full of fear. They're shining with relief.

Voices build, rising in excitement.

"We aren't alone!" I call out, feeling bold. "And we don't have to fear." I lock eyes with a woman who looks uncertain, confused. But real slow . . . she smiles. At my words, my Discovery.

There's movement at the top of the steps.

Brother Stockham steps away from the pulpit. And it seems my eyes are playing tricks on me, because his face has changed—from shock to wonder. He tilts his head, measuring me. And then . . .

Then it seems he's made up his mind. He steps toward the lacquered box that lies on the side table.

Inside is our commitment to life, or to death.

He reaches into the box. Pulls out a sawed-off shotgun.

My breath stops.

The crowd goes still.

"You are quite right, Emmeline." His voice is clear in the quiet. Mild and deadly. He reaches into the box again. His eyes are soft, like some giant weight has been taken off his chest. "I can no longer lead." His right hand loads the gun. One bullet. Two.

I'm frozen, staring at him as he hefts the gun from one hand to the other, his eyes tracing over the two short barrels. Then he draws back the hammer. He shifts his weight, grasps the gun solid in his right hand. "And I can't have you—"

Frozen thoughts, frozen tongue.

"Leave her be!" My pa pushes out of the crowd.

"Pa!"

Pa holds up a hand to keep me back, drawing his stooped shoulders up square. He faces Stockham. "You just leave her be."

Stockham's eyes widen. He cocks his head, weighing something.

My father taught me many lessons.

There's a clatter of sounds inside my head: the roar of the river, the whispers of *les trembles,* the soft drop of Tom's fishing line onto the water, Kane's heartbeat.

Stockham holds the gun steady, looking between my pa and me. Then he smiles. A real smile. Like . . . like he's relieved. "You have lifted the burden," he says.

Then he spins the gun and puts the barrel in his mouth.

I squeeze my eyes shut. A deafening crack shatters the air.

Someone cries out.

And then there's dead silence.

No whispers, no river, no heartbeat.

Salvation and survival can be at odds.

When I open my eyes, Brother Stockham has fallen and Brother Jameson is screaming. "Heathen! Devil!" He stares around at people, willing them to action. "She is back from the dead! She brings death! Seize her!"

But no one moves toward me; they begin to retreat, backing toward the doors like they want nothing to do with Jameson, with the horror at the pulpit. There's a ruckus at the back of the hall. My heart is tight, a heavy stone in my chest. That look in Stockham's eyes . . .

But then Pa turns back to me and I forget my despair.

310

His scruffy hair and crinkly eyes—he's confused, but underneath that is relief. Love. His mouth moves, silent. *My girl,* he says. He smiles that smile I remember from years ago. I want to stay in it forever, but a flash of movement distracts me.

Jameson. He disappears behind the pulpit and straightens back up with the gun.

Pa freezes at the look on my face. Turns. And as Jameson draws the hammer and takes aim at me over the pulpit, my pa surges forward. "No!" He scrambles for the stairs, his weathered frame an impossible blur.

A second crack echoes through the hall.

And Pa's body jerks backward before me.

My mind winds the spool of that moment backward a split second, lets it loose, winds it in again. Everything is mute, everything moves slow.

And then Pa is falling, falling, drifting to the floor like a poplar leaf, his trembling hands grasping at the air before him, his head striking the ground.

A low din in my mind now, a thousand bees angry in their hive. The crowd behind screaming, shoving, scrambling backward. Hands grab at my cloak. I pull free. I'm swimming through the river again, deep and thick, pushing hard as I can for the other side. For Pa.

My knees bang against the floor. His chest is a gaping wound, torn open like a withered, hollow tree. The boards beneath him are sticky with bright red blossoms. I take his head in my hands, search his glassy eyes for a glimmer of life. For any hint of that look I've been seeing for weeks but didn't understand until now.

You're worthy, my girl.

That look is gone; his eyes are dark as the coldest river. When I look up, Jameson is reaching for the box again, fumbling for more bullets. His hands shake as he grabs one and drops it in, reaches with his thumb to pull back the hammer.

I'm dead in his sights.

I cover Pa's body with mine and look away, back at the people who are scrambling every which way. Mothers grab children, men shout and shove. They surge away from Jameson, desperate to get to the back of the hall, to the doors that now hang open.

I see Kane.

He's pushing people behind him, straining to get to the front. People duck and stumble aside and I see there's a knife glinting in his hand. The look in his eyes is both desperate and dead sure. He shoves the woman in front of him aside and bursts through the crowd, leaping high and bringing his elbow up.

He whips his arm forward and sets the knife free.

And Jameson squeezes the trigger one last time.

33

LA PRISE.

Her winds sound like an animal. At times a shrieking eagle, at times a bleating lost lamb. Always there. Always battering the walls of our quarters, always blowing inside my head. Gusting, railing. *Always there,* until I can't tell silence from wind, whether it lets up, whether I'm dreaming.

Some days I go outside and stand in the ice-cold winds, let them slap at my cheeks and steal my breath. I hold tight to the lead rope that runs from our kitchen door to the woodshed. In this blinding snow, letting go would mean I might never find my way back. Just ten steps from our door, I might lose my way; freeze to death.

I hold tight to that rope, my fingers stiff beneath my mitts, my skin burning in the cold.

Trying to remember what I'm holding on for in this smothering dark.

Because there comes a point during the winterkill when

you can't remember it being any different. You can't imagine it being different.

You can't imagine you ever felt the sun-filled breeze warm your skin. Can't imagine that your heart swelled at the sounds of birds and trees around you. Can't imagine that you ever felt those warm hands in yours.

And you can't follow the thread in your mind back to those moments, because it's all too far away, and the days are too short and the darkness too long.

The despair is too deep.

Always there. Gusting. Railing.

The loss is like a sickness. It hangs about you, pulls at your skin, muddies your thoughts. Makes you want to give up, let go of the lead rope, head into those death winds.

Give yourself over to *La Prise* for good.

And yet.

The very blackest depths of that sickness, the furthest bottom of that hole—it has something to tell you. Hollowness means there was once a fullness; suffocating absence means there was once a presence. And if you let yourself listen, and think on that, you remember that it used to be different. You realize something more was possible. *Is* possible.

And in that howling silence, you can hear it: your secret heart beating.

Hold on. Hold on.

So instead of losing your path, instead of letting the winterkill have its way, you hang tight to that rope. You pull yourself hand over hand back to the warmth.

You wait out the dark.

You wait for the Thaw.

34

"EMMELINE!"

I turn slow from my perch on the bank, my eyes reluctant to leave the swallows that dip through the new cattails on the swollen river. The sun blinds me for a moment and she's just a shadow striding across the green flats in her calm way.

I pick myself up from the bank awkward-like before I remember I don't need to favor my bad foot so much. Matisa and Soeur Manon have figured a kind of tincture to help with the pain.

Matisa knows lots of things that can help us: ways to make stores last longer, cures for certain kinds of ailments. Most of her ways come from the land, though some of the supplies they brought have also helped with sicknesses and wounds.

Course, some wounds are beyond healing.

She reaches me and stops. "You've been out here all morning."

"I know," I say, looking at the woods beyond the flats. "Can't help watching everything green up."

We look around at the trees budding out, the small pockets of snow melting slow in their crooks and shadows.

"Talks are in an hour."

I sigh real deep. "Again?"

She smiles. "Talking is good."

"If it gets us anywhere."

She shrugs. "I'm sure we're close."

We're quiet again. The swallows swoop and dip.

She tilts her head at the river. "Being out here—does it bring you peace?"

I swallow hard against the stone that settles in my throat. "Suppose."

We stand there a moment, listening to the chirrup of the birds, the soft wind. Matisa turns to go. "You'll be needed at Talks," she says over her shoulder.

"I'll be there," I murmur, looking at the river. "Matisa?" She looks back. "You have that dream again?"

She nods, her eyes serious. I watch her turn and walk back to the fortification, carrying the weight of it on her shoulders. We'll have to speak on that dream at Talks.

Now that the Thaw is here, we've got some decisions to make. It was a hard Ice Up, even with Matisa's help; we lost three people and had barely enough stores to survive on. Can't imagine Jameson's family fared any better after being cast out—doubt they're still alive.

And Matisa's been dreaming on a war. A big battle, coming in along the horizon, setting the river on fire. She tells us there are bigger weapons out there—more deadly than rifles and bows and arrows. There are weapons that can turn people to ash, poisons that can destroy their insides, addle their brains. She had the war dream all *La Prise,* and Isi's pushing hard for the three of them to return home.

I stare across the bulging waters and up the bank, picturing the sweeping prairies greening up in the sun. Matisa says the land is vast, bigger than we could ever imagine. There might be other places to Discover, other unknowns. I know Matisa's hoping I will go with her so she and I can figure our dreams.

But there are some people I won't leave without.

I look back at the fortification. Two forms stand on the top of the north wall. Tom's blond hair catches the sun as he bends to look at whatever Frère Andre is pointing out.

They're up there every afternoon now, looking at the woods, at the hills beyond.

He's Tom again, but better. That spark of curiosity I used to see in his eyes is back, and it shines when I talk about journeying beyond our settlement. He can feel change coming too. And he's looking toward it with his head high.

I close my eyes a minute and take a deep breath. The memory of *La Prise* lingers in the breeze, but there's the smell of new willow budding out and a softness to the wind that comes with the Thaw.

I head back.

When I reach the east gates, he's leaning against the wall, arms crossed, waiting for me.

"Find anything new out there?" Kane says, that funny smile curving his mouth.

I nod. "Everything."

He takes my wrists and pulls me to him.

"Careful," I say as he wraps my arms around his back. "Sister Ann's been eyeballing us. Fixing to bind us."

"You can't be kept. She doesn't know that by now?"

I want to smile—it's there, deep down—but I can't find it.

His eyes search my face. "Em?"

I clear my throat. "She says . . . she says my pa would've wanted us bound." It's been months, but talking about him still makes my chest ache.

Kane studies me a moment. "You think that's true?"

I chew on my lip. I think about Pa telling me how he chose my ma and didn't care what anyone else said. I think about holding on to that rope in the killing cold. Think about heading back into the warmth. And Pa's face, the very last time he looked at me. "I think . . ." I bring my eyes to meet Kane's. "I think he'd want me to be happy," I say, "however that looks."

Kane smiles. And my stomach dives as he leans in to kiss me.

When he pulls away, I trace a finger across the nick on his temple, where the shotgun shrapnel grazed him. He grabs my hand and brings it to his mouth, drowning me in his black eyes. We stand there clasped together in the bright afternoon, the earth swelling and warming all around us.

The Lost People are gone now, but the breeze pulls wisps from my plait, creeps soft fingers along my neck, whispers in my ear.

And it sounds like hope.

La fin

318

ACKNOWLEDGMENTS

Sincere thanks to my inimitable agent, Michael Bourret, for championing my book and finding it the very best of homes. Thank you for advising me to go with my gut. I'm so glad I did: it partnered me with the kindest, smartest, rockstarriest agent I could imagine.

Deepest thanks to my incredible editors, Maggie Lehrman at Amulet and Alice Swan and Rebecca Lee at Faber & Faber, for asking the questions that transformed this manuscript and for guiding my choices so graciously. I feel so fortunate to have had your advice and expertise.

Thanks to the entire team at Abrams/Amulet, including copyeditor Nancy Elgin and proofreader Kat Kopit, who treated my book with swoon-worthy fastidiousness, and the marketing team, including Nicole Russo and Jason Wells, and cover designer Maria Middleton. Thanks to the entire team at Faber for all of the enthusiasm and support, including acquiring publisher Leah Thaxton and cover designer Emma Eldridge.

Many thanks to Lauren Abramo and the foreign rights department at DGLM for sharing my book with readers around the world, thereby ensuring *international fanciness*. Thanks also to Caspian Dennis and Kate McLennan at Abner Stein Agency for securing my Faber home.

I owe an enormous debt of gratitude to my critique partner, the talented Dana Alison Levy, who reads my work, helps me see it with new eyes, and is always around for a phone call to commiserate, celebrate, or *mull*. Thank you for your tiny-armed hugs and giant help, TD.

Thanks to all of my wonderful early readers: Bethany Griffin (who advised me to go with her gut. Apparently we share a gut?), Sarah Harian (who loved this book at a critical moment), Angela Sparks, Rachael Allen, Jennifer Walkup, Lindsey Culli, and Debra Driza (who all offered wonderful feedback and encouragement). Amazing writers and women, all!

Special thanks to my best friend, Amanda Marshall, for early reading and general cheerleading (also for not looking askance when I announced that day in the mall that *I shall write fiction for a living*).

Massive thanks to Jaki Campeau for childcare at the drop of a hat, for your encouragement and support. I am so lucky!

Thank you to Josie C. for gifting me the blanket-dream story back in grad school.

Thank you to Dr. Rosalind Kerr for teaching me to be careful with my words.

Moral support awards go to Kim Iampen (holder of my hand) and my Edmonton girlfriends and Rimbey girls (fillers of my metaphorical and literal cup). Giant thanks to Pamela Anthony (photo-safari-er and checker of reality) and Joel Higham (designer of all things pretty and genius).

Merci beaucoup á Marc Piquette pour votre patience avec la conjugaison et la traduction. Merci á Thérèse Romanick pour répondre á mes appels aléatoires. Vous êtes très gentilles! Thank you to Becky Pickard for *les trembles*.

Thanks to my online writing friends, particularly the lit-bitches, who provide a landing pad for all things manic and hilarious, writerly-related and not. Without you I would be a lonely little writer indeed.

Thank you to my entire family for your love and support.

I'm particularly grateful to my mom and dad for instilling in me a love of reading and for encouraging me in my fantastical imaginings (also for adoring and entertaining my children when deadlines get crunchy).

My baby brother, Tim, deserves special thanks for setting my feet on this path and encouraging me down it by being willing to speak all things world-building whenever I need. My brother Jeff, too, for listening to my rants.

I'm filled with gratitude for my husband, Marcel, who always believed I could do it, and who provides me the time and support to keep writing. I love you.

To Matias Alex and Dylan Asha, who make each day joyful and new: thank you for being the wonderfully weird little creatures you are. You are beyond my best imaginings.

Finally, thank you to my big brother, John. My grief could fill an ocean, but my gratitude for the strength you showed is equally deep. You were true Bravery. I miss you.

DISCOVER WHAT LIES BEYOND THE SETTLEMENT
IN *DARKTHAW*, THE SEQUEL TO *WINTERKILL*.
TURN THE PAGE TO CONTINUE THE JOURNEY . . .

DARKTHAW

RISK THE UNKNOWN PATH

A WINTERKILL NOVEL BY

KATE A. BOORMAN

1

THE RIVER IS SWOLLEN AND VIOLENT.

The dead lie beneath.

I fix my eyes where the banks close to a narrow gap and the river rushes through in a torrent. Where the trees bud out with soft green tips, bending in the springtime breeze. Where they sent my pa to his peace.

They did it quick, that very day he died to save me, before *La Prise* howled in and blinded us, before the world went dark. Wrapped in cloth tied at each end, his body was thrown to the deadly chunks of whirling ice. I had the memory of those waters deep in my bones, the hollow scream of the river loud in my ears, and I went with him, swirling down that giant hole of black.

Then Kane put his hand to the nape of my neck and pulled me, gentle, to his chest, his woodsmoke warmth. I heard the winter winds whistling through the trees, Kane's heart beating loud in my ear. Matisa put her unfamiliar, familiar hand in mine.

We took shelter. The dark rushed in. The river froze.

And our dreams began. Matisa's of death: river on fire, shattering bone, deafening sound. A war destroying the people she and I love. Mine of life: tall peaks of rock, snowcapped trees, shining waters. A valley where warm winds drift across an impossible lake: blue like a robin's egg yet green like the newest poplar buds. And all of it, calling out to me.

Matisa says we're the dreamers of her legend—two dreamers from "different times" who were meant to find each other. Last fall, I dreamt about Matisa every night. I dreamt she was out in the woods beyond our fortification, and the pull, the desire to find her, was so strong, I risked my own life to do it. She was dreaming of me, too. She left her home and searched these woods, a forbidden place among her people, to find me. All winterkill long, my dreams have been about life—my new life, out there. A small part of me wants to cling to that idea, wants to believe that this alone is the reason she came.

But I know different. The disaster Matisa dreams: she believes we will prevent it if we stay together. And even if I don't rightly know how, I plan to try. I'll leave this place and journey to her home, that strange and beautiful place in my dreams. Find out how our dreams connect, how they can prevent death.

I fiddle the balsamroot in my hand. It grows much closer to the fortification, but I can't help but come out here to pick it. I bend low to pull some more from the bank, shifting my weight to my good foot before I remember it won't hurt to lean on my other, thanks to Matisa's tincture. She says I'll forget the habit soon enough.

The voices that used to whisper at me from the trees are silent. My Lost People, the ghosts of the First Peoples who once lived on this land, are here now. They have been found; we have been found.

But I hear new voices murmuring beneath the rush of river. Way down in those cold depths. Clamoring under the surface.

And they don't speak of life.

I close my ears to the murmuring and breathe the soft wind that sighs through the willows. The sun shines on the spot where they cast my pa. My pa's body, so still. I push the memory away and let my eyes fill up with the silver light gleaming off the waters. That once solid ribbon of frozen river is now a glimmering rush, feeding the thirsty willows and cattails, helping the trees burst into all shades of green.

With the Thaw comes promise.

I put that idea in my secret heart and hold it there. I cling to the truth that this river's melt brings new life, new beginnings.

I try to push away a different truth that creeps cold fingers across my chest: once ice thaws, what is hidden in its depths can resurface.

My world is changing. I have to believe it's changing to the good.

"Em!" A child's voice comes from far off, behind me.

I turn. Kane and his little brother Daniel are making their way from the fortification. The morning sun bathes them in a warm glow, but the walls loom dark behind them.

Kane's head is bare, and his shirt is open at the neck, like always. He walks casual; hands in his pockets, like he has all the time in the world to get to me. I know better; I know neither of us can get near the other fast enough.

Stolen moments from this past winterkill wash over me in a heat: desperate kisses and fumbling hands in the dark woodshed. Kane's breath on my skin, his woodsmoke scent all over me.

Nothing about those secret meetings was slow. And they were always far too short . . . heartbeats in time, only.

Tom's ma, my self-appointed guardian, would look on me hard when I stamped back into the common area, shaking snow from my winter cloak, hoping my cheeks looked flushed from the biting cold.

I watch Kane approach now, cabbage moths fluttering around in my belly.

Daniel breaks away from Kane and races toward me, his five-year-old legs pumping furious. "I got to feed them today!" he calls.

I pull my gaze from Kane and notice Daniel's bright eyes. "Feed them?"

He skids to a stop before me, dark hair all mussed. "The horses!"

Of course. Daniel plain loves those beasts. None of us had ever seen horses before Matisa and her cousin, Isi, and brother, Nishwa, showed up on them in the fall; such animals were taken by the sickness when our ancestors arrived. Matisa's horses are like something from a fairy-tale picture book: all long lines and sleek muscles.

I reach out my hand to smooth Daniel's hair. "You been wrestling with Nico?" Kane's other brother, Nicolas, is eight, but Daniel is the sort to bite off more than he can chew.

Daniel shakes his head but looks at the ground, a mischievous smile on his face.

"Why are you so messy?" I prompt.

Kane strolls up. "He lets Dottie snuffle his hair," he answers for him.

"Dottie?"

Daniel looks up, pleased. "Matisa's horse!" he says. "I named her."

"Did you now." I'm distracted, with Kane so close. His sleeves are rolled up, and the tilt of his head, his dark eyes on me . . .

"Yep. Dottie. Because of her spots. And she thinks my hair is grass!" Daniel giggles and grabs at my hand. "Come on, I'll show you!"

"Hang on, Daniel." Kane puts a hand on his shoulder. "Remember I told you Em and me had some things to speak on?"

Daniel drops my hand, his face crumpling in disappointment. "But—"

"That was the deal, right? You could come out to the river so long as you let me and Em talk?"

Daniel nods, reluctant.

"I'll come soon as we're done," I reassure him, smoothing his hair again.

"You pull some feed for her," Kane suggests, pointing to the pockets of new grass growing on the banks. "She'll love that."

Daniel's off and pulling grass in a heartbeat. I feel a pang. He's going to be so disappointed when we take those beasts away. Never mind his older brother.

Kane's dark eyes are studying me. I turn toward him, passing the balsamroot one hand to the other, keeping my fingers busy so they don't wander where they'd rather be—up near the open collar of his shirt.

"You've been out here a while," he says. They're nothing words—idle talk. But his voice is softer, huskier. The cabbage moths in my belly are furious.

"Just getting some things for my medicines," I say. I shrug like I'm at ease. "Mayhap I lingered a bit."

That funny half smile pulls at the corner of his mouth. "You and these trees," he says. "You've always loved them best."

"Not best. Just prefer them to being inside." I glance at him from under my eyelashes. "I love other things best."

His eyebrows arch. "That so?"

"Sure." I put the herb into my satchel and make my eyes go wide. "Spring strawberries, for instance."

He frowns to hide a smile. "Strawberries."

"Delicious," I say. "Better than trees."

"Ah," he says. "Well, I hear the ones out there"—he tips his head at the woods—"are the very best."

I smile, a fluttering starting in my chest. *Out there.* It's all so near. "Matisa says we'll leave this week," I say.

"She can tell?" Kane asks.

I nod, but guilt stabs me. "She says Soeur Manon will go soon." Soeur Manon, the healer woman who was teaching me her craft, the only one besides my pa who ever cared for me, is lying in her bed in the Healing House. Dying. I promised myself I'd stay to see her out. "She's barely opened her eyes in days," I say. "Don't think she even knows I'm there."

Kane's eyes search my face. "She'd be happy to know we're leaving," he says, gentle. "She'd want you to." His brow creases. He rubs a hand across the back of his neck. "Wish everyone were so inclined."

"You talked to your ma again," I guess.

He nods.

"And?" I cross my arms, like it'll shield me from the answer I don't want.

He shakes his head: it didn't go well.

"She's not worried about the *malmaci*, is she?" Before Matisa and the boys discovered our settlement, before this past winterkill, most people believed we were alone—mayhap even the last people left alive anywhere—living under the threat of the *malmaci*, an evil spirit, in the outlying forest. It attacked those who explored too far, turning them into rivers of blood, ravaging them from the inside out. It snatched people who wandered out beyond our borders. We know now it was lore, superstition only. We know now it was a sickness, one that Matisa's people had suffered with and fled from long ago. And that the Takings—the disappearances—were started by Brother Stockham's pa to protect his position as leader of the settlement. People shouldn't fear it anymore, but there's a sliver of doubt left in some.

"No. It's the fact of me going at all."

I sigh, though I don't rightly know what I was expecting. Did I really think she'd send him off with her blessing? His pa died years ago, and he has two little brothers; she counts on him for all manner of help. But . . .

She can only expect that so long.

I look over his shoulder at the tall wooden walls of the fortification, my gaze tracing up to the empty watchtower. Used to be a Watcher in there at all times, day and night, surveying the woods outside the fortification, ready to report any sign of danger, any sign of Waywardness. Things are different now. We can make our own decisions.

"You're . . ." I have to force myself to meet his eyes. "You're sure you still want to come?"

"Em." He reaches out and grasps my forearm. The way he says my name—my breath gets fast. His touch is fire.

"I'll go anywhere with you."

His hand slides down my arm, and I lace my fingers in his, drowning in his gaze—the gaze that sees straight into me, sees all of me. Our fingers tighten, and it pulls us closer. I throw a quick look at Daniel, but he's busy, his head bent to the grasses. Kane reaches for me with the other hand, and I let him draw me toward the heat of his body. I place my hand on his chest, my fingers grasping at the open laces of his collar. His mouth is so close. I could kiss him here, in the fresh air of the Thaw. It would be right . . .

Over his shoulder I see a figure emerge from the fortification gates. It's Tom, and his blond head is lifted like he wants to speak as he hurries toward us. Kane follows my gaze and turns, pulling away.

I miss the feel of Kane straightaway, but I'm distracted by the way Tom is moving, crossing the distance in long, loping strides.

For days he's been busy tending to his pa, who took ill at the end of *La Prise*. We'd been talking about the Thaw for months, talking about my dreams, about Matisa's people, but with his pa unwell, there's a chance he won't be seeing any of it. More likely, we'll be leaving without him.

My heart clenches tight at the thought. He should be coming; there's nothing for him here. It's not just that he's curious about what's beyond, it's what lies out there for him. Here, he'll be expected to find a life mate and produce children. But Tom is *ginup*, and his heart would only ever belong to another boy. Matisa has told me that such a thing isn't strange to her people and surely not persecuted. He should come with me, find a new life out there, one that doesn't have to be a secret.

But he would never leave with his pa sickly the way he is. And that thought washes me in a muddled wave of sadness, anger, and pride.

As Tom pulls up, I see his cheeks are flushed and his blue eyes are serious.

My stomach knots. Is the tea I've been giving his pa not working well? I start rifling my brain for my medicines knowledge, wondering what Matisa and I might be able to come up with in its place—

"It's Soeur Manon," he tells me. "Matisa says you need to come."

The Healing House is silence and shadow.

Isi and Nishwa stand on either side of the door. Nishwa offers me a soft smile as we approach, Isi inclines his head, his eyes unblinking. It's always the same these days: Nishwa with the easy look, Isi with the look that makes me feel tested—tested and found wanting. He's been pricklier ever since the Thaw began. Ever since I insisted we wait on Soeur Manon.

I ignore his weighty gaze. Heavy clouds are gathering above us, blocking out the morning sun. Surely that's what sets the tingle on my skin. I cross between the boys and push the door open.

Matisa sits beside the bed, her hand resting near Soeur Manon's snowy hair. The rest of the healing woman is covered by a mound of wool blankets—our futile attempt to chase away her chill. Futile, because it's not a chill that comes with cold.

Matisa beckons me close, her calm presence spilling out like much-needed light in the dingy hut. I feel Tom and Kane linger in the doorway.

"It's all right," I say over my shoulder. "I'll come get you . . . after."

Tom touches my elbow—a gesture of brother-like love—and leaves. Kane's parting look washes me in a different sort of love: fierce and protective.

The door shuts, sealing out the crisp air, the beam of sunlight. In the candlelit space, the room feels smaller. I cross to the bed, pulling a chair from the corner of the room with me, and sit.

Soeur Manon's wrinkled face is dwarfed by the bed and blankets; her eyes are shut, her breathing shallow, irregular. She's been this way for days. I search for some sign that she is near her end but find nothing different.

I look to Matisa. "How do you know?" I ask under my breath. Doesn't seem proper to be speaking on a person's death in their earshot.

"I have seen many people go," Matisa replies. "I know when it is time."

I study Matisa in the flickering light. Her dark-brown braid shines against the blue of her shirt. Her face is open, reassuring. Course she's seen people come into this world and leave it; she's a healer, like Soeur Manon. Like I was training to be. She and Soeur Manon spent months sharing what they knew with each other, taught me what they could. I turn my eyes back on Soeur Manon, reach out, and place my hand on the blankets that cover her shoulder. Matisa places her hand on my arm, rubbing her thumb back and forth in a soothing rhythm I'm glad for. It helps steady my racing heart.

Soeur Manon was always kind to me; she understood me in a way I didn't realize until it was near too late.

"Did anyone else stop by?" I ask. I wonder if everyone understands who—and what—we're losing. All of her knowledge, her methods, her cures.

Course, they probably assume I'll be here to take her place.

"Frère Andre," Matisa says. "He brought another blanket. It was covered in embroidered flowers. It was Soeur Bette's, I think. I didn't tell him that she is beyond all of that."

I think of the old Watcher with his wiry beard and failing eyes, offering the blanket that once warmed Soeur Bette—the life mate he lost not two months back. He's another who was kind to me, helped me see that I was worth being kind to. He was the one who opened the sealed fortification gates for me even though *La Prise*—the deadly winter storm—was howling down upon the settlement. Even though I was supposed to be dead. He told his Watchers not to be afraid, and he locked the weapons away so they couldn't do something foolish when Matisa arrived. If not for him, my Lost People wouldn't be here; Matisa wouldn't be here.

As if recalling that memory, the wind picks up outside. A soft patter of rain starts on the thatched roof above us.

"Rain is good," I say. "Greens everything up."

Matisa nods, her hand still tracing a soothing pattern on my arm.

"It'll be real pretty out there," I say. "Don't you think?" Don't know why I'm babbling like this. Feel a need to fill the silence. Fill these last moments. I pat the old woman's shoulder and clear my throat, forcing down a lump. "She'll be glad we're on our way. Last week she opened her eyes long enough to look straight at me. You know what she said? *Emmeline: allez-vous-en!* Go already!" I force a laugh, but it's cut short by the sob building in my chest.

"She always knew what was truly in your heart." Matisa's voice is gentle. Her hand is warm.

I blink back tears and nod. "She knows my new life lies beyond."

Matisa's hand stills.

I look at the old woman's snowy head. I keep the rest of what Soeur Manon told me to myself. About freedom bringing choices—*les choix que vous ne voulez pas*: choices I don't want.

Can't see how that can be. After years of being eyeballed, years of having no choices at all, the freedom waiting out in those trees has to be good.

"Em," Matisa's voice breaks my thoughts. "I want you to know something."

The winds pick up, gusting against the little shack.

I look at her.

"Our dreams led us to each other," she says.

I nod.

"You know that I believe we should stay together," she says. "But"—she clasps her hands together—"I will not ask it of you."

I study her face, trying to figure where this is coming from. Matisa knows I want to see what lies beyond. She knows I've always planned to leave this place with her. She saved my life last fall, risked her own to pull me from the river, but this is about more than repaying a debt to her: it's about starting a new life. It's about choosing a new life.

But she wants me to recognize it *is* a choice.

I look at Soeur Manon, my thoughts whirling around her last words to me.

She's still as ice.

I watch for the rise of her chest, listen for a rattling breath. Nothing.

Matisa puts her hand on my arm once more. "She's gone," she says, soft.

And, like they're answering my heart, the heavens open and the rain thunders down on the roof above, washing the Healing House in sorrow.

The soil shifts beneath my dream fingers as I dig. The river sings with the voices of the dead. I'm beneath the dogwood, a place I know so well, a place I've been dozens of times to dig roots for Soeur Manon.

But why?

We sent Soeur Manon to her peace. I glance up, across the Watch flats to the fortification. It's silent. Everyone has gone.

Suddenly Matisa is on the ground before me. Her eyes are closed tight, her skin is mottled an angry red and swollen with purple bruising. A trickle of blood streams from her nose.

I am digging, fast and furious, grabbing huge handfuls of soil.

And then, a rush of hoofbeats is tearing down upon me. Gunfire. Horses. Screaming.

The dead in the river sing out, telling me to hurry, hurry, hurry.

I wake in a sweat, the dream bleeding out into the chill morning air. Sitting up, I scrub my hands over my face and shiver. The screaming echoes in my mind. Shrill. Constant.

No. Not screaming. The Watchtower bell is ringing.

The Watchtower bell?

I leap from my bed, pushing off the wool blanket, my bare feet slapping against the cold wood floor. The sound of the bell doesn't send the same spike of fear through me it once did. We haven't abandoned Watch fully—there are still a few Watchers up on the walls each night, but they're not watching for an attack from some spirit monster from the forest. The alarm bell is kept as a way to get the settlement's attention in the case of something else urgent: a fire, a coming storm, a wild animal.

I dress quick, my pulse racing. As I pass my pa's old room, I notice Matisa is already up and gone, like always. I grab my cloak from a hook beside the door and push outside. There are people rushing toward me, headed for the east gate. At the wall, a crowd is gathering. I push through the people who are assembling in a silent semicircle. I notice a few weapons clenched tight in weathered hands, but no one seems to notice me jostling them aside. Everyone's craning their necks at something but hanging back, like they're reluctant to get too close.

When I get to the front of the crowd, I pull up short.

A man stands outside the east gates.

ABOUT THE AUTHOR

KATE BOORMAN is a writer from the Canadian prairies. She was born in Nepal and grew up in the small town of Rimbey, where she developed a fondness for winter. She has a master's degree in Dramatic Critical Theory and a résumé full of assorted jobs, from florist to qualitative research associate. She lives in Edmonton, Alberta, with her family, and spends her free time sitting under starry skies with her friends and scheming up travel to faraway lands.

CHECK OUT THESE OTHER GREAT READS!

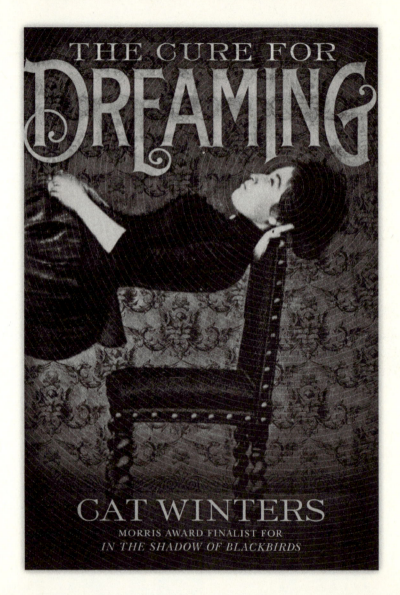

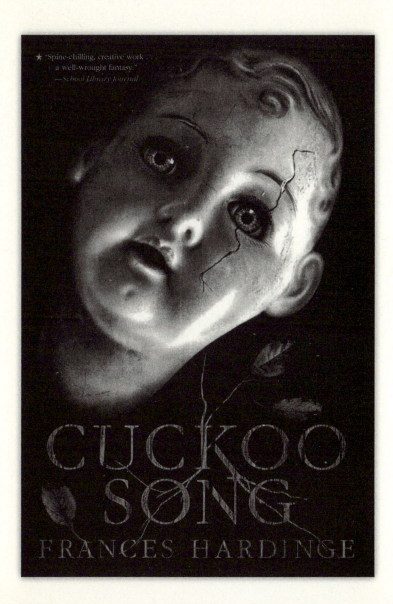

★ "Spine-chilling, creative work . . .
a well-wrought fantasy."
—*School Library Journal*

CUCKOO SONG

FRANCES HARDINGE

SEND AUTHOR FAN MAIL TO:
Amulet Books, Attn: Marketing, 115 West 18th Street, New York, NY 10011.
Or e-mail marketing@abramsbooks.com. All mail will be forwarded.

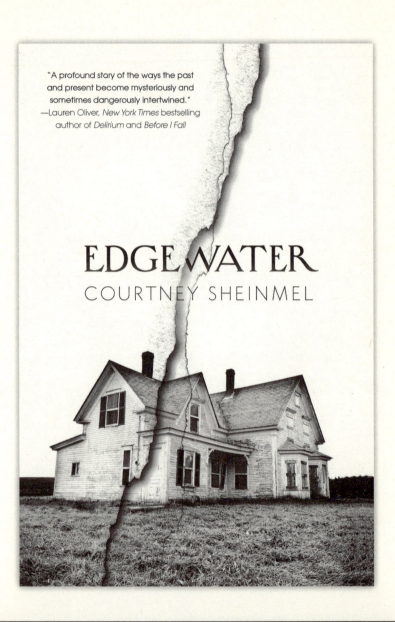

"A profound story of the ways the past and present become mysteriously and sometimes dangerously intertwined."
—Lauren Oliver, *New York Times* bestselling author of *Delirium* and *Before I Fall*

EDGEWATER
COURTNEY SHEINMEL

Amulet Books
An imprint of ABRAMS
WWW.AMULETBOOKS.COM

SEND AUTHOR FAN MAIL TO:
Amulet Books, Attn: Marketing, 115 West 18th Street, New York, NY 10011.
Or e-mail marketing@abramsbooks.com. All mail will be forwarded.